Caffeine Nig

LIVE

3 4144 0098 3815 8

Luk

Hometown

Fiction to die for

Published by Caffeine Nights Publishing 2016

Published in Great Britain by
Caffeine Nights Publishing
4 Eton Close
Walderslade
Chatham
Kent
ME5 9AT

www.caffeinenights.com

British Library Cataloguing in Publication Data.
A CIP catalogue record for this book is available from the British Library
ISBN: 978-1-910720-57-8

Cover design by
Mark (Wills) Williams

Everything else by
Default, Luck and Accident

ACKNOWLEDGEMENTS:

Thank you to my family and friends for their encouragement and understanding over the long years I've spent writing. I'm also deeply grateful to Darren and Caffeine Nights for bringing Hometown to (dark) life, and to various writers and film-makers who've inspired and/or frightened me since I was a kid. Last but by no means least, thank you to my wife Rebecca who convinced me I had something special with this tale.

This is for Rebecca. The light of all lights.

LIVE
BORDERS

One

Inside Stu Brennan's head, a dead woman screamed his name.

Stu's hand jerked, his cup flew and smashed against the sink. Coffee splashed the floor. The crash of the breaking cup rang around the little staffroom and the scream filled his head again.

He slammed his hands against his ears, closed his eyes and held his breath. For a beat of a few silent seconds, there was nothing but his own interior voice, desperate to reassure him with simple noises of comfort. Then he heard his name a third time, a horrific bellow behind his eyes.

Stu collapsed; his hand struck the splashes of coffee and a piece of his broken cup.

He knew who was calling his name.

This isn't happening.

The thought was so solid, so comforting it was easy to think it was true.

This isn't happening. This is not happening.

Right. He was at work; this was a Tuesday morning; the other shops and the rest of Dalry were all right outside and everything was where it should be so there was no way this was happening.

His legs refused to work properly and he had to move somewhere between a crawl and a shuffle for the short distance towards the toilet. Pulling himself up and using the edge of the sink as leverage, Stu staggered a couple of steps to the toilet door. Breathing much too quickly, he pushed it shut, locked it and dropped onto the lavatory.

The thud of music from below on the shop floor pounded in steady beats. Stu held on to the sound with as much focus as he could. Through his panic and confusion, he tried to picture Rich downstairs, Rich sorting the tills, Rich probably tapping on the counter to the rhythm of the music as he readied the shop for opening.

Stu took a few deep breaths. Doing so helped to bring some small degree of focus and rational thought.

Stand up. Wash hands. Sort out the mess he'd made with his coffee. Make another drink. Sit in front of his computer before anyone else arrived at work. Talk to people. Be normal.

Rational thought spoke again while he remained perfectly still. Sandra was in the cash office and the only reason she wouldn't have heard the breaking cup was down to her door being shut. There was nothing to stop her from needing the loo or coming out to make her own drink. What would she think if she saw the mess and nobody cleaning it up? How could he explain it?

Sorry, boss. I just heard my name shouted inside my head by someone who can't be speaking to me and I needed a sit down.

Stu shook and swallowed the ugly taste of vomit. He closed his eyes again. Images swam in front of him and his eyes flew open. The images remained.

He saw a house and his first thought was this was *his* house. The thought was wrong.

He stood in front of his parents' house, close to the wide front garden, the low wall bordering his mother's flowers and the healthy green of the grass. Their car sat on the long drive and that was normal. What wasn't normal were the broken windows, the black stain of fire damage on the bricks and the spray paint covering the smashed in door.

Stu heard his shout of horrified negation despite being aware of his lips clamped together and his tongue immobile with shock. His feet moved, forcing him to back away, and he tripped on the uneven pavement. He dropped, landed heavily and his hands slapped down on dark stains. Wet stains.

Cold blood covered his fingers and palms. And still the horror arguing against this filled his head, still he couldn't do a thing but see it all here, all right in front of him: his parents' house, his childhood home like something out of a horror film, while the moon shone and his breath rose and the rapid thud of running feet drew closer.

Running to him. Dozens of people by the sound of it, their shoes and boots thundering on the ground as they sprinted towards him. Stu lunged upright, panic swallowing him.

The runners were coming from both ends of the road. The only way to go was forward, into the house.

Into the black of the house.

They were coming closer. They were coming and they were coming for him.

'Stu?'

His eyes jerked open and strained to focus on the white of the toilet wall. The toilet, the little sink, the window behind him, open to let in the cool air of a normal October day. Everything was as it should be.

Apart from the faraway echo of the final scream in his head and the crash of all the running feet from somewhere else.

'Stu?'

Stu did his best to control his panicked thoughts. It was Rich outside. He was at work in his record shop, in the toilet at work, and Rich was outside the door.

'Stu? You in there?'

Rich's voice edged close to panic, a ridiculous idea but a fact with which Stu couldn't argue.

'Yeah. Out in a sec,' Stu said, aware of the tremor in his voice. 'Miles away. Sorry.'

The double meaning of his last few words hit him and he swallowed a mad laugh. He gripped the sink as hard as he could and pulled himself up. His face in the mirror was much too white, much too strained.

What the hell is this?

'Want me to clear up your mess?' Rich asked.

'No. I'll do it.'

'All right. Just make sure you open the window if you've done a stinker.'

Stu listened to Rich walk from the staffroom to the stockroom and he glanced at his watch. Quarter to nine. Less than two minutes had elapsed since he'd picked up his coffee and heard the first scream.

No scream. There was no fucking scream.

He had to phone Kirsty. Had to tell her.

Tell her what?

He tried to formulate an answer, tried to force one to make sense. The effort was too much and the attempt collapsed into nothing.

Call Kirsty. Of course. And tell her he'd either gone nuts or he was being haunted.

A scent breathed, faint but unmistakeable. Against his will, he inhaled.

The aroma of perfume filled his nostrils before fading. Memory came to life and Stu's shocked whisper followed it in one breath.

'Oh my God.'

The perfume shop. Three days before her twentieth birthday. Going into the shop with Will; Will talking to the woman behind the counter, telling her what he wanted and it was a birthday present so he needed a big bottle, needed it in a nice bag.

Stu placed a gentle finger on the bridge of his nose, remembering the smell of the perfume, remembering catching the scent of it three days later when they'd all been in the pub for her birthday. A warm night in September, the lights from traffic outside striking the window they sat opposite and ...

'Poison. She liked Poison. It was her favourite.'

Staring at his reflection, Stu struggled not to weep.

***

She's in her bed, arms around herself and she can't stop watching the shadow grow in front of her window. It moves millimetre by millimetre over the carpet towards the wall. Eventually, she knows it'll reach the wall and slide over the paper towards the ledge, and then it'll be on the glass and night will be here.

She can't move and more than that, she doesn't want to. If she remains utterly still, then nothing happens and nothing will have happened. That'll be the best thing in the world.

Sweat slides in narrow trickles from her neck down her back; her t-shirt sticks to her skin and there's no need for a duvet, not in August. Even so, she doesn't remove the bed covers. Her head's still visible as well as a little of her neck. The rest of her is secure in the dark and heat and stink of her bed.

She watches the shadows and the red light of sunset. Lying here perfectly still, it isn't hard to picture her window open wider than it is, open fully to let in the warmth here at the end of the day; not hard to think of herself climbing up to the ledge, dangling her feet and legs over the edge into the space of air and jumping down to the bushes at the front of the house. She did that once before a few months ago. Easter holidays. The house empty, sunshine doing its best to break through the clouds, and Stu and Andy laughing, calling to her, telling her to come out and she'd jumped right down to the bushes without considering it or wondering if the impact would hurt. Easy to remember that, just as it's easy to picture the shocked circle of Andy's face as he watched her launch, watched her fly and watched her fall, laughing, into the deep green of the bushes.

She could do that again, launch, fly and drop. Then stand and run to the road, run to the pavements and grass and run all the way into the centre of Dalry where she'd never been by herself. She could walk through the little side streets, take shortcuts through the old part of the city she knew only vaguely and run from those little streets and squat buildings into the wild and secret spaces of the fields and trees in the Meadows.

Be in there.

Be in the secret places where there were no shadows and no creeping sunset trickling into her bedroom.

She could do that. She could be away from this bedroom and its dark and heat and stink. All it would take was one quick movement of the duvet thrown back. Do that and it would take nothing to run to the window and jump. Do that and leave this all here behind her, be rid of it, be someone else without this dark and heat and stink.

She remains utterly still, eyes on the growing shadows, and she thinks of the heat of the ending summer, of jumping from her window, of Andy's face as she flew down to the ground.

Two

The darkness blew apart without a sound.

Andy Pateman turned in a circle as quietly as he could and tried to make sense of his surroundings just as he had three times before.

Fourth time lucky, his mind whispered. He wanted to punch that voice as hard he could, silence it.

'Get a grip,' he whispered which didn't help.

The light wasn't overly bright by any means, but it illuminated his surroundings enough for him to place them.

St Mary's Court.

How long's it been?

Fuck off, Andy thought back and the voice miraculously fell quiet.

He knew how long it'd been. He didn't need any interior voice to ask him.

'Twenty-eight years,' Andy whispered.

The time didn't matter. The years he'd spent away from this building were gone. The past was here now and it had brought all its grim squalor with it.

The layout of the building was close to how he remembered it. A wide door, lined by single pane of glass, opened to a gloomy foyer. Two lifts ahead, graffiti covering both doors; stairs at the far end of the foyer. The stairs curved sharply, eight steps up and darkness peeked around the corner.

Flat nineteen.

The thought came without any sense of nostalgia and that didn't surprise him. Whether this was actually happening or not, he had few happy memories of the flat he'd lived in for two or three years all that time before. While he'd been too young to understand his mother's financial state after his dad left her, he'd known enough to know the building they'd moved to was a horrible place full of banging doors, bad smells, raging people and grey days that stretched ahead as far he could see. Getting out of St Mary's Court soon after his eighth birthday had been probably the happiest day of his childhood.

And now here it was. St Mary's, back as if he had never been away.

From somewhere not too far above, a door banged and Andy heard the first scream.

Flat nineteen.

The short plank of wood lay where it had three times before. He took it from beside the foot of the stairs and wondered who'd left it there and why.

For you, idiot.

Andy took the first few steps, paused, then rounded the corner before his nerves could stop him.

Another scream. It was of fear, not pain. There wouldn't be long before that changed, though.

Andy counted the steps as he ascended. Twelve steps to the next floor. Then there'd be another ten to the corner, and twenty after that to the front door of his old flat. All those steps in the thin light coming through the occasional broken window.

If all the windows were broken instead of just dirty, I'd be able to see where the hell I'm going.

Ahead in the dark, someone yelled, the words lost to Andy. He gripped the plank as if it was a club and took the steps to the corner. Murky daylight brushed the hallway ahead at irregular intervals. None of it was sufficient to show anyone hiding. Andy remained still, gathering his nerve. During the first vision, he'd stood at the corner for much longer, an hour, maybe; stood there while harsh screams broke out. The second time he'd moved forward when the screams began but lost it after five steps. He'd sprinted back to the ground floor, shrieking as he ran.

The third time, he'd made it halfway to his old flat before the screams changed into something awful, something full of more pain than he could imagine. After those three times, he'd come to in the real world of his own flat, his cries silent while he wept.

Now he'd do it. Get to flat nineteen and stop whoever was causing the other person's pain.

Simple.

A crawling sensation ran down Andy's back and he registered the trickles of sweat as if he'd never felt the touch on his skin before.

A squeal, then a laugh, then the sound of someone being struck. The squeal fell into a choke which was followed by more laughter.

Andy walked to where he guessed the centre of the hallway to be, held his plank and counted the steps. He made it six before the shouts became distinct words. Andy froze.

'Fucking bitch. You love this. I'm telling you. All the girls do.'

More screams, slightly muffled, and Andy's stomach took a lazy roll. The words were definitely from a man, but there was something wrong with them. They'd been more barked than said, more guttural than a normal voice.

That's someone who isn't all there.

The man's voice rose in terrible rage.

'Suck it. Bitch. Fucking telling you.'

Jesus Christ, Andy thought and a sliver of wood stabbed his index finger. What came instead of pain was a sickened anger, a need to punish the man somewhere ahead.

You bastard.

He trotted forward and reached his old front door. It announced itself with no fanfare. It was just there like all the other doors in the building.

Not quite, Andy realised.

The door to flat nineteen was ajar. Not by much, but enough for him to see a patch of the yellow, floral carpet he hadn't thought of in years, and the thin crack which ran the length of the wall an inch or so above the skirting board.

The man in the flat was still ranting; Andy eased the door open and gazed at his old home. The hallway stretched ahead; half of the open plan kitchen was visible from his position. In the living room, a man squatted over a naked woman. His jeans were down enough to expose his backside; one hand was at his front and he leaned on the other as he attempted to lower himself to the woman's face.

'Last chance. Bitch. This. Or this.'

He lifted his free hand and Andy realised he wasn't leaning on it. He'd been holding a bottle. Liquid sloshed inside it. Andy stared at it and a nameless fear crept over his skin.

'This,' the man said and jerked his right shoulder. The woman whimpered. 'In your mouth. Or this. Goes on your face.'

The man waved the bottle of liquid and Andy understood.

He ran forward; the man rose, bringing up the bottle of petrol, mouth open in shock, and Andy saw the woman's battered face, the blood on her thighs, the dirt and debris covering the sparse furniture. He swung his plank down to the man's hand while still running; wood struck hand and the bottle flew to crash into the wall. Instantly, the stink of petrol rose from the wall and carpet. Andy brought his plank around to strike the rapist in the face. Pain exploded in his back and he collapsed onto the mucky carpet.

The man who'd been hiding in the kitchen stood over him with a baseball bat. He was naked. The man grinned, exposing his broken teeth, and the woman sobbed as the first man levelled his foot with her face.

Then the cry filled Andy's head like a klaxon.

Save her. Please, Andy. Save her. You have to. You have to, Andy.

The world fell apart and when it came back together some time later, he lay on the floor in front of his chair. In the evening light, he jerked upright.

Andy, save her. Please, Andy.

'No more, all right? I can't do that. No more.'

Please, Andy.

A breath touched his cheek and brought the faraway sound of a girl weeping.

'No more,' he whispered.

He crawled to the window and eventually managed to stand. West London, coloured red by sunset, lay before him. He gazed at the familiar buildings, at the streets and people below. None of it made sense. Not anymore.

Save her, Andy.

A final touch of breath on his cheek came and then nothing.

His vision blurred. Tears fell and, through them, he stared at the trembling shape of his mobile.

I'll call Stu. If it happens again. One more time.

The phone mocked him with its silence and a desperate voice told him he didn't have to call Stu.

Call Katy. She'll understand. She'll help you.

A wordless noise of mocking dropped out of his mouth. He couldn't lie to himself. Calling his ex and telling her what he'd seen was insane. Even if they'd spoken at all in the last couple of months, how could he expect her to believe this?

You don't need to expect her to do anything. This is nothing to do with her. This is before her.

Away from the horror of his vision and St Mary's and back in the normal world of his nice flat with its impressive views, Andy slid against the window and dropped to sit in as small a ball as he could make.

***

She's at the pub half an hour after finishing with him. She's drunk her first drink two minutes later and she's studying the crowds thirty seconds after that.

Busy tonight. Christmas is long gone; the feel good time of the week between it and the end of the year is gone with it. Now it's the beginning of February. Last week's snow is dirty slush and there's been no sun in a fortnight.

So what, though? So fucking what? This is about her. This is her night tonight, and who cares about the cold or the snow or Will's face when she made the mistake of looking back from his front door?

What matters is here in the pub with the heat and the bodies and the noise. She gets another drink and knows she's only being served so quickly because she's leaning over the bar, exposing her cleavage. And so what about that, as well? Like it matters.

An invisible knife stabs her stomach and she breathes it out. Karen's face comes to mind and there's a dizzying second of vertigo while she thinks of her friend. It tells her to leave, to get away from the pubs in the centre of town and get back to the quiet and peace of her streets. Get back there and get to Karen's. They can talk about him, about Will; they can play some music, drink some wine and maybe she'll cry and maybe she won't. Maybe Karen's dad will give her a lift home at some point gone midnight and he'll tell her to take care like he always does, then maybe she'll wake up in the morning, ready for a Sunday of nothing at all.

Maybe.

Fuck maybe.

Another face fills her mind. Mick. Big Mick. Fat Mick. He'll understand. He's a good guy. He'll know the right things to say. He always does. She can call him and go round and talk to him and ...

She cuts the thought off before it can develop. Ending it with Will was bad enough. She can't think of Mick that way. All she'll achieve by getting in the middle of two friends is to make a bad situation even worse.

She turns in a slow, lazy circle and surveys the crowd of Saturday night drinkers.

There, at the end of the bar. Three men, all at least ten years older than her. All laugh and one looks her way.

She holds his gaze for long enough, then leans over the bar again. The barman is with her despite the other people who've been waiting for minutes. She orders two bottles of Foster's Ice, grips them by the neck and turns back to the man at the end of the bar. He speaks to his two friends and advances to her, sliding through people as if they're made of air.

She has to swallow. Her chest is too tight and the sensation is as uncomfortable as it is welcome.

Sunset, she thinks and hammers at the thought until it's dead.

'Hi,' he says.

'Hello.'

He speaks over the noise of the drinkers and music. She doesn't catch his words and he leans closer to her.

'I know it's a really bad opening, but can I buy you a drink?'

He's smiling, showing even teeth. The gel on his hair and the mint on his breath merge into one unpleasant scent.

'No. I can buy you one.'

She hands him the bottle; he takes hold of it below her hand still gripping the neck.

'I'm Dave.'

She smiles and doesn't say her name. She taps her bottle against his and sips, not looking from his eyes.

Somewhere in her past, shadows grow towards a window while twilight winds down to night. She's under the covers, deep in the dark and heat and stink while sweat covers her back.

'Who are your friends?' she asks and any thoughts of Karen, of Mick, of Will and of the sweat on her back are buried below her question.

This is her night and she's in control. The morning and all that it means is faraway. Shame and regret don't matter now she's in charge.

She tightens her grip on Dave's hand and moves ahead of him to lead him back to his friends, and for those few steps, she can ignore the wish that Mick was here instead of this man and his friends; the wish that she could talk to Mick and laugh with him and use his help to find a way of undoing this night.

Three

Mick Harris opened his pack of cigarettes and gazed at the last two in the packet. Jodie watched him without speaking.

'My last two fags,' Mick said. 'You know what this means, don't you?'

'What?'

'I'll have to start drinking more.'

She laughed and he welcomed the sound. Lately, a week or more could pass without him making her laugh. The thought stabbed at him and expanded before he could stop it.

Bollocks to lately. It's been for the last six months.

Right. But so what? Moving to Leeds hadn't been his choice. There hadn't been a choice, not if he wanted to keep his job.

Mick buried the thought and told himself coming out tonight appeared to have helped. Jodie definitely seemed happier, more relaxed.

He watched her sip her drink, then glanced at the other people in the pub. Not many out tonight. The weather probably hadn't helped. Rain, that annoying kind. Drizzling all day rather than chucking it down for fifteen minutes. Despite a decent September, summer was definitely long gone. To be expected, he supposed. October was on its way out.

'You can definitely take time off for the scan?' Jodie said. She placed a hand on her stomach.

'Yeah, course. When is it?' He smiled. 'Next Friday at ten, isn't it?'

'Ha, ha. Funny man. Monday at two. And if you really did forget, you'd be sleeping in the shed.'

She pretended to throw her orange juice at him. Mick flapped his hands in mock panic, then sipped his lager. Her eyes remained on his and he took her hand.

'Course I wouldn't forget,' he said.

'Not if you know what's good for you, you won't.'

Mick swallowed another mouthful of beer and started talking. The words came easily as they always did when he needed them to. And he needed them especially at times like this when he and Jodie were going through it. He told her about his two customers who'd come in after lunch, the ones who'd wanted a mortgage which was easily thirty grand more than they could actually afford; he asked her about the upcoming scan and told her she'd have to borrow one of his bras if her breasts grew any bigger.

They drank; other customers drank and left the pub and Mick deliberately kept his eyes off the TV. So what if the snooker was on? He'd told himself two weeks before he needed to make an effort now; she was past six months, there was no getting away from what would be here in just three months and it was about time to get himself sorted.

The cigarette packet was looking at him.

Jodie caught his gaze and laughed. Again, Mick heard his girlfriend's honest laughter and he smiled, glad to feel it on his face.

'Go on. I'll let you,' she said.

'Last two.'

'Where have I heard that before?'

Mick pocketed his cigarettes and fished in his other pocket for his lighter. 'Last two, I'm telling you. After this, it's no more.'

'If you say so.'

She tilted her head back so he could kiss her and her hand traced over his hip. A pleasurable tickling sensation ran across his skin.

'Don't take too long,' she told him.

'Don't steal my pint.'

He headed to the doors, standing aside when he reached them so a couple could enter. The man held the door, Mick passed through, nodding his thanks and moving his cigarette to his lips.

He stood against the window beside the doors, sheltered by an overhang, and watched the traffic pass. Two more smokers left the pub and stood together away from him. He glanced their way, wondering if there would be any small talk but they were involved in their own conversation. Mick faced the window and made out a little of Jodie's profile. She drank her orange juice and pulled her mobile from her bag. Probably texting her mum. Mick smiled, thinking of the scan next week but only in the practical sense. He pictured the hospital, the staff, the time it would take to get there and back and didn't let his thoughts develop from those images. His smile faded and he studied the buildings and people on the other side of the road in an effort to take his mind from hospitals and the pregnancy.

A passing bus caught his eye. It stopped in the traffic, revealing dozens of faces pressed up against the windows. Mick paused in reaching for his cigarette and stared at the bus.

Everyone in the bus was staring outside. They were all staring at him.

He took an involuntarily step backwards and hit the window. It shook behind him. The bus moved forward and there were no faces pressed up against the window. The vehicle moved through the lights, the cars and vans behind did the same and Mick had a clear view of the opposite side of the road for two seconds before traffic going the other way blocked it.

Every single person on the other side of the road was still. All of them were looking at him.

'What the fuck?' Mick said before he was aware the words were coming. He dropped his cigarette, glanced at the two men and both were looking at him. Despite their frowns, both men showed obvious concern.

'You all right, mate?' one asked.

Mick stared across the road and saw nothing but moving traffic. The wind abruptly changed direction and the rain struck his face. He swore and shifted position so he was out of the rain. The other smokers gazed at him for another moment, then returned to their conversation.

Relax, you knob. All is cool.

He pulled his cigarette packet free and gazed at the remaining smoke. One for tonight, after dinner, and that would be it. No more fags and a little less beer. Time to focus and definitely time to go back inside.

His mobile vibrated in his jacket pocket.

'Bollocks,' Mick whispered although he knew it could have been worse. The phone could have rung while he was still at the table with Jodie.

He moved his finger to answer the ringing phone and paused. There was no number displayed on the screen. There was nothing at all displayed on the screen.

The mobile continued to ring. The other smokers watched him stare at his phone; Mick glanced at the nearest man, then at the cars on the road.

They were staring at you. Everyone on the bus. Everyone across the road. They're watching you.

Something was wrong.

Right here, right now. Outside the pub with the smokers and the cars and the rain. Right here and right now, something was wrong.

Don't answer it.

The whisper in his head seemed much further away than it should have been. It was more like a memory than a thought.

Mick took a few steps away from the smokers and answered his phone.

At once, a blast of summer heat struck him. Sunlight much brighter than a few months before bashed into his eyes, blinding him; his cigarette fell to the wet ground and he smacked against the pub window.

What the hell is this?

The heat wasn't just sunlight. It was each long, hot summer day he'd ever known rolled into one savage fire. Anything good in those long days was burned into a dead husk.

A sound came: a crying child. The weeping wasn't due to physical pain. This was a child deeply upset.

A voice spoke from somewhere in the blinding light. Mick caught two words—*all right*—and wanted to bellow that no, he wasn't all right. Nothing was all right and ...

up ...

Jesus Christ, it was so fucking bright; it was so hot. It ...

summer, the end of summer, the end, Mick, please help me, please, you have to help me ...

vanished and Mick was left holding his silent mobile to his ear.

Up. Oh my God. Cheer up. Cheer up.

Wet. His hand. Wet.

Still with his mobile against his ear, Mick gazed at his other hand. The rain hadn't touched it but he could still feel wetness on his fingers, on the tips. Something warm. A solid surety told him the warm wetness had a salty tang to it.

Cheer up. Cheer up.

'I said that. I told her to cheer up.'

One of the smokers spoke to him and his words lived on the other side of the world.

'You okay, mate?'

I told her to cheer up. And I touched her face. She was crying. I touched her cheeks.

Mick lifted his free hand and stared at it, stared at tears from almost thirty years ago on the tips of his fingers.

Then there were no thoughts while the other smokers asked if he was okay and the October evening eased its way down to cold, damp night.

***

She concentrates on the wind in her hair and nothing else. She knows the headstones and grass are all around and the vicar's words come to her but they're a meaningless noise and the headstones are indistinct shapes at the edge of her vision.

The wind is a steady breath in her hair; loose strands lift from the side of her head, just above her ear, and the sensation is as if someone has whispered to her.

She glances at her father. His head is down, both of his hands holding one of her mother's. Still, the vicar's words are a drone. It's not even that he's speaking a foreign language. He's simply making a noise in the same way a bored child would.

The wind drops and, for the first time on this long day, something new registers. It's the smell of the wet grass. A great deal of rain fell in the night, and despite the rising temperature of the late morning, the grass remains wet. The aroma fills her nostrils and says this is spring. This is good spring. Here is the start of warmer days, longer hours since the clocks changed, and sudden rain showers to bathe the flowers and grass and bring the smells of freshness to the world.

Spring, and summer coming ahead.

Winter's done and summer is coming again.

She can't think of that. Not here. Let all thoughts of summer stay away in its dark and heat and stink.

I wish Will was here.

The thought comes out of nowhere. Shock or simple surprise doesn't come with it. She knows what the words mean and she can picture Will's face as easily as she can see the church across the grass. She knows the words, the name and the face but she doesn't feel them. Will isn't here and wishing changes nothing.

Her eyes move without her telling them to. She sees the headstones and she knows what they are despite the shifting and blurring of their shapes. She knows the church isn't really a drawing of a building, that its old stones are as solid as the ground below her new shoes. She could touch them if she wanted to. She could press the tips of her fingers against the centuries old stones and that would convince her it was a real object and this was a real day.

But that would mean leaving this ...this ...what is this called? All these people she stands with and isn't part of, all standing on the wet grass while this man makes drone-like noises and the long brown shape in front of that man is ...

Is.

It is a box.

No.

It is more than a box.

It isn't a big box. It doesn't need to be. Even though she'd been ...she'd been ...she'd ...

The thought chases itself into nothingness. It can't be completed. All it can do is chase itself. All she can do is stand in this pretend drawing of church grounds and wish Will was here.

The vicar's words are a note, a buzz. The smells of the cemetery and its grief and wet grass belong to someone else. And when her brother's hand slides into hers to give a reassuring squeeze, she's already feeling nothing but the breeze again playing in her hair.

Four

Will Elton slid his glasses off and rubbed his eyes. The signs that work was over for today were all with him: the smell of the ink on his fingers, the dull ache in his lower back and the rumbling in his stomach which he had ignored for too long.

He gazed at the drawing, studying it with equal parts criticism and pride, as always wondering what Karen would think of it. The monster's face wasn't perfect, but the landscape of scorched fields and the sun attempting to break through blood-red clouds was pretty decent. He'd done a fair job with the hero's posture, too. The young man on the page stood tall against the monster, sword raised in an attacking movement and the faint curve to his legs suggesting a man ready to run should the monster prove too fierce.

'Darren will like it,' Will told himself and imagined his agent's response—*nice job, Willy. You're a natural.* Karen would like it, too. With a bit of luck, the author and publisher would as well. And most importantly, it only needed a little more work before the kids would like it.

And that was job done.

Will stood, stretched and relished the cracking in his spine. He chucked his pencil onto the table and typed a quick email to his agent to tell him the work would be done in another few days. With the email sent to Darren, he studied the drawing for another moment, noting it could do with some more colour in the monster's body and the broad expanse of the hero's shoulders might need developing.

'Job is done,' he told himself, fully aware that unless he called it a day now, he'd carry on for another three hours. Amused, Will left his studio. In the kitchen, he filled the kettle, ate a couple of biscuits and spooned coffee into his mug. The microwave clock caught his eye. Just gone five. Karen would be home within the hour.

The kettle boiled; Will filled his cup, stirred it and went through to the living room, ready for a quick break with the news and his coffee before the evening ahead.

His halt in the doorway was abrupt enough for coffee to spill over the edge of the mug and splash on his fingers. He hissed, barely hearing it.

The living room was alive with aromas despite the window in the kitchen being the nearest open one. Will inhaled, attempting to name the scents. Various flowers and grass, definitely. More than those, the smell of sweat, good sweat that came from exercise.

Not exercise. Running for the sheer joy of running, playing, rolling in grass with mates and the sky above as blue as the grass below was green.

Will closed his eyes and counted to five. The phantom smells faded. Will opened his eyes.

A large sheet of paper rested on the sofa, white against the brown. Two of the cushions supported it just as they'd supported him that morning while he ate his toast. Nobody had sat there since. Nobody else had been in the house. Will gazed at the paper for a moment, not yet ready to name the apprehension in his stomach as fear. Moving with mannered steps, he set his coffee down on the table, crossed to the sofa and picked up the sheet.

A great wave of nausea flowed over him and the muscles in his legs locked, preventing him from dropping.

'What the hell is this?' he whispered in a child's voice.

Trembling rose from his legs to his stomach and up to his arms. The sheet of paper shook as if in a wind. The mixed fragrances of various flowers, grass and sweat returned, filled his nose and mouth as if he was outside somewhere miles from his house. Unwillingly, he inhaled and smelled running water and the thick stink of algae.

Sweat and grass filling a sunny day. All stuck to him in his living room. All inside his house.

The soft murmur of a girl's laugh flowed by, someone enjoying a good joke. The laughter faded as the scents of flowers and grass had. The taste remained, coating his tongue and lips.

With slow care, Will dropped the sheet back to the sofa and eased himself down to a chair at the table. The drawing was still visible from where he sat. Taking his eyes from it took a massive effort. He stared at his coffee and welcomed the white noise in his head. A car passed the house and Will glanced through the window, aware of his staring eyes and unable to relax them. Not Karen. The paper remained on the sofa; the drawing mocked him.

'This is …'

He had no words.

Will blew out a shaking sigh and squeezed his eyes closed to stop the tears. A wave of grief hit him and he did his best to think through it.

Call Karen.

Yeah. Sure. And tell her what? A drawing had magically appeared in their house? A drawing that wasn't one of his?

'Not a good plan.'

So. Okay. What then?

The drawing remained. Will stared at it and managed to croak one word before the tears fell.

'Geri.'

***

She stands utterly still despite the wind. It's much stronger up here in the car park than down on the street. Down there, it's all about the shops and the Christmas lights, the crowds and the streetlights on already. Up here, there's the darkness; there are the secrets in the car park, and there's the cold she doesn't feel.

Up here, she's untouchable.

Her fingers brush against her coat and squeeze the material. She presses harder and feels the weight of her fleece below the coat. Below that, her t-shirt. Below that, her skin, her flesh and blood. The only thing that the wind can touch is her coat and that's all right. The rest of her belongs to her.

Her eyes water when the wind changes direction to blow into her face. Her vision blurs as she attempts to focus on the Christmas lights below, and despite her watering eyes, she doesn't blink. She welcomes the blurring. Easier to not see, easier to think of below like something off a Christmas card. Streets filled with snow and people hurrying to their homes as night closes in and all is right because it's Christmas.

Briefly, the sensation of laughter fills her throat and mouth before falling apart. And isn't that how it should be? Isn't that all right?

Yes, she tells herself. This is just how it should be because this is the only way things can be made right. She made mistakes. She held it all inside when she should have let it go. If she'd done that, if she'd let it go all that time before, she wouldn't now be standing here on the edge of the car park.

Everything would be all right. Everything would be exactly as it should be.

She can fix it, though. Even now, fifteen years later, it's not too late.

She giggles, aware she's crying but not caring, not giving a shit.

Not too late? Not true. It's much too late in one respect. In the most important respect.

But still, she can make it as right as it ever will be. One little step. Just one step and all will be as it should be.

Karen's face comes to her out of nowhere, Karen from a week before, when she last saw her.

Tell me what's wrong, Karen said.

Talk to me, Karen said.

She didn't tell Karen what was wrong.

She didn't talk to Karen.

And now Karen's a week behind. She's back there and this is above the world, above the Christmas streets.

She stares straight down.

Her breathing slows.

Stops.

She closes her eyes.

There's no darkness now. Only light. She welcomes it as she would an old friend. It bathes her. It blows away all shadows and her name comes from the other side of the light.

One little step and the light is her friend.

One step.

The snow filled streets, the winking lights, the traffic, the shops and the people finishing their shopping in the middle of the Christmas card below all welcome her on the way down.

27

Five

Karen Elton closed the staff room door and checked her bag. Mobile, keys, purse. All good. With her other hand, she balanced a small box against her hip: assignments ready for marking by Monday morning. They could wait for tomorrow afternoon, though. This was all about Friday and the postponed staff meeting now finally over. Half past five and the weekend had come once again. Hallelujah and amen and so on.

Checking the mobile was locked, she crossed the corridor into the main bulk of the almost empty maths department. At the far end of the block, a cleaner vacuumed the hallway while another washed a classroom floor. The noise of the vacuum cleaners echoed along the corridors, and the scent of air freshener and bleach made a pungent aroma on all sides.

Karen headed to the doors, waved a goodbye to one of the cleaners and exited the department into cool air, thankfully free from the bleach smell behind. She inhaled, scenting the promise of a chilly night ahead. As she followed the pathway, the car park rolled ahead, mostly deserted. The last members of staff had left as soon as the meeting finished, leaving her to clear up the coffee cups. Their cars were now gone and the car park looked strangely bleak with so few vehicles on it.

Karen shook off the unexpected melancholy and listened to voices coming from the playing field. A dozen kids, all year seven boys by their look, were on the grass kicking a football around. Their jackets lay in untidy piles, their ties off and their shirts loose and untucked. One of the boys saw her and waved. She couldn't identify him well enough to name him but returned the wave anyway. He slapped another boy's arm, pointed to Karen and both children waved, then laughed together.

Holding back her smile, Karen gave them a quick wave and continued walking.

'How to make me feel old, boys,' she whispered but felt no real annoyance. The early years of her teaching career were far behind. If that meant the days of teenagers giggling at her were gone as well, then so what? Twenty, twenty-five, even thirty were behind her, now.

Letting her smile come now the kids were out of eye line, Karen crossed the school grounds, thinking of the evening ahead. Still a couple of hours to get showered and dressed before they were due at Brian and Debbie's for dinner, a couple of hours to let go of the working week and relish the two days away from the school.

'Half term soon. Thank God,' she said and laughed at herself for speaking aloud. Another week to go before the break of half term and she was already wishing that week away.

'God forbid,' she muttered and laughed again, grateful she didn't mean her cynicism. She and Will had spoken about taking a few days off to go away; the plans hadn't come to anything and she didn't mind too much. He had a lot of work on and she could do with a few days of as little as possible. A couple of days of the odd pub lunch and the odd shopping afternoon.

Smiling at the mental picture, Karen shifted the weight of the box under her arm and saw the figure standing beside her car.

She jerked to a lurching stop. A babble of thoughts sped through her mind, telling her there was no way anyone could have reached her car in the few seconds she'd not been looking at it; there was nowhere for anyone to hide on the mostly empty car park; the figure beside her car wasn't one of her students and definitely wasn't a colleague.

The sun broke free from the clouds for a moment. Light shone. The figure beside her car shone. Her hair glowed like fire.

The box under Karen's arm dropped and hit the ground. The lid fell to the side and the wind ruffled through the top few pages. Karen's feet moved, taking her forward despite the explosion in her stomach that made her want to collapse. She broke into a jog, not hearing her little, whispering breaths or the tap of her boot heels on the ground. The figure beside her car remained motionless and didn't grow into sharper focus the closer Karen got to it. She stopped at the edge of the car park, thirty or forty feet from her car and the figure. Fear announced itself, and with it, the realisation it had been with her for the last few moments. Despite being in the familiarity of the school, a panicked whisper inside told her to back away, to get away from the figure.

Karen didn't move.

Will.

Her husband's name failed to calm her down. Fear filled her chest; her breasts ached and a familiar flavour, unpleasant with its suddenness and invasion, filled her mouth.

She bent double, coughing hard, doing her best to clear her throat and mouth of the invading taste. It eased after a minute, she stood straight and the figure beside her car remained as motionless as a statue.

Karen screamed at her legs and feet to move. They did nothing. Her eyes could move even if her head couldn't, and she tried desperately to look to the side of her vision as if she had any chance of seeing the boys on the field. They were completely out of view and the only sign of life was the figure ahead of her.

Clouds passed over the sun for a moment; light broke through again and struck her. The wave of bitter cold that had enveloped her seconds before remained, despite the abrupt warmth. Wind traced the goosebumps covering her entire body.

A weak breath followed the breeze, a sigh that wasn't the light wind and Karen thought:

Oh my God. You haven't changed.

The figure beside Karen's car gazed at her; the sunlight covered her, covered *her,* not it. *Her.* Her hair. Her face. Her mouth, opening to form a shape.

Karen's name.

The car park and school grounds became a meaningless tremble. Karen's last clear sight before her legs dropped her to the ground was the figure in the car park, beckoning her.

Six

Half an hour passed in silence. Will remained on the chair at the table, coffee untouched and gaze stuck to the drawing. Normal sensation faded from his legs to be replaced by stabbing pins and needles when he shifted slightly. The pain meant nothing. Not with the drawing close enough for him to touch.

A new sound registered in slow waves through the fog around his head. He heard Karen's key in the lock and didn't move. A silent moment passed before he realised that although the front door had opened and her boots had clumped a few paces on the wood of the hall floor, nothing more had come since.

Still with his eyes on the drawing, Will spoke.

'Karen?'

He forced himself upright and the pain in his legs announced itself eagerly. Will hissed and rubbed the muscles in his thighs.

'Karen?'

Will blinked a few times, rubbed his eyes and focused on the door to the hallway.

'Karen? You all right?'

Wincing with each pained step, Will left the table and crossed to the living room door.

Karen stood in the hallway, leaning against the front door, car keys still in her hand.

'Karen?' Will said.

Her eyes moved, but much too slowly and an ugly thought muttered to Will.

That's what she'll look like when she's old.

Light coming through the frosted window in the door lit her hair but not in any way that brightened it. It was easy to picture Karen's hair grey, her skin lined and her eyes slow and tired.

'Karen?' Will said again and took lumbering steps towards his wife. Her hands rose and she was in his arms and weeping against his neck.

'I saw her,' Karen said. 'Jesus, I saw her.'

31

Will embraced her and kept his eyes closed. His mind threw up images and memories he didn't want to touch. Karen's hand found one of his and held it with a desperate tightness. Opening his eyes and not focusing on anything, Will let Karen pull him into the living room, neither speaking.

Karen fell into an armchair and Will rested on its arm, holding Karen's hair and staring out of the window into the garden. From their angle on the chair, they couldn't see the drawing and that could only be a good thing.

'What happened?' he asked and took Karen's hand. He rubbed a fingertip over her wedding ring and she gave him a ghost of a smile.

'It was …it was like it wasn't real when I knew it was completely real at the same time. Like I was asleep *and* awake. I was here and I was somewhere else at the same time. And that makes no sense at all.' Karen let out a noise somewhere between a laugh and a sob. A long pause followed; Will waited for his wife to find the words.

And while he waited, a name bled inside his head and heart.

Geri.

Seven

Karen's voice faded into silence. She'd been holding Will's hand from the moment the words broke free. She eased it from his grip in the silence and flexed her fingers. Blood filled in the white flesh. She gripped Will's hand again, holding it as tightly as she could and turned it over. Tracing the ink stains on the tips of his fingers and seeing it on his skin was no surprise although it was a comfort.

'What now?' she said and watched him debate his reply. Dull amusement filled her. Ten years of marriage and she knew her husband in ways that nobody else in the world did, and here he was trying to find a way of telling her she needed to take a break from work.

What about the picture? He can't tell me that's down to stress.

It sat on the table exactly as it had for the last fifteen minutes, mocking her by existing.

'Someone having a joke?' Will said abruptly and she gazed at him, aware he saw the flaw in his own idea. Even so, she verbalised it.

'Who?'

'God knows. Someone from Dalry? From school?'

'Who?' she said again. 'We don't know anyone who'd do something so shitty. Even if we did, why now?'

She gazed at their furniture, at the big TV, and at the patio window. Here they were in their nice house with its nice garden and their nice jobs in nice Cambridge and here they were with something that made no sense.

She glanced at Will, meaning to say something that would be as comforting as she could make it and saw the look in his eyes. All at once, she felt as if she stood a hundred feet up on a tiny ledge.

He looks young.

The panic vanished. Dismay took its place. She fought it and gazed at Will. While it might have made sense for this—whatever *this* was—to have aged him, it had done the opposite. A wildness

33

shone from his eyes. The muscles in his face jumped and one hand gripped his knee to keep his leg from jiggling. Tendons stood high on his forearm, but more obvious than those things was the something new in his face.

Not new. Old. She hadn't seen it for years.

He looks young. Oh God. What the hell is this?

Panic and fear raced through her and in an attempt to ignore both, Karen registered a third emotion. Jealousy.

She cleared her throat and remembered the taste that filled her mouth in the car park. She hadn't told Will what it was, hadn't been able to bring herself to do so.

It'll be a long time before he gets another blowjob.

Horrified laughter rose and she coughed to hide it. Ignoring Will reaching for her, she stood and her gaze landed on the drawing on the table.

It was looking at her.

There's no way we can stop this.

The thought didn't make any sense and it didn't matter. What mattered was the look in Will's eyes.

'I need to call Stu,' he said.

His mobile rang.

Eight

'Elton, you fairy,' Stu said.

His eyes were closed, had been from the moment he'd pressed a thumb over their number on his phone. Even though he'd closed his eyes and the kitchen door, he'd been unable to block out the outside world. The sound of the TV was a meaningless drone from the next room, occasionally punctuated by Lucy's giggles at Kirsty's singing. Despite the closed doors and his closed eyes, he saw his wife and daughter as easily as he would have done had they been right beside him.

He didn't want them beside him now, though. Not with this conversation.

'Stu?' Will said. And was there something other than surprise there? Yes. There was definitely *something*.

'The one and only. How's it going?'

'I'm okay. You? Shit. This is strange. I was just about to call you. How long's it been?'

Nothing since Christmas. How about that, Big Willy?

'Long time. I saw you were on Facebook a couple of weeks ago. Anyway. How's Karen?'

'Good. I'll pass you over.'

'Hold on a second, Will. Need to talk to you.'

Stu opened his eyes, gazed at the window over the sink and wished that night had come so he wouldn't be able to see the pavement and road.

'Why? What's up?' Will asked.

'You were about to call me?' he said and the pause was long enough for Stu to wonder at the fear making goosebumps rise on his arms and shoulders.

Eventually, Will managed to reply. 'Yeah. Been a strange day.'

'Been a strange few days here,' Stu said before he could stop himself.

'Why?'

Will asked his question after another pause and Stu imagined Karen beside him, listening to half a conversation. Although he hadn't seen Will or Karen in best part of a year, picturing them was oddly easy.

She's cut her hair shorter; it's at her neck now and lighter than it was. She's lost weight. So's he. Needs a shave, too. There's ink on his fingers. The tips are black.

Stu's stomach rolled. The thought wasn't his. How the hell could he know that Karen had cut her hair or that Will needed a shave?

What the hell is this?

'Stu? You there?'

'Here, Willy. Stupot in the house.'

Stu said the words before he realised he'd even thought them and a burst of pain came with them.

Will laughed and, thankfully, it sounded real. 'Shit, it's been centuries since I heard that.'

'About that long.'

There was another pause, one that still hurt but a hurt he could handle. Stu inhaled deeply several times. Brief tears fell. He wiped his eyes and said: 'It's Geri, Will. It's about Geri.'

And when Will replied, there was no surprise in his words. There was only an ache.

'Yeah. I know. She's come to see us, too.'

Nine

Andy stood beside the doors ten minutes before the train arrived in Dalry. His luggage pressed against his shins and he kept glancing at it as if expecting it to have vanished. Maybe disappeared here and returned to London without him.

Why not? Stranger things had happened lately.

He watched the fields and trees grow more sporadic as houses and roads took their place. Then industrial estates, seemingly asleep this afternoon; then roads busier the closer they drew to the centre of the city.

Andy gave it a minute's thought and decided at least eighteen months had passed since he'd last been in Dalry and that had been a quick weekend trip to see his mother. The little he'd seen in a few minutes didn't look much different to how he remembered it. A couple of tall office blocks were now flats and there looked to be some work going on beside the river, although it was hard to be sure as they passed over the water and the great clacking rose from the bridge. Beyond that, it was Dalry as he'd known it for the first twenty odd years of his life.

The thought was pleasing and Andy realised he was smiling as the train closed in on the station. He saw a tiny fraction of Thorpe Road and was unable to stop himself picturing that long road curving into the suburban areas of Dalry, of the streets he'd known, of the houses and his school.

I think I'm getting old.

The thought made him smile a little more. That smile died as he remembered the day before. Stu had called him for the first time in God knew how long and got into it without much warning.

I just spoke to Will. He said I should call you. It's about Geri, Andy.

No pause. No chance for him to think of a reason why he couldn't go back to Dalry. No time to think of the most convincing way to tell Stu he was full of shit. Only time to wonder if he was going to vomit, then time to say he'd get the train and see them all tomorrow night. As soon as he'd hung up, he shouted at himself he should have got out of it. Why not tell Stu he couldn't make it or that the whole thing was stupid or he'd be there next week? At least that would have given him some time to think.

Andy had smacked the window and relished the throbbing in his palm. It shut the voice up. Even if it hadn't, he knew why he hadn't said any of that stuff to Stu.

He'd seen. He'd been back in his childhood flat. It was real just like Will's drawing was apparently real. Having a go at Stu or saying he couldn't make it wouldn't make either less real.

Andy knew that. And still he wished to be back in London, to be anywhere but closing in on his hometown.

'Shit,' he breathed and pressed his forehead against the window. The train passed a retail park, then greenery. Andy stared at the fields, at a herd of still cows and pictured himself getting off this train in Dalry and getting straight on the next one to London. The picture was as clear as the fields and cows.

Get off the train. Get on the one going back to London and call Stu. Tell him there'd been a change of plan. He saw it as if it had already happened.

Bollocks, he told himself.

In his jeans pocket, his mobile rang. He glanced at the screen but didn't recognise the number. He answered it, raising his voice over the noise of the train wheels.

'Hello?'

'Andy?'

A woman's voice, disturbed by a crackle of interference.

'Yes?'

'It's Karen.'

'Hey, Karen. How are you? Everything okay?'

His voice sounded normal to him. And never mind about the sudden increase in his heartrate. This was Karen. This was Karen and Will and what was frightening about two people he'd known forever?

'Yeah, we're fine. Where are you?'

Another crackle came, loud enough to make him flinch.

'Almost in Dalry. What about you?'

'Almost ...' *crackle* ' ...tunnel. Should be there in an hour.'

'Good stuff. Where are you staying?'

His mouth was too dry to get the words out properly. The train was slowing and it could only be seconds before the other passengers were right behind him, pressing into him.

'Will's dad.' More interference broke Karen's voice in half and Andy flinched again.

'Karen?'

'Yeah?'

Her voice sounded clearly and Andy laughed for the first time in days.

'I'm looking forward to seeing you. Is that strange?'

She laughed as well and repeated his words to Will, then Andy caught a murmured reply. Karen came back to the phone.

'Looking forward to seeing you, too, although Will says "Pateman, you're a big poof."'

He laughed, more static crackled and it was no longer important. His fear had lessened and that could only be a good thing.

'Karen, this is a pretty bad line. I'll see you tonight, okay?'

He caught her goodbye and pocketed his mobile with relief. As he pressed it into his pocket, a soft voice asked why Karen had called him. To say hello? Not likely. Not when they'd be together in a few hours.

Behind, people filled the narrow corridor and took their luggage from the racks. Andy let the thought go. He held his bag, gripped the handle beside the door and tried to control his breathing. Through the little window in the door, the edge of the shopping centre came into view, then the bulk of it. On the surface at least, it hadn't changed at all in eighteen months. As the train passed, he kept his eyes level with the building, picturing the shops inside, the escalators, the wide seating areas and the daylight shining through the skylights. For a moment, it was easy to pretend this was just a trip to the hometown for someone's birthday or maybe a wedding. Getting off the train, squeezing through the crowds around the exit, grabbing a taxi, get to his mum's house, a shower and some food, then to the pub to see old faces and tell stories of old days.

Fat chance.

The train eased to a gradual halt. Andy tightened his hold around the handle of his bag as the door slid open and there was the platform, just a few steps away, waiting for him.

Move now or you won't ever move.

The thought sent him forward before anyone behind had chance to comment on his lack of movement. He stepped down to the platform and crossed quickly to a bench. Around, people strode from all directions, passing him, suitcases and bags wheeled on the ground. Andy pressed himself against the bench and fought the urge to throw himself back on the train and go anywhere that wasn't Dalry.

'Get a grip, you ponce,' he whispered and the words were so like Stu's that he laughed. Nobody heard it; the sheer volume of people prevented the sound from carrying. He covered his mouth with both hands as if blocking a cough and laughed again.

'This is mad,' he said and that also helped. Made it feel as if this was happening to someone else.

He glanced at his watch. 4:19. Plenty of time to get back to his mum's, shower, eat, get changed, speak to the old dear for a bit and then find out the plan. Stu hadn't specified anything during their brief conversation the day before. There'd been no need to. And definitely no need to say Geri's name. They knew what this was about.

'Course you do,' he muttered and realised he'd spoken aloud. With that realisation, another crowded in. He was more terrified now he was back home than he had been during his visions of St Mary's.

Still wishing he was anywhere but Dalry, Andy took his bag and joined the flow of people to the station exit.

Ten

Mick sat on a bench opposite the taxis and studied his mobile. Behind, the shadow cast by the Station Hotel buried him and the bench. Although the afternoon wasn't much beyond mild, the coolness in the shadow was welcome. This little spot seemed quieter than the pavements and roads. There was space to think here.

For the third time, Mick read the text he'd typed. Telling Jodie the train had been delayed and that he'd only just arrived; telling her a lie and it came easy. Telling the truth that he'd been sitting on the bench for almost an hour was just stupid and he couldn't have that. There was no way to explain it because it didn't make sense. Better to lie.

He read the text a fourth time, decided it wasn't personal enough and added three X's at the end. Putting their standard end to a text was a sham act. Adding a kiss for her and a kiss for the babies, that was something another bloke would do. *That* guy wouldn't be sitting here in the shade; that guy wouldn't even be in fucking Dalry.

'Fuck it,' Mick said and sent the text. The delivery report arrived a few seconds later. Mick deleted it and slid his mobile into his coat pocket.

Okay. Text sent. Now what?

That was obvious. Get the fuck out of here.

Mick grinned, wondering if anything had ever seemed less funny. He watched a group of teenage girls exit the station, all of them laughing, their shadows long, and their voices high. One saw him looking, nudged a friend and they both appraised him as he studied them.

Mick gave them a sunny smile, expecting abuse. The girl who'd see him first returned the smile and Mick allowed himself a snigger when she walked on with her friends.

'Girls,' he muttered.

All the pretty girls. All the smiling girls who'd come his way back in the old days. He pictured their faces, said their names in his head and said Geri's name aloud.

Geri. The one who got away.

He didn't smile at that thought.

He stood and his gaze landed on a man outside the station entrance. The man shielded his eyes from the sun and stared across the road at him.

'Andy?' Mick muttered with dumb surprise. His mind flipped back to a day that had to be over a year before, a wedding reception. Him, Andy, Stu and Will all drunk, all laughing and all promising to keep in touch.

Neil and Sarah's wedding, a voice said. *April last year. You never kept in touch.*

Andy crossed over the road, dropping his hand from his eyes to offer it to Mick to shake and Mick grabbed him, held him hard.

'Pateman, you fucker,' he said.

Andy slapped his back. 'Nice to see you, shithead. Been too long.'

The men stared at each other, luggage at their feet. Abruptly, Mick let out a great burst of laughter.

'It's been a long time, me old fruit,' he said.

'Got to be a year. Neil and Sarah's wedding, wasn't it?'

Over a year. You never kept in touch, Mick's mind whispered to him again and he wished for the voice to die.

'Yeah, probably.' He managed a smile which felt pretty close to genuine. 'Looking good.' He grabbed at Andy's beard. 'Not sure about this, though. Giving it the Peter Sutcliffe look?'

Andy sniggered. 'Fuck you.'

They stared at one another, silent for a moment.

'Stu phoned you?' Andy said.

'Will did. Said he'd spoken to Stu.'

The laughter, seconds gone, felt as if it had never been. Mick searched for something to say that would bring it back, a mention of the teenage girls, more insults. Anything.

'What happened to you?' he muttered.

Andy shook his head. 'Long story. And I need at least a few pints to tell it.'

'Yeah.' Mick pulled his mobile from his pocket, gazed at it for a moment, then put it away. 'I got a phone call. I hope I never get another one like it. I was with Jodie. We were having a drink and my phone rang.' He wiped his lips. 'Jesus, I'm sweating just thinking about it. I heard her, Andy. She was a kid. She was crying. And I heard myself. I was telling her to cheer up. I heard us as kids.' He shook his head. 'Jodie thought I was taking the piss for a minute. I wish I had been.'

They gazed at the ground, neither speaking for a moment.

'You staying at your mum's?' Mick asked.

'Yeah.'

'Share a taxi?'

Andy laughed, a healthy, honest sound. A few seconds passed during which Mick believed this was all utterly normal. They were back in town for a wedding or something like that. They'd all get together and they'd all get drunk and all would be as cool as it always had been.

'Yeah,' Andy said.

Mick lifted his bag and swung the strap over his shoulder. Andy gripped the handle of his case. An abrupt burst of fresh wind blew over them and scattered leaves.

This isn't normal. Not at all, Mick thought and tried to ignore himself. He could focus on the shitty business that had brought them here. He could think of that and be miserable and frightened. Or he could talk to his friend and be glad to see him.

He made his decision in a heartbeat.

'So,' he said. 'You still like little boys?'

The men gripped their luggage and crossed over to the taxis, both talking as the wind grew stronger.

Eleven

Stu closed the door to his daughter's bedroom and remained still, listening. He pressed an ear against the door. No sounds emerged from inside and he let out the breath he'd been holding for the last few seconds. Getting Lucy to sleep easily tonight was a huge stroke of luck. Stu knew he could have been with her for another hour at least, in and out of her bedroom while she cried or needed her nappy changing. Tonight, though, she'd dropped off in minutes which gave him plenty of time to get ready and get to the pub.

He counted to thirty silently and walked to the downstairs hallway. Kirsty stood at the kitchen door, arms folded over her breasts.

'All right?' Stu said.

'Yes.'

Stu attempted a smile. 'Yes said like that means no, you're not.'

She didn't return his smile and Stu tried to think of a way around this. There wasn't one and that was close to a relief. It meant he didn't have to think up any lies Kirsty would never believe.

He crossed to the kitchen and pulled the door shut.

'What's up?' he asked.

'I don't know. I just know something's wrong and I know you're not telling me what it is.'

Kirsty hadn't dropped her arms and there was something so horribly severe in her posture and her lack of smile that Stu wanted to lower his eyes from hers, to stand abashed like a scolded child.

'I told you. It's just a few beers with Will and the others. I told ...'

'I know what you told me, Stu. But what aren't you telling me?'

Stu gazed at his wife. Behind her, the dinner plates were still in the sink. Usually, he'd wash them, give the kitchen a clean up after putting Lucy to bed. Not tonight, though. Not enough time if he was to get to the pub by eight.

'Something's wrong, isn't it?' Kirsty said and finally lowered her arms. They hung by her sides for a moment, then her hands linked and twisted together. She didn't seem to be aware of touching her wedding ring. 'Something happened a couple of days ago.' She wouldn't look at him. 'When you came in from work on Tuesday, I knew something had happened then.' Her eyes rose to his for a fraction of a second and it was long enough for her to spear him with a look.

'Is there someone else?'

The words were beyond insane; the idea, nonsense. Stu floundered for a reply, loosely aware that doing so made it appear as if was stalling. With a huge effort, he forced the words out.

'Christ, no. Shit. There's nobody else. This isn't about that.'

She sniffed back her tears. 'So it's just you and your mates in the pub?'

'Yes.'

'Don't lie to me, Stu.'

Her words weren't a shout. Even so, they possessed more power and more anger than Stu had ever heard from Kirsty before. He stared at her, tasting the words, the truth, but unable to let it out. Fear swallowed those words. Fear for his wife and their normal life. Fear that the truth meant their normal life was finished.

'If this is just a drink with your mates, why didn't you ask me if I wanted to come?' she said.

He floundered again, aware as he spoke that he should have thought of this.

'I didn't think you'd fancy it. Plus getting a babysitter and ...'

'That's such bollocks. Any other time, you'd want me there. I know they're your mates more than ours. I know you've been mates with them for years and I don't care about that. I like them. I see them with you, and I know you like to see any of them sometimes on your own, but this still doesn't make sense. You've specifically not asked me if I want to come out. Why?'

Her anger had been replaced by hurt and confusion. Both were worse than anger.

Stu closed his eyes for a moment and discovered a new emotion. Relief. He hadn't lied to her. Not exactly. Even so, he hadn't told the truth and he shouldn't be too surprised that she'd known something was wrong.

'This isn't about anything like that. It's nothing to do with you. It's about something I heard and something Karen saw, and a phone call Mick got and Will's drawing ...'

The words trailed away. Behind Kirsty, the last of the day's sun had become dusk. Outside the open window, the breeze played over dead leaves.

'What did you hear?' Kirsty said and Stu crossed to her. He held her, hands linked around her waist. She resisted for a moment.

'I'll go out tonight, speak to the others and find out what's going on. As soon as I get home, I'll tell you all about it.'

'What did you hear?' Kirsty said again and Stu knew there was no way around this, no way to get out of it. Kirsty never let go when she had hold of something. He knew that like he knew he didn't want to see any of his old friends.

He said the words as if they were weighed down with an anchor.

'A ghost. I think I heard a ghost.'

Twelve

Will placed the four pints of lager on the table. 'This place hasn't changed in the slightest,' he said.

'Sure it has. They cleaned the toilets for a start,' Mick replied.

Will sat; Karen placed a soft hand on his leg and he welcomed the touch.

'All right. Other than cleaner bogs, it's pretty much the same.'

He glanced around. From their table close to the windows at the front of the building, he had a fair view of the whole pub. There was a small crowd at the bar although he imagined it would become busier later. Three staff served them quickly, another fifteen or twenty people sat at the few tables and in the long line of booths built into the opposite wall. He studied the floor, glad to see it hadn't changed from the same scuffed wood he'd known years ago. Still faded, still sticky, still pretty manky.

Good. So it should be.

He held back his smile, sipped his lager and watched a few people pass by on the pavement. The temperature had dropped in the last couple of days; his breath had been visible once or twice during his and Karen's walk here from his dad's house and he'd concentrated on that rather than saying much to Karen. Despite the chill, the young men outside seemed not to notice. They wore their smart shirts and trousers and didn't care about the cold. Will looked away, feeling abruptly old and tired.

The clock over the bar read 7:45. It was either time to start talking about it or time to just drink and drink and pretend none of this was real. He gazed around the pub again and then at the long seat upon which Mick and Andy sat opposite him and Karen.

'We filled this dump, didn't we?' he said and wished he hadn't. It was too early for nostalgia.

Karen laughed. 'Yes. When we weren't old enough to be in here.'

'And the beer was cheaper,' Will said.

'And all this were fields,' Andy said and laughed. Will forced out his own laugh, aware it sounded as fake as Andy's had. He sipped his lager, Karen did the same and silence fell over their table. Mick tapped his fingernail against his glass and glanced at the doors as they opened. A woman entered and Mick looked away.

'He said eight, didn't he?' Will said. He knew the answer but some words had to fill the silence.

'Yeah. Thought he would have been here by now,' Andy said quietly

'Probably helping Kirsty put Lucy to bed,' Karen muttered.

Will drank, and without conscious thought, he ran a hand over the side of his jacket. Mick caught the movement.

'The picture?' he asked.

'Yeah.'

'Can we see it?'

Will reached for his jacket and Karen pulled his arm back.

'Wait until Stu gets here. Best if we all see it together.'

Will lowered his hand from his jacket and nodded, unable to meet her eye. Mick took a large swallow of his drink, set it down and grinned.

'A bag of peanuts if any of you can tell me the name of the guy who worked here who all the girls fancied,' he said.

Karen let out a little laugh. 'Jimmy Eccles. God, I haven't thought of him in years. He had a cracking arse.' She eyed Will, grinning around her glass.

'That guy?' Will said and gave Mick a quick look. Mick dropped a wink that was fast enough for Will to wonder if it was genuine. He swallowed the urge to silently signal his friend he was grateful for such a meaningless topic of conversation.

'He looked like a bell end,' he said. 'With his designer stubble and his leather jacket.'

'And his nice arse,' Mick said and Will flicked beer foam at him.

'You've got me to fantasise over,' he said to Karen and she thumped his arm.

'Yeah. Fantasise you wash the dishes and stop pissing on the toilet floor.'

'Or wash the floor and piss on the dishes,' Mick said.

Relaxed for the first time in two days, Will laughed. He caught Andy looking at him and a flash of a thought that they shouldn't speak of what had brought them together lived and died in a heartbeat.

'We really going to wait for Stu?' Andy asked and Will's laugh fell away.

'Probably should,' he said.

Andy tapped on his glass as Mick had. He spoke without any emotion.

'Why did you phone me, Karen?'

She frowned. 'When?'

'When I was on the train. You called me.'

Her frown deepened and she drank her beer for a moment. 'To say hello. To see how you were.' She shrugged. 'No big reason. Why?'

Will knew he should keep his eyes on Andy's, keep in control rather than let the lie show on his face and in his downturned gaze. Even so, he couldn't look from the table and his beer.

'Really?' Andy murmured.

'No. Not really,' Will said and forced his gaze up to Andy's face. 'Stu asked us to call you.'

'Why?'

Will glanced at Karen. She nodded.

'He was worried you wouldn't come back,' Will said and wished it sounded even a little less shitty to say such a thing.

Andy remained still for a moment. A slow, unwilling smile trickled over his face before he let out a harsh laugh.

'Well, I've heard funnier one liners,' Mick said. Andy ignored him.

'I wondered if that was it. What's it been? Eleven, twelve years since we all lived here, since we did this.' He waved a hand, encompassing the pub, encompassing Dalry, Will realised. 'And he hasn't changed. Still the one in charge of all of us. Sad thing is, he was right. On the train, I was about three seconds away from getting off it and getting on the next one back to London.' He sighed, a weary breath that trembled from his mouth.

'Why didn't you?' Karen asked.

'How could I? Not with all this. Not when it comes to you lot.'

Mick cackled and clinked his glass on Andy's.

'Not when I keep seeing the flat I lived in when I was a kid,' Andy whispered.

Mick shifted in his seat but didn't speak.

'We should wait for Stu,' Karen said quickly and Will kept his mouth shut. Something had come to their table in the last few seconds; something made of why they were back. And if Andy wanted to tell his story, then he would tell it whether Stu was here or not.

'I'm seeing it like I see this table, all you lot, the windows. It's all real, not like I'm just thinking about it or looking at a photo. It's completely real. And it's a rough place. I mean, a proper dump. The sort of place you see in films about drug dealers and dodgy bastards.' Andy's gaze remained fixed on his pint. Will stared at the bubbles in his friend's lager and wanted to be anywhere else.

'There are broken windows and graffiti and all that everywhere. The lifts are broken and I can hear screams from upstairs. So I go up there; the screams are coming from my old flat. Number nineteen.' Andy laughed hollowly. 'I go down to it and there's a guy in there, raping a woman. He tells her to give him a blowjob or he'll pour petrol on her face.'

'Christ,' Mick whispered. His fingers were wrapped around his glass tight enough for his knuckles to have turned white. Andy still hadn't looked away from his drink and Will wondered if his friend could still see the pub and the people around it.

'I run into my old flat, smack the guy with a plank of wood and another guy comes out of the kitchen and hits me with a baseball bat.'

He took a deep swallow of his lager and wiped foam from his lips.

'It's happened a few times. I only had the balls to go into the flat the last time. I came back to my own flat when the second guy hit me.'

Will realised he was squeezing Karen's hand only when she winced and eased hers from his.

'Sorry,' he said. She gave him a distracted smile and rubbed her fingers.

'What would have happened if you hadn't come back to your own flat?' she said to Andy and he shrugged.

'God knows. They probably would have bummed me.' Will heard the forced humour in the words just as he'd seen Andy's forced smile. 'They looked like the sort of nasty bastards who'd do anything to anyone just for the hell of it.

'The question is what has that got to do with Geri?' Mick said. Will flinched, unable to stop it. Mick saw the movement.

'Come on, man. We have to really talk about her sooner or later. This is all about her, isn't it? I mean, I get a call from her; I hear her crying and then I hear myself telling her to cheer up. Stu hears her calling his name inside his head. You get your drawing, whatever it is, and Karen sees her at school. What's Pateman's old flat got to do with her?'

'You say that like the rest of it makes sense,' Will said. His hand trembled as he reached for his drink.

'None of this makes sense,' Mick shouted and stared at the people on the closest table when they glanced at him.

The pub doors opened and Stu was there. He stood, framed by the doors. Illumination from a streetlight ran ahead of him onto the dirty floor.

Silence, long and thick, span out. Then Will was up, arms outstretched to embrace his friend.

Thirteen

They encircled the table, the pub busier now, louder. The background music had increased in volume and they needed to raise their voices to be heard. Surprising herself, Karen welcomed the noise. It all made the pub feel like a pub should on a Friday night. Months had passed since she and Will had been to a pub on a weekend night, but even so, the noise, the bulk of people and the smells of different drinks all joined together to make everything feel as it should be for friends in a pub on a Friday night.

'How's Jodie?' Stu asked Mick.

'Good. She's good. Getting fat. You know how it is.'

'As fat as you?'

'Not quite. Working on it, though.'

Stu squeezed the flesh on Mick's chest. 'You could do with one of her bras,' he said.

'Na. She won't let me wear her underwear, anymore.'

Stu laughed and lifted his beer. 'Cheers, all. Good to see your asses again.'

The others lifted their drinks and a mutter of *cheers* ran around the table. They tapped their glasses together, and for a second, Karen let herself feel happy. It passed and a suggestion of fear took its place.

'Lucy all right?' Andy said.

'Yeah. Fine. Almost lets us sleep for a whole three hours these days.'

'Kirsty?' Karen said.

'Yeah. We had a few words before I came out.' He paused and appeared to consider. 'I had to tell her the truth about tonight. She didn't believe it was just a drink and a get together.'

He dropped his gaze from Karen's and sucked his teeth. He took a long swallow of his beer and nobody broke the silence.

'So, what's the scores on the doors?' Stu said, placing his glass down. 'We all okay?'

Karen noticed a look pass between Mick and Will. She leaned forward, resting on her elbows.

'We've done all that, Stu. The catch up.'

'Without me?' he said, pretending hurt.

'Afraid so. We need to talk.'

At once, all his pretence vanished. He looked scared and tired. 'Yeah. I know.'

Will slid the folded sheet of paper out of his jacket pocket and didn't open it. 'This was in our house yesterday and it isn't one of mine.'

'You sure?' Mick said and Will raised an eyebrow, still holding the sheet. 'No, I mean, maybe it's like that writing thing.' He mimed writing in the air. 'You know. Those fruits who think if they hold a pen to paper, then something comes through them and writes. It's not them writing. It's someone else.'

He dropped his eyes and chewed his lower lip.

'Automatic writing?' Karen said.

'It's not that,' Will said.

'Yeah, but hang on a sec.' Andy raised a hand. 'It *could* be. Say you were in a trance or something like that. You wouldn't know you did it, right? You could have drawn that and not even know it.'

Will's jaw clenched and Karen mentally told him to calm down. With great care, he unfolded the sheet of paper.

'You know my stuff. How I draw. My style.' He swallowed a few times before he managed to get the rest of the words out. '*That* isn't how I draw at all, so even if I *did* draw it without knowing it, it still means it's someone else's work.'

Every line of the drawing had imprinted itself on Karen's mind since the day before. Even so, she stared at the image with the same sense of wonder and fear as she knew the others felt.

The girl at the window. The building. The grounds around the building. And the day, summer in all its glory, all its warmth and colour soaked into the paper through simple ink. The naked blue sky, the streaming yellow, the trembling in the air as heat rose from the ground, baking as it flowed upwards.

The girl at the window. Her face. Her smiling face, full of love, full of hope. The gun in her hands.

Mick leaned back into the seat, hand over his eyes but not before Karen had seen all the colour gone from his face.

Stu reached a shaking finger to the figure at the window and touched the lines of the face.

'Geri,' he said. 'Jesus Christ.' He stared at each of them. 'It's her, isn't it?'

'Yes.'

Karen felt the weight of her one word and wanted to take it back, to deny what she was looking at.

Geri. What is it? What do you want?

The face at the window, framed by her red hair. It was like looking at a photo.

'It's her.'

Stu withdrew his finger and rubbed repeatedly at his mouth. Will folded the paper and didn't put it back in his jacket.

'Let's talk,' he said, facing the table.

Andy barked a mirthless laugh. 'Fine. Let's talk. What the fuck are we doing here? What the fuck are we doing in Dalry? What's this about?'

'Chill, Pateman,' Mick said and Andy rounded on him fast.

'Chill? Bollocks. This isn't just mad. It's impossible. It's ...'

'It's true,' Karen said. 'And you know it.'

'How can it be true? Geri's dead. She's been dead for best part of ten years.'

Karen heard her next words as if they belonged to someone else. 'That doesn't seem to matter to her.'

Fourteen

Andy eased his way through the crowded bar, two pints held tight against his chest. Stu spoke behind him and the words were lost below the sound of the Friday night drinkers. He stepped nimbly to the side when two teenage girls walked towards him fast. One of them might have apologised; it was hard to tell in the noise. He pressed himself against the underside of the stairs in the centre of the pub floor and Stu joined him.

'Okay?' Stu said.

'Yeah. Just trying not to get knocked over.'

A laugh bubbled up from somewhere far below and he wanted to ask Stu if the night seemed as insane to his friend as it did to him. To go from discussing their dead friend to fighting their way back to the table in a crowded pub was utterly surreal.

A gap opened in the crowd; Stu marched forward, holding three pints, and Andy followed. He sat close to Mick who pushed at him in mock disgust.

'Queer. You trying to sit on my lap?' Mick said.

'Knobber,' Andy said and managed a real laugh. It was wonderful to be able to do this, to laugh when nothing made sense, and to slip back into old habits that had died years before.

A scream rang out from somewhere above. Andy jerked his head up, stared at the steps and saw nothing unusual. Coldness crept up and down his body.

The scream had been the same as before. Exactly the same. He studied the others. None of them had reacted to the noise which made sense. It was his vision, after all. His share of Geri.

Relax. They're all here. You're all part of this.

'One thing that occurred to me earlier,' Karen said and looked at Stu. 'Geri's parents.'

'Diane and Gary, wasn't it?' Andy said, still watching the stairs.

'Yeah.' Stu nodded. 'They moved years ago. Got to be seven at least. Maybe eight.'

'I thought it might be worth, you know, speaking to them.'

'What? To ask them if their dead daughter has been in touch?' Andy meant his words to come out light. Instead, they were waspish. He lowered his head. 'Yes, I know I'm a twat.'

'Yeah, we know.' Mick shoved him. 'Don't change.'

Andy managed a little laugh. 'What about her brother? What was that guy's name?' he asked.

'Phil,' Karen said. She glanced at Stu. 'Any ideas?'

'I think he moved, as well. Don't know where to.' He gripped his pint and spoke without meeting anybody's eye. 'One thing I thought of earlier. Maybe it's worth going to Geri's grave.'

He drank his beer as if embarrassed.

'Why?' Andy said and did his best not to sound peevish.

'Why not?' Mick said, shrugging.

'No. I mean, it's not like she's going to be there, is it? We can't talk to her there any more than we can talk to her here.'

'Where else is there to go? Her house? Even if her parents still lived there, we could hardly knock on the door and ask to come in, could we?' Stu spoke without anger and Andy wondered if anger might have been better than the tiredness in Stu's voice.

'When did you last go to her grave?' Karen asked.

'Last year. Went on her birthday. Felt like I should, you know.'

They drank for a moment. The doors opened and closed as a crowd left to be replaced by several women.

'Is that the plan, then? Go to her grave?' Mick said.

'Now?' Andy said, unable to hide his surprise.

'Could be an idea,' Will said and Andy knew his face showed his dislike of the idea. He couldn't help it, though. Will spoke again.

'I know it sounds nuts, but what else can we do? We've all had some kind of contact with Geri and it doesn't matter that she's dead. She's still got in touch with us. She obviously wants something and it seems pretty clear it's to do with this.'

Will tapped the sheet of paper.

'But Geri with a gun, that's just bollocks,' Andy said. 'Who the hell would she want to kill?'

'Maybe we should ask her,' Mick said.

Andy traced the tips of his fingers over Will's paper.

'Can I?' he said.

Will nodded and Andy slid the paper over the table. Watched by the others, he opened it and studied the drawing again.

Despite knowing the situation was crazy, he couldn't get away from the drawing. While he wasn't an expert on Will's style, he knew enough about his friend's work to know this wasn't Will's. While this drawing definitely had the detail in Geri's face and the building she was inside, it lacked Will's attention to the rest of the scene. Whoever had drawn this was an expert at faces and identity and colour, but they weren't too fussed about background.

It's not about background. It's about Geri with a gun.

Andy folded the paper in half and slid it back to Will.

'Best put it away,' Mick said. For once, he didn't sound as if he was joking.

'Yeah.'

Will pocketed the drawing and took Karen's hand. Andy studied Will and Karen and the firmness with which Will held her hand. Briefly, Andy wondered if they had spoken about Geri and what the situation meant to Will in ways it didn't to the rest of them.

'So say we go to her grave. Then what?' he said.

'Bollocked if I know, but it has to be worth a go,' Stu replied.

They talked for another few minutes. Andy listened to their conversation, wishing he was surprised that their words didn't seem to mean anything. He finished his drink, watched Stu and Mick do the same, and pulled his coat on.

'Okay. Let's go and see our dead friend.'

He'd meant for his statement to be a joke, to be as light as something Mick would have said. Instead, it belonged to the voice of a bitter man, unable to believe what had happened.

'Sorry. That sounded different in my head.'

'Knob jockey,' Mick said and gave him a loose hug. 'We'll let you off.'

Will and Karen pulled on their coats; Karen swallowed the last of her drink and nobody moved from the table. Stu glanced at the others and pointed towards the doors, now hidden by Friday night drinkers.

'We go, we get a taxi, we see Geri's grave and we go from there. If nothing happens, we come back here and get shit faced. How's that sound?'

'That's a plan and a half,' Mick said.

Stu led them towards the doors, sliding between people, conversation impossible in the noise. A few steps from the two bouncers, Stu pressed himself against the wall and faced them.

'We're all okay with this?' he asked, voice raised over the mix of music and conversation. He looked at each of them in turn and Andy stuck his hands into his jeans pockets to stop them shaking. 'We all know what we're doing?'

'Yeah. Sort of,' Will said.

Stu scratched at his mouth. 'We all believe this, don't we?'

His mouth trembled and Andy couldn't think of a time he'd seen Stu so miserably frightened.

'Yes. I don't think we have any choice,' Karen said.

'Yeah,' Will murmured.

'I'd rather eat my own leg than be here because of this,' Mick said. 'But doesn't look like I have much choice.'

'Is that a yes?' Karen asked him.

He smiled, nodded and wiped at his damp eyes.

Will appraised Andy and the words were coming up, furious words at Will, telling him to fuck off, telling him this was all a load of shit.

'Yeah,' he said and his vision wavered with his tears. He inhaled sharply, held the breath and let it go.

The world changed.

Stu was walking to the doors, the bouncers were opening them and the cold of the night was coming to them.

The world changed.

Karen and Will were following Stu, hands linked. Mick was turning to him, hand reaching for his shoulder and his mouth opening.

The world changed.

All the colour fell out of Mick's face and out of Will and Karen's coats, then out of the walls, then out of the floor. Everything around him became a dead grey. The steady beat of the music dropped into a tuneless drone; the men and women around him and crowding the long bar became transparent. Andy stared through them, tasting the cry in his mouth and wondering from far off if it would be as faded and ghostly as everything around when it finally arrived. The drinkers became shadows and the sounds of their voices and laughter were the distant rumble of thunder.

The grey of the floor vanished. The floor was gone. Andy stared at an endless black that dropped into nothing. He stood over it, a meaningless mote in the void.

His cry finally broke free and he fell into the nothing, Mick beside him, Stu, Karen and Will above, then below. Black swallowed him.

The world was darkness.

Darkness lit with little lights.

Fifteen

Mick threw himself upright, staggered a few steps forward and fell to his knees. Momentum carried him further and he dropped to the grass. His breath pounded in his chest; he coughed and tried to ignore the dizziness spinning in his head. He pushed himself upright and gazed at his surroundings. Dim moonlight shone on the grass for a circle of a few feet.

'Grass,' he said.

His mind made no attempt to explain the situation or to accept it. The small part of his consciousness that seemed to be outside this told him there was no way of explaining it. It just was and there was nothing more to it.

'Right,' he said and stood.

Pain rolled up his legs. He rubbed the fronts of his thighs. The pain must have come from a sharp impact. The ache suggested it had been a few minutes before.

'Right,' Mick said again and studied the area.

There was little to see. The moonlight didn't stretch far; the grass was more or less featureless. Not wanting to take his eyes from the land, Mick pulled his mobile from his pocket and quickly checked the screen. No signal. He stared at it. No time, either. Knowing it was pointless, he selected Stu's name. Nothing happened.

Mick pocketed his phone and hugged himself. Wherever the hell he was, the temperature had fallen a few degrees since he'd left the house. Earlier, it'd been maybe ten or eleven degrees. Not too bad for the third week of October, and he'd gone to the pub in a jacket over a chunky sweater. Now, his big coat, the one he'd bought for his and Jodie's holiday to New York last Christmas, would have been handy.

Mick jammed his hands in his pockets. With little thought, he walked in the same direction he faced, taking slow steps over the grass. The plan, such as it was, meant walking to a recognisable landmark, see if he could find a phone or get a signal and call the others. Then get back to the pub or Stu's house or somewhere that made sense and find out what the fuck had happened between standing beside the pub doors and finding himself here.

Geri. What the hell is all this?

His breath danced ahead of his mouth and tightness embraced his chest. It couldn't be more than five or six degrees out here. More like late November than October.

He stumbled as the grass vanished and he stood on a path.

It ran to his left and right, curving away out of sight after a few steps. Mick squatted, placed his hand on the cold ground and traced a finger over the cracks that filled it.

A path goes somewhere.

True, but this path didn't look particularly well-travelled. The moonlight shone on cracks and lines. Grass grew over its edges and tatty weeds jutted from many of the cracks. Mick stood again and gazed ahead. From the little he could see of the grass, it appeared to rise and dip a little just ahead. He stared straight in front and wondered if he could actually see a shape or if his mind was simply making shapes out of nothing because it desperately wanted to place his surroundings.

Only one way to find out.

He moved forward again, counting his steps. After fifteen, he stopped and gazed at the fence. Like the path, it was full of cracks and obviously old. Mick scratched at it. The night air filled the wood with its cold. Mick lowered his hand and stared at the houses on the other side of the fence. No lights shone in windows. No sounds came from them.

He knew where he was.

'Atherstone Road,' he whispered and the chill in the grass ate into his boots.

The grass of Atherstone Park.

Twenty-four years, a voice said to him and there was no need to argue or debate. The voice was right. Twenty-four years since he'd been here, standing on this field as a twelve-year-old boy, playing football with his mates while his home was visible on the other side of the fence.

Staring at his childhood home, Mick pictured the road, the houses and the small patches of grassland all a matter of feet away. He hadn't walked on them in over half his life and that didn't matter. They were here, right in front of him.

Mick's fear had been with him since he'd begun walking. Now it spoke, asking where were the others and why were no lights on in any of the houses?

Everyone's asleep.

Right. Because everybody went to bed at half nine, didn't they? *You don't know what time it is. Could be later than it was in the pub.*

That didn't help. If time he couldn't account for had somehow passed between their last conversation in the pub and finding himself here, that changed things.

How come nothing's changed here?

He stared at the fence, then the silent houses. The thought was right. Not only did the park appear exactly as it had when he was a kid, the houses also looked the same.

Mick jerked around at a sudden sound, saw nothing and strained to hear. It came again: a scraping. Something on wood. Something on the fence.

Mick backed away fast, attempting to look in all directions at once. Nothing moved in the dark. He clenched both hands into fists, stood still and listened. The scraping muttered again, a pause, then a thud.

Someone had just jumped over the fence.

Mick's fear exploded into terror. Still straining to hear, he trotted back towards the path, stood on it and faced the fence. Something moved over the grass. A man dashed towards him, hunched and silent. Mick threw himself to the side as the man lunged at him and stumbled. The man dropped and swung his baseball bat. It hissed in the air, missing Mick's stomach by an inch.

'Christ.' Mick kicked the man in the thigh. The movement was clumsy, the blow only a weak connection of boot to leg.

The man let out a hacking wheeze that descended into a laugh. A stink of dirt and waste hit Mick's nostrils. He gagged. The man smelled as if he lived in his own shit. Mick jumped backward as the bat came close again.

'Who the fuck are you?' Mick shouted. 'What the hell is going on?'

The man wheezed. His face wasn't completely visible. He wore a scarf over his neck and mouth, leaving only pale cheeks and dark eyes exposed. Lank hair covered his forehead in dirty curls. With a fast, unthinking eye, Mick noted the man's clothes of a long coat, torn in many places and stained, black jeans full of holes, and battered boots below his jeans. Options sped through Mick's mind. The nutcase was drunk, stoned or just mental. None mattered as much as the bat.

'Put it down.' Mick's voice shook. 'The bat. Drop it.'

The guy wheezed another laugh. His hand shot around, bringing the bat towards Mick's feet. Mick jerked back and the man leaped upright.

'Kill,' the man said. 'You.'

'Fucking drop it,' Mick shouted.

The attacker jerked forward with a stabbing movement. Mick stepped back and sprinted across the grass. At once, the man ran after him and primitive survival kicked into Mick's brain.

The fence to his right had been a hundred feet when he was a kid, then the slope, then trees, then the embankment down to the dual carriageway. He had to get to the trees.

Behind, the loon closed in; Mick streaked to his left, then back right. Bitter air burned in this throat. He upped his speed to the maximum and felt the ground rise. He veered left again and the trees, all bare and dead, were right in front.

There'd be nowhere to hide in the little wood. Mick shot back to the right, then threw himself into the trees. He crashed against one, ducked, and the man with the bat raced towards him. Mick's foot lunged, the man hit it and flew forward. Mick leaped, crashed into the cackling figure and they both dropped. Screaming, Mick pummelled at the man's face, fists breaking skin, blood on his knuckles, skin split. Still screaming, Mick pounded at the man's head until fire made his hands cook. Sobbing, he crawled backwards and leaned against a dead tree trunk. His hands burned with pain. He lifted them to his face; blood coated his fingers. Wincing, he flexed them. They moved but not without a deep, throbbing hurt.

Nothing broken. Nothing but that guy's face.

Mick's stomach rolled. Not looking to see if the man was conscious, he grabbed the baseball bat and gripped the cold handle. A splinter stabbed his thumb. He wiped a thin line of blood on his jeans and walked down the slope, breathing as quietly as his panting breath would allow, sobbing as quietly as he could.

Sixteen

Will's first thought:

Karen. Where's Karen?

The second:

Fire.

He rolled, hit a wall and groaned. He made it upright by holding on to the wall, and stared into nothing. Shapes surrounded him, all too indistinct to identify. None of them mattered, though. Something was burning. Something below.

Heat rose to his feet, then up. Will squatted, touched the ground and withdrew his hand quickly. The floor, wherever he was, was too hot to touch. Moving like a blind man, Will stretched his arms out, splayed his fingers and felt his way forward. Three steps took him to the edge of a piece of furniture. Metal. Cold. Low down.

'It's a bed,' Will whispered, leaned forward and felt a soft mattress. He pressed and his fingers hit something damp, something he instinctively knew to be unpleasant. He wiped them on the frame and heard the crackle of the fire below. Smoke hadn't reached the room yet. Even so, the sound was enough to push Will close to panic. He edged along the end of the bed and his feet hit a pile of soft things. He kicked them gently and some fell to the side. Steeling himself, Will bent and felt the soft objects. Wool, maybe. Something old. And was that denim?

Clothes? What the hell is this?

It was a bedroom. He was in someone's bedroom and the room below was on fire.

Will wiped sweat from his forehead, tried to think clearly and heard a great bark of laughter from straight ahead, high and excited.

Still with his fingers splayed, Will stepped forward and hit a long line of some thick material. He pulled at it; dust and dirt coated his hands, and he pulled again. The dust played over his mouth and nose. He recoiled, coughing, and yanked hard. A brief burst of cold air hit him from somewhere in front and the rumble of the fire pulsed in reply.

'Karen,' Will said without hearing the word. He pulled again; more ugly laughter rang out, then the unmistakeable sound of breaking glass below. Cheers.

Cold air. Rough material.

Curtains. And a hole in the window on the other side.

Yelling, Will yanked again. The material tore, dust flew and the curtains collapsed. He threw them off, coughed the filth from his mouth and gazed at the moonlight breaking in through the hole in the glass.

It shone on him and the curtains. It shone on the mess of broken furniture and old clothes on the floor. And it shone on the ghastly stains on the bed.

His bed.

He was in his bedroom, the bedroom he'd slept in for the first twenty-one years of his life, the bedroom his dad now used as a study.

It was exactly as it had been the day he'd left home, down to the posters on the walls. Only back then, they hadn't been torn and defaced. Back then, there hadn't been illegible graffiti sprayed on each wall, drawings and words that didn't make sense.

'Fuck this,' Will whispered and stared through the hole in the window. The stink of the smoke had grown stronger. His panic, muted for a moment by shock, returned and he shouted through the hole.

'Hey. I need help. There's a fire.'

Movement below. Will saw a few figures, then others, come from the front of the house. Ten of them. Maybe twelve. They gazed up at him. None reacted to his cry.

'Hey,' Will roared.

One of the figures took a few steps forward, pulling an object from their coat pocket.

It was a bottle.

A second figure joined the first's side. A spark in their hand and the rag in the neck of the bottle was alight.

The bottle flew through the air, a little fire rising, then falling towards Will's bedroom window.

He screamed once and dropped. The bottle passed his window, then fell. Glass broke; a soft woof of fire and more laughter, high and childish, followed it.

Will managed to stand. A small patch of the grass at the side of the house was aflame. The figures ran back to the front of the house and Will finally saw how small they were. The kids ran to his front door, coming through the fire they'd started, all coming to him.

Will moved without any conscious thought. He grabbed a chunk of wood from the floor, didn't think of it as a piece of the desk he had used for homework and threw it at the window.

Glass exploded and dropped to shower the grass. Will took another jagged piece of wood, smashed more glass and boosted himself up to the ledge. Fiercely cold air coated his skin.

'Karen,' Will whispered.

There were no figures on the grass. The fire from the Molotov cocktail they'd thrown at him had almost extinguished itself. The conflagration below had become a full roar and there could only be seconds before the kids made it up the stairs and smashed through the bedroom door.

Will jumped.

He hit the bushes, fell and lay winded on the grass. Above, a full moon shone from a deep black sky. There were no stars.

'Karen,' Will croaked.

He rolled and realised he was still holding the piece of wood he'd used to smash the window.

Voices above. Shouts. Jeers.

Will stood and ran drunkenly. The shouts changed from excitement to anger. Will dashed alongside his burning home, reached the front garden and raced for the path ahead. Following it brought him to a cycleway. He left that, took a cut lined by black hedges and smelled water. Despite the cold, the water was gorgeous compared to the reek of smoke and dirt which still clung to him.

Will ran in a straight line, crossed another cycleway and hit grass. The aroma of water abruptly grew sharper. Will crossed the grass, wood against his leg and realised where he'd unconsciously been heading for safety. Monk's Cave was straight ahead. Picturing the creek which ran from the boulders and shallow pond of the cave to the river was as easy as it had been when the burning shell behind really had been his home.

Will reached the trees which grew around Monk's Cave and bare twiggy branches stabbed him. Brushing them aside, he crept into the shadows of the Cave and squeezed between two rocks. Behind, a metal gate blocked access to the interior as it always had and thinking of the complete dark inside sent waves of coldness through Will.

Relax. Just stay quiet.

As if on cue, the laughter of the kids who'd burned his house answered him.

Will pushed himself further down between the boulders. His jacket shifted upwards, taking his shirt with it. His skin pressed against the rock; he jerked in shock at the cold and grazed his back.

A hiss escaped his mouth. He clamped his lips together, reached to his back and pulled his jacket down. The cold clamped on his arms, chest and face, eating into him, and his breath was fog in the air. Will ducked his head and did his best to still his breathing. The voices drew closer and there was something wrong with the words, something that made them sound like gruff barks more than actual words. One of the kids, a young boy by the sounds, said *water*. Another replied with a shouted *no*, and their steps drew closer to Monk's Cave. Below the steps, a soft crackling rose. Will squinted through a tiny gap in the rocks. The kids carried flaming torches. Four of them. The sticks were simple makeshift lights, casting shadows in a wavering circle around the group.

Someone barked *water* again and the group headed to the river. Will readied his legs to launch him. If he made it to the grass and back to the path, he could outrun the little bastards and get somewhere safe, find some help.

A scream rang out, sexless, full of fear.

Will jerked upright, exposing his location. The torches lay on the grass close to the edge of the river. He saw running shapes, heard a tremendous splash of water. Someone shrieked, and then silence. The torches burned on the grass. Nothing moved.

With shaking legs, Will crept out from the boulders and edged along the creek a few yards. With the thin light cast by the moon and the glow of the torches, a small fraction of the river was visible. The surface didn't move. Holding himself, shivering with cold and delayed reaction, Will crossed to the nearest torch. Not comfortable with taking his eyes off the water even for a second, he fumbled picking up the torch and came close to burning his hand. Swallowing repeatedly, he moved a little closer to the water.

A massive, howling laugh crashed over him, booming out of the river and from the opposite bank.

Will dropped the torch and ran for his life.

Seventeen

Mud pressed against Stu's face. He shoved his hands down against the cold ground and pushed himself up. Mud stuck to his lips. In disgust, he brushed it off and blew the remnants from his nostrils. The smell clung to his nose and he wiped at his face, shivering.

He rose, staring at the house in front. It was instantly familiar. 'Mum? Dad?'

His voice sounded as if it belonged to someone much younger. Stu took a few tiny steps to study the little of the garden he could see. He finished by facing his parents' home. It appeared to be normal other than the lack of lights in any window.

'Normal?' he whispered. 'How the hell is this normal?'

A memory hit him and he swayed as if blown by a strong wind.

This was what he had seen a few days before at work. His parents' house like something that belonged in a warzone, the whole street nothing but empty houses with smashed in windows.

He stared at the fence on one side and the high row of bushes on the other, expecting the others to be with him, expecting the pub to be there and their conversation about Geri to continue as if it had never stopped. The cold bit at him; he was vaguely glad he'd been wearing a decent sized fleece despite the night not really calling for it. This was winter, not autumn.

'Will?' he whispered and didn't even get the breeze as a reply. 'Karen?'

A ghastly mixture of panic and fear made his stomach cramp. There were too many corners and dark patches in the garden. Anything could be inside them.

Fighting his fear, Stu crossed the garden towards the house, planning on knocking on the back door, getting inside and calling the others. He stopped after a few steps and gazed at the remains of the kitchen window.

A jagged hole spread from the middle of the pane, leaving sharp teeth of glass poking in and out. His gaze moved to the living room window, then up to his parents' bedroom. All the windows were broken. And there was something on the back door.

Stu moved closer. Spray paint. Covering the width of the door, a smiling face gazed at him with mocking humour. Seeing the childishly drawn graffiti on the door to his parents' home brought a new emotion to Stu. Anger. It mixed with his fear and fermented in his mid-section.

Keep calm, he told himself.

He moved alongside the house to the side passage. The moonlight didn't reach that far and the few steps to the gate were horribly black. Stu paused, one hand touching the brickwork of the house.

Mobile.

Cursing himself for not having thought of his phone, Stu took it from his pocket and cursed aloud. No signal. He pocketed it, then pulled it free again.

'No time. No date. Handy,' he whispered.

Moving forward, he slid his phone into his pocket and kept his other hand on the side of the house. His foot hit the gate; it rattled with a sound that was too loose. Stu fumbled until he found the handle and opened the gate. It let loose a tired creak which didn't stop until Stu held the gate still and gazed at the front garden.

It was a scorched mess. Even with a lack of light, Stu could see the burned grass, the flowerbeds ravaged by flame, and the remnants of the tree trunks. The garden hadn't simply been burned. It'd been torched.

Stu closed the gate behind himself, walked to the centre of the garden and studied the front of the house. Like the back, the windows were broken. The same smiling face had been painted over the door.

'Bastards,' he whispered and had no idea at whom the word was aimed. Wind gusted; he shivered and considered entering the house. At once, horror rose and he rejected the idea. Wherever the hell he was, it wasn't outside his parents' house. This was a nightmare place and he wasn't going inside the building in front of him. No chance.

'Where to, then?' he asked himself and knew the answer.

Back to the pub. Back to the place he'd been with his friends. Stu pictured the route. At a fast walk, he'd need fifteen minutes to return to the pub.

A rhythmical sound, something tapping, reached Stu. He walked to the pavement and named the sound. Running feet. Lots of them, coming closer. Exactly as they had during his vision of this place.

Another whisper spoke, this one from a long-silent corner of his mind concerned only with survival. The whisper muttered with a nameless fear that told him to run before whoever was sprinting closer reached him.

The sound grew louder. Whoever they were, they'd arrive in seconds.

Stu jogged to the pavement, faced both ends of Huntsman's Walk and jogged to his right. Within a few seconds, his jog became a run. He crossed over the road, hit a wide stretch of grass and stopped beside an oak tree.

The runners were still coming closer.

Stu ran over the grass and reached the end of Huntsman's Walk. A short line of paving slabs marked the way between gardens and opened up to Winslow Road shops. A glance told Stu there'd be no shelter in the shops. The few which didn't have graffiti all over the shutters covering their entrances were full of smashed windows and doors. They were all abandoned.

Running feet behind and drawing closer.

Stu dashed past the shops, reached Cromwell Road and ran right, heading towards his old school, a squat building set a fair way back from the road. Stu ran towards the main entrance, panting hard, and looked back. The runners had to be in sight.

Nobody was visible. The heavy slap of dozens of feet on the ground echoed up and down Cromwell Road all the same, and Stu understood that the invisible runners were almost at him.

He sprinted into the main grounds and saw a flickering light in a window. It vanished a moment later as if aware he'd seen it. Out of breath, Stu tore towards where the light had been, barely aware of the word *please* falling from his mouth over and over as he ran.

Eighteen

There was someone beside her.

Karen stayed utterly still. She hadn't moved in what felt like hours but could only be minutes. Dark pressed on her eyes. The hard seat on which she'd found herself pressed against her back, and there was someone beside her. They hadn't spoken. Neither had she. There was no need. Even though she couldn't hear their breathing, she knew they were beside her.

There was no way of knowing how long it had been since she'd …what? Appeared here? Woken? Whatever had happened in the pub had brought her here and all she could do now was hope the others were somewhere close. The problem was, even if they were close, she couldn't rely on them to get her out of this.

Karen lifted her left hand, held her arm steady and eased it down. There was a table in front, not wide by the feel of it. Dust coated it and her forearm. She grimaced at the touch, lifted her arm again and gingerly felt the air beside her level with her head. Nothing there. She pulled her arm back, tensed her legs and prayed there was nothing behind.

With a massive shove, Karen used her legs to push her chair back and leaped to the side. Her chair hit something hard, clattering as it fell. She ducked, struck a wall and lunged forward.

The clattering fell silent. Nobody spoke. Karen's coat brushed against old wallpaper as she stood upright. She rubbed her chest as if to decrease her heartbeat and felt her way along the wall for several seconds until she reached what could only be a door. Something sticky covered the handle. She jerked her hand back, pushed the door with her foot and it eased open to a silent corridor. Karen peered as far as she could to either end and faced the black room again.

'I know you're in here,' she said, shocking herself with the sound of her raw, naked fear. 'You make a move and I'll run. Think you can find me in the dark?'

The words wanted to sound tough, in control. They wavered, though.

'You tell me what's going on here,' she shouted.

Silence came back.

Holding her breath, Karen lowered her head to the door, pressed an ear against the wood and strained to hear anything.

The corridor was as silent as the classroom.

Will, where are you?

An idea gleamed.

The door. This was a room. The door. A light switch.

Karen's hand crept back to the wall, found the doorframe and rose. She felt nothing but the old wallpaper lined with splits and cracks.

'Want to talk?' she said, still searching for the switch. 'Want to tell me what's going on?'

Nothing. No switch. Only a shitty wall.

'Nothing to say?' she said and hated the tremor in her voice just as she hated the feel of the wall on her hand.

Her fingers hit a small square with a switch in its centre. She rested her index finger over it.

'Nothing to say?' she cried and hit the switch.

Light exploded above. It lasted no more than two seconds before it fell into a tired spluttering that cast crazy shadows and angles to each table and chair.

Karen slapped a hand over her mouth to keep the scream back.

She was in a classroom. Three rows of tables were before her, five tables in each row.

At each table, two mouldering corpses sat waiting for the day's lessons to begin.

Nineteen

Andy slid a foot forward and froze when he heard the scrape, much too loud in the dark.

He counted to thirty, moved a step forward, counted to thirty again and took another step.

Where are you guys? What's going on?

He played back the last few moments in the pub: the conversation about going to Geri's grave, moving through the crowds in the pub and stopping close to the doors; Stu asking if they believed it, all of them saying they did and the world changing, the floor turning into a black hole.

Now this.

Where the hell are you?

Panicked tears formed. Furiously, Andy blinked them away and hugged himself. Wherever he was, it was much colder than the pub. This was like being inside a fridge.

Above, someone screamed and Andy felt no surprise at all.

St Mary's Court.

At least he knew where he was just as he knew what to do.

Oh, Geri. This better be for the last time. And you better tell us what this is all about.

It didn't matter that the thought was nonsense. All that mattered was going upstairs, stopping the woman from being raped and then getting back to the others. Anything else could sod off for now.

But he didn't have to go upstairs. He could just run.

Disgusted horror rose inside and Andy cursed himself. Even if this mad business didn't have something to do with his dead friend, he wasn't so much of a fucking coward that he'd let a woman be raped.

Holding on to a bravado he didn't feel, Andy faced where he guessed the stairs to be and walked with his arms outstretched. He hit the wall before he expected to and swore under his breath. Using it as a guide, he moved step by step and eventually found cold metal. A moment's blind exploration told him he'd come to the lifts. Andy passed them and stopped when the wall ran out.

So, the stairs.

He crouched and searched on the stone floor for the plank. His fingers found it gratefully and he stood again.

'Up,' he whispered and felt for the wall. Andy made his way to the corner eight steps up, barely breathing, found the outline of the window and eased the filthy curtain back. Moonlight fell in, not illuminating much. Dirt covered the glass; Andy leaned close to it and attempted to see outside. What might have been a couple of cars were parked close to the side of the building. There was nobody in sight.

Andy dropped the curtain, moved along the wall again and ascended to the first floor. The screams hadn't come again and the shouts weren't audible yet.

This is fucking mad.

The thought was an automatic one; it didn't detract from the reality of the situation. The outlandishness of what was happening, of what had brought him here, the impossibility of being back in his childhood home after seeing it in visions— none of it meant anything now. All he had here was the plank of wood in his hand and the silence ahead.

Andy eased his way forward, peered down the corridor and made out faint light. Although he couldn't be sure, it seemed a couple of the doors were open and dim illumination coated the walls and floor. It flickered and wavered and with a gradual increase in his fear, Andy realised the light was candlelight.

This is mad.

'Bitch. Fucking bitch.'

Andy jerked his head back at the shouts and tightened his hold on the plank. He closed his eyes for a moment and thought:

Don't forget the guy hiding in the kitchen.

He slid along the wall, walking low. And there it was. Flat nineteen, the door slightly ajar.

The woman's sobs reached him, muffled, choked. As it had during his final vision, Andy's stomach rolled.

You fucking bastard.

He peered through the crack between door and frame and could just make out the line of the woman's legs, white in the moonlight. The man was straddling her stomach, leaning forward, calling her a fucking bitch, telling her to take it in her mouth.

Andy shifted his angle. The man's left hand wasn't visible. From Andy's point of view, the man's arm stretched beyond the doorframe with the bottle of petrol presumably on the dirty carpet.

His heart was thunder in the centre of his chest, was a tremendous pounding in his ears.

'Take this. Bitch. Or get this on your face.'

All thought ceased in Andy's head. He shoved the door open, dashed through the hall as the man on the floor moved, hand coming up. Andy ran, swung his plank and hit the man's hand dead centre.

The rapist screeched, the bottle flew, hit the wall and exploded. In one movement, Andy smashed his plank against the man's head, swung himself one hundred and eighty degrees and ducked.

There was nobody in the kitchen.

The figure on the floor made a noise somewhere between a word, a shout and a scream. Andy jerked around, inhaled the stink of the petrol soaking into the wall and carpet and brought his plank down on the bastard's face.

Bone broke and blood splattered the wood. Andy hit him again and the woman's screams bashed off the walls in a ceaseless note. Movement spun at Andy's left side.

He ducked and swung and missed a rat dashing through the kitchen. Andy entered the little room, swinging his plank and quickly checking each still corner. No second man was visible; he dashed back to the woman and the rapist. The woman had slid to the wall below the window and had pulled her legs up to her chest. Andy's words—*it's okay, you're safe*—lay stuck in his mouth and a distant voice mused in his head that the woman was really only a teenage girl. He stared at her and wondered briefly if she looked slightly familiar. She lowered her head, weeping, and lank hair covered her face. Andy prodded the figure on the floor. The man's arm fell from his chest, he loosed a sigh that made blood bubble from his mouth and that was all.

Andy squatted. No emotion came upon seeing that the attacker was dead. His nose was a pile of broken bone, blood and cartilage. The wood had stabbed one eye; a large sliver jutted from it, and a slight dent marked the middle of his forehead.

Andy stood and realised his legs were about to collapse. The woman's screams ran around and around and movement hit Andy's eyes. He spun and swung at the same time; a punch struck his stomach and he shoved his plank downwards as hard as he could.

It hit bone and something that made a hollow clang. Andy's other hand shot up, hit the thing that made the strange sound and pushed.

The knife slid into the man's mid-section. Blood immediately coated Andy's hand in a hot puddle. The stink of the man's breath coated his face. Weight pressed Andy's forearm and pushed him forward; the man fell back, coughing, howling. He hit the wall, slid along it to the hall and disappeared towards the front door. Andy took a few lurching steps as if to follow, saw the open cupboard door and realised the second man had been hiding in there.

'Bastard,' he whispered.

His legs gave way as the woman in the other room fell silent. Something hot and wet touched his hand. He lowered his gaze.

Thank you, Andy. Thank you so much.

You're really here?

Yes. I'm sorry.

No worries.

More wet stuff touched his hand. He sensed the woman standing in the hall, watching him. He wanted to speak, to tell her to be careful. The words wouldn't come. With a huge effort, Andy lifted his head, focused on the woman's face in the little moonlight and managed a final smile.

He fell to the dirty carpet, hands still on the handle of the knife deep in his stomach.

Twenty

Stu crashed against the window. It rattled but held. Inside, flickering light bounced against the glass.

The running steps were still coming. Images, not words, told him when the sound of the steps changed from hitting road to pounding on the stretch of tatty grass behind him, he'd have a few seconds before they reached him.

'Hey. Inside. Open the fucking window.'

A shocked scream answered him.

'Open the window,' Stu yelled.

He hammered his fists against it again and someone bellowed from the other side.

'Who are you? What the hell is going on?'

Karen. That's Karen.

'Karen? It's Stu. Let me in.'

Inside Karen struggled with something, then coughed as she pulled curtains out of the way. He caught sight of her for a second. Her face was a strained, white shape. Dirt coated it in streaks.

'Karen,' Stu shouted.

She pushed against the window. It held firm. She pushed at the bottom of the frame and the window slid up a few inches.

'More, Karen. Let me in.'

He gripped the frame as she did. Together, they pushed and the window rose with a ghastly scrape. Behind Stu, the crash of the running steps changed and terror exploded in his chest.

They were on the grass.

'Up, fucking up,' he screeched.

They pushed together. The window jammed.

That's not even a two foot gap, Stu thought.

He boosted himself up, shoved his arms through and Karen took hold of his hands, crying, shouting his name.

Freezing fingers pulled his ankles.

Stu screamed his horror, his outrage. Karen yanked him. His stomach scraped against the window frame and the pain was a world away.

The hands were moving higher, seemingly dozens reaching for his knees and beyond. Fingers dug into his shin muscles, then his kneecaps. Karen's hands were on his arms, then his shoulders. She howled against his ear; he wrapped both arms around her, bent his knees as much as he could and kicked backwards.

The hands behind lost their hold for a fraction of a second. Stu shot forward when Karen pulled and they both crashed to the floor.

'Up,' Karen panted, pulling his hand.

They ran in a bizarre crouch before making it upright close to the door. Stu saw the dozens of corpses at the tables. Karen yanked on his arm. He faced her, dumb with fear.

'Come on,' she shrieked.

Dead kids, he thought with stupid wonder. He looked back to the tables and each body had vanished, leaving empty chairs all thick with dust. Then they hit the door and corridor beyond.

'This way,' Karen shouted, pulling him.

They sprinted as a crash rang from behind. Glass smashed. They reached the corner and ran to the halfway point of the next corridor. It opened to a foyer, then the school's main entrance.

Karen stopped and Stu tried to speak through his gasps. She pressed a dirty finger to her lips, then kicked at a door. It swung open. Holding Stu's hand, Karen pushed gingerly at the main doors. One opened and fresh air hit Stu's face. Behind them, the door Karen had kicked showed an office and more windows. Praying the decoy would work, Stu let Karen take him outside. They ran alongside the school building, reached an empty car park, then grass. Without speaking, they sprinted hand in hand across the field to the large hedges.

Stu collapsed there, panting and fighting the pain of the stitch in his side. He spat excess saliva, studied the main building and listened for the sound of running feet. There were none.

He fell against Karen, buried his face in her neck and welcomed the warmth and simple scent of her.

'What the fuck is this?' he said. Her heart thrummed against his chest and her arms wrapped around him. 'What the hell is going on? Who were those kids and where the hell did they go?'

Karen said nothing for a moment. Stu held her tighter. The cold dried the sweat coating his body. Then Karen spoke in the whisper of a frightened child.

'They were dead, Stu. They were all dead.'

Her arms encircled him and the heavy smell of their sweat and fear filled Stu's nose. He breathed as slowly as he could.

'We need to find the others. We should get back to the pub,' he said.

'They were dead,' she whispered.

Stu stared at the shape of the school, the building he'd known as well as his own home for seven years. The school had always been familiar even after the remodelling they'd given it a few years back. It had always been a welcome sight because of what it meant and what it had been to him.

Now it was a sleeping beast across the grass and its broken windows stared at them.

Dozens of running feet smacked on the tarmac.

Without a word, Stu and Karen linked hands and ran.

Twenty One

Mick shifted position in the flowerbed, pressing himself against the low wall that blocked the grounds from the pavement and road. He couldn't be sure of it, but suspected he'd been there for at least twenty minutes, sitting in the cold, surrounded by dead flowers, desperately trying to think. None of this made sense; there'd been no sight of any other people since the guy at Atherstone Park, and his mobile was a useless chunk in his pocket. He couldn't even check the time let alone phone anyone. Even so, he'd kept looking at the blank screen while running from the park, praying *something* would show on the display.

Praying didn't help. He'd got this far and been forced to stop through exhaustion. Cursing his lack of fitness, Mick shifted position again. His head was only an inch or so from the top of the wall. He had to hope the thick shadows in the garden covered him from view.

He craned his head around and gazed at the house behind him. He knew where he was and he knew these houses even though he hadn't walked on Thorpe Road in God knows how long. The road and therefore the house had been part of his life for years. That didn't seem to matter now. This wasn't Dalry.

But it was on the surface. It was exactly Dalry. Same streets, same buildings, same green spaces. It was exactly Dalry in its skin. Below, though, it was somewhere else, somewhere wrong.

There were no lights anywhere. Most of the streetlights he'd passed were smashed as were many of the windows in the houses. No cars had passed, so he hadn't seen any headlights. This version of Dalry wasn't his hometown.

It's a nightmare, he thought and shivered. The cold bit into his flesh and the constant drip from his nose had congealed to a frozen layer on his upper lip.

Mick hugged himself and planned the rest of his journey. From here to the foot of the bridge would take a bare minute if he ran it. Getting over the bridge and beyond the roundabout, another two minutes, maybe. Then from the road, around the multi storey car park to Long Gate in four minutes.

He could be back in the pub in less than ten minutes. All he had to do was get moving.

'Simple,' he whispered and grinned bitterly. Simple? What the hell was that when you were taken from the pub to a nightmare in a second and then maybe killed a man in self-defence? Simple was bollocks.

Something new caught his attention. Mick rose as much as he dared and listened.

Someone was coming

Mick dug his fingers into the cold stone and gripped the end of the baseball bat with his other hand. The person was coming closer. Mick pushed himself through the earth to the end of the wall and risked a look around the corner. There wasn't anything moving on Thorpe Road and the only sound was the advancing runner. Whoever they were, it sounded as if they were coming towards the bridge which meant they'd pass his wall in a matter of seconds.

Mick pulled back behind the wall and held his breath.

Feet striking pavement met the runner's panting breath. Then they were level with the low wall, passing by without a pause. Mick counted to ten, looked out at the road again and saw the runner crossing to the other side. Their arms were tucked tight against their side, their long legs clad in black jeans, a tree branch held in one shining white hand.

Dumb wonder filled Mick and the word fell out of his mouth before he could stop it.

'Will?'

The man whirled around, wood coming up. He lowered it and a great burst of gratitude exploded in Mick's heart.

Weeping, he jumped over the wall and ran to Will. The men embraced, Mick rubbed at his eyes and held Will hard.

'Jesus Christ, man. This is nuts. This is fucking nuts,' Mick said.

'No shit,' Will said and Mick laughed. It didn't matter that his laugh was too loud. Will was here and he was all right.

'Karen,' Will said, pulling away from Mick and staring at him. 'Have you seen her?'

'No. Nobody.' Mick waved his bat around. 'Well, almost nobody. There was a guy ...I ...he came at me with this, man.' He waved the bat around.

'He's dead?'

Mick struggled for an answer. The word *dead* meant nothing. For now, that was.

'I think so. I didn't check.'

'Where?' Will said.

'Atherstone Park. I was there. No idea how. I was there; I could see my old house, but it was wrong. Everything's wrong here. And this guy, he jumped over the fence and came at me. I got the bat off him and ran.'

'Shit,' Will whispered. He stared at the silent houses. 'I got attacked by a bunch of kids. It was in my old house. I mean, where my parents live.'

He took a breath and told Mick his story. As Will described the mocking laugh rising out of the water and from the other side of the river, an ugly fear turned Mick's testicles cold and then slid upwards through his body.

'This isn't right, is it? I mean, *none* of this is right. We should still be in the pub, talking about Geri, not in this fucking ...' Mick trailed off. Words seemed like too much effort.

'I need to find Karen,' Will said and an implacable hardness covered Will's face. Mick understood it. He would have felt the same if Jodie had been involved.

'They'll go back to the pub,' he said.

'How do you know that?'

'Where else is there to go?'

He watched Will's face and prayed the others were safe and already in the pub.

Eventually, Will nodded. 'I hope you're right, fatboy.'

Mick managed a laugh. 'So do I, Elton.'

Together, they crossed to the other side of the road and headed to the bridge that would take them back to the pub.

Twenty Two

Karen stood beside the window, not wanting to touch the frame or the narrow ledge in front of it. Both were cracked, the dirty wood split in several places. Through the glass, she made out a little of the pavement and the sight was dispiriting. Pavement and road were full of holes; rubble lay in piles and rubbish presumably from overturned bins drifted past the pub when the wind blew.

Inside the pub was no better. Most of the seats and tables had been smashed apart or removed; horrendous stains covered the floor and nearly all of the bottles behind the bar had been smashed. Stu had pointed out that whatever had happened here must have occurred a while ago. There wasn't any scent of spilled alcohol and no wet patches near the broken bottles. His theory hadn't helped to calm her. If whatever was going on had happened a while ago, then where the hell were they? More, where was everyone else?

And most of all, where was Will?

The thought wouldn't go. It stabbed into her head over and over, a million pricks of the same needle. She folded her arms over her breasts and focused on her breathing for a moment. It helped a little.

Stu crossed to her from the wrecked bar, clutching a bottle of water. Karen took it, noting how cold it was and realised that was down to the outside temperature and not because it came from a working fridge.

'I don't think it's fresh,' Stu said and Karen lifted the bottle up to the moonlight. The illumination wasn't strong enough for her to read the label.

'Not fresh like you'd get normally,' Stu said. 'I think it's been refilled from a tap.'

Karen smiled; it felt thick and greasy.

'I'll give it a miss, thanks,' she said. Stu took the bottle and placed it on the remains of a table.

'What time have you got?' he asked.

She checked her watch, staring at it until she could be sure what it read.

'9:30,' she said and saw her thoughts on Stu's pale face.

'Around the same time we were talking about Geri, wasn't it?' He gestured to the wall above the bar. Karen followed his finger. A clock was nailed to the wall, the face cracked but the hands still visible.

'Just gone eight?' she said.

'I think so.'

'We've both gone nuts, haven't we?'

'I honestly don't know if I wish that was true.'

'Do you remember *anything* after the pub and before this?'

'Not really. We were in the pub, near the doors. Then it's like ...it's like everything faded. All the colour went like we were in a black and white photo.'

She shook her head, frustrated.

'It's okay. I know what you mean,' Stu said.

'That's all I know. Then we're here and it's like we're in a nightmare.'

Stu sniggered and a forced note darkened the laugh.

'What?' she said.

He ran a finger over the cracks in the wall. 'I feel like we're in a film. Something like *Escape From New York*. You seen it?'

'Kurt Russell?'

He nodded. 'Snake Plissken would get us out of this.'

Stu rubbed his mouth and in the little moonlight, she saw how close he was to tears. The forced jokey comment hadn't helped to calm him at all.

'What about Bruce Willis? He'd know what to do,' she whispered and Stu stared at her. A sickly grin spread over his mouth.

'I'd prefer Bruce Lee,' he murmured.

Karen hissed laughter. 'Chuck Norris. He'd roundhouse kick us out of here.'

In the quiet of the ruined pub, they laughed as softly as they could and for a few glorious seconds, worry over Will left Karen's mind. Stu held her.

'We'll work this out,' he said.

'Yeah.'

Tears fell; more threatened and she furiously blinked them away, mentally yelling at herself to stay calm.

In one quick movement, Stu cocked his head.

'What?' Karen whispered, abruptly afraid.

Stu placed a finger to his lips and leaned close to the window. Karen strained to hear, heard nothing for a moment but her own heartbeat, and then someone walking fast.

More than one person.

She joined Stu beside the window, the footsteps closed and the figures outside were right in front.

Joy exploded through her. She ran to the main doors, skidding on the stone floor, Stu right behind her, and her hands hit the handle just as the door opened.

The movement pulled her with it and she fell against Will, crying, laughing and attempting to kiss him at the same time.

Twenty Three

They took one of the few whole tables which gave them as much of a view of the pub as the moonlight would allow. Will glanced from shadow to shadow, wishing that more of the open floor was visible and doing his best to not think of what could hide in those shadows. The wall against his back was a comfort despite the cold seeping through his fleece. It helped for him to feel slightly grounded, or as grounded as he could given what had happened.

'So nobody's seen Andy?' he said, still watching the shadows.

They'd told each other their stories, his hand hadn't left Karen's, and there was no sign of Andy.

'Not seen anyone,' Mick replied. 'Only that mad fucker with this.' He tapped the bat.

'It's pretty safe to say whatever's going on, we're somewhere people don't like us,' Will said.

'We're in Dalry,' Stu said. 'I mean ...' He gestured to encompass the pub. 'We know this, don't we?'

'Mate, I hope I never get to know anywhere as shit as this,' Mick said in a flat voice.

Stu shook his head. 'Christ on a bike.' He met their eyes. 'What's the deal? What do we know? All of us have seen or heard or had some contact from Geri, right? Our dead friend has been trying to speak to us and ...' He paused and Will replayed Stu's last sentence. As mad as it sounded, as completely unrelated to the real world, their situation boiled down to those few words. The probability of their situation wasn't the issue. It was all about the reality of it.

'She's been trying to speak to us, we get together and we end up here. It looks like Dalry, it's got the same buildings and roads and stuff but it's a fucked up, nasty place, right? So the thing is, how do we get out?'

'The thing is, where's Andy?' Karen said.

Mick shifted. 'Can I say something?' he said, eyes on the table.

'Of course,' Karen replied and took his free hand. Mick wrapped his fingers around hers and spoke without making any eye contact.

'I'm scared shitless. When that guy came at me, it wasn't just being scared because, you know, here comes a nutter with a baseball bat. It was because I had no idea what was going on. I still don't. Why did that guy want to kill me? None of us have a fucking clue. And we don't know where Andy is. He's somewhere here, somewhere like we are. If this was normal, I'd be out there like a shot with this.' He lifted the bat for a moment. 'You know that. He's a mate despite of the last couple of years. You all are. I know things have changed and we don't see that much of each other, but that doesn't matter. If I wasn't so shit scared, I'd be out there right now, looking for him.'

His voice fell into a few hiccupping sighs. He freed his hand from Karen's, rubbed his eyes and still made no eye contact.

'I think all we can do right now is hope Andy gets here soon,' Will said and hated the taste of his words.

'I ...' Stu said and Will spoke over him.

'If he's not here by the morning or if we haven't worked out what's going on, then we look for him, all right?'

No words had ever sounded so ugly.

Stu looked away.

'All right,' he muttered.

'It could be a plan to see if we can find somewhere that's a bit more of a cover,' Karen said.

'We haven't seen anyone here,' Stu replied and Karen raised an eyebrow.

'How do we know that means anything? Even if there isn't anyone around here, they'll see us if they go past.'

She pointed to the window and its smashed panes. Stu nodded although it was with reluctance, Will thought.

'Where to?' Stu said.

'Upstairs?' Will suggested. 'At least we'll be out of sight of the street.'

They stood. Will pulled Karen close. Stu and Mick were watching him. Waiting for him.

Who made me a leader?

He knew.

Karen had. He had her to worry about, to keep safe. Stu didn't have his wife here; Mick didn't have Jodie. Illogical or not, sexist or not, he was in charge because he had the most to lose.

'Stick close,' he said and gave the others an uneasy smile to say he knew it was a horror film cliché.

They bunched together and a freakish mixture of dismay and sorry humour filled Will for a moment. He swallowed it back and walked towards the centre of the pub, hand holding Karen's. The shadows he'd watched earlier looked as if they were growing larger the closer he drew to them, growing into the cracks on the floor, oozing through the smashed chairs.

A tickling sensation touched the back of his neck: hairs rising. Will struggled to stay calm and to concentrate on the weight of his wife's hand. The shadows moved with him, matching him step for step.

Bollocks. All bollocks, he told himself.

The shadows moved, he reached for the stairs and grimaced at the feel of the muck coating the rail.

'Ready?' he whispered and glanced upwards.

A little more moonlight shone at the top of the stairs and fresh air kissed the sweat on his face. Despite the cold, it was welcome.

'Get a move on, Elton,' Mick whispered and Will sniggered.

He led them up, watching his step and watching the moonlight draw closer. As he placed both feet on level floor, he moved closer to Karen and saw the body lying below the closest table.

Twenty Four

Stu crouched a little way from the table and gazed at the corpse. It was sexless. Decay had eaten its features and there was nowhere near enough flesh on its remains for him to take a guess whether it was male or female. Even the remnants of the clothes didn't help. They were simple rags that exposed white bone and mould.

'Shit,' he breathed and stood. Will had dropped his branch and wrapped his arms around Karen. Both stood against the wall. Mick remained at the top of the stairs as if unwilling to come any closer.

'It's very dead,' Stu said. 'Probably for ages.'

'Is that supposed to be a good thing?' Will said.

'How the fuck should I know?' Stu wiped sweat from his mouth. 'Sorry. Been a long day.'

Mick cackled laugher that was too close to hysterical for Stu. He glanced at his friend. Mick subsided and Stu faced the body again. Now that they knew it was there, its smell couldn't be ignored. As odd as it seemed, the stink hadn't been noticeable downstairs. Up here, it was all around them.

'We up for finding somewhere a little less grim? An office or something? I don't think anyone's going to mind if we go into the staff areas,' he said.

Keeping in a close group, they moved towards the upstairs bar, crunched over broken glass behind it and reached an open door. Stu glanced around. A line of moonlight illuminated beyond the door a few feet. He had no idea what was further inside. While he could picture a storage cupboard somewhere ahead, a little space for them to crouch inside and hide like animals, he had no way of knowing where the corridor would take them.

'Maybe we should stay out here?' he whispered.

'Sounds like a plan,' Will muttered and sniffed several times. 'What the hell is that stink?'

'Your arse?' Mick whispered and Karen thumped him. Stu placed a hand over his nose and mouth and breathed slowly.

Where's Andy?

The interior voice was horribly shrill, the sound of a nagging old woman.

We'll find him or he'll find us, he told the voice and it subsided into mutterings.

Mick nudged his arm. Happy to leave whatever was beyond the door, Stu walked with the others back to the centre of the second floor. The smell, a rich, meaty stink, seemed to have grown stronger. He studied the floor but saw nothing other than dirt and broken furniture. Mick nudged his arm again and jerked his head towards the nearest row of windows. Silently, they crossed to them and peered down to the street. It appeared as ugly and as abandoned up here as it did on the ground floor.

Stu inhaled fresh air and shivered.

'I think we might be dreaming,' Mick whispered and glanced at him. Stu wanted to see humour on his friend's face, even a bitter kind. There was just a tiredness he'd not seen before, a look that belonged on the face of an old man.

'No. I don't think so,' he replied and Mick made a noise somewhere between a sigh and a hiccup.

'You're probably right.' He laughed a little. 'But I prefer my idea.'

They returned to the others and Stu gestured to a nearby table which was relatively whole. There were no chairs. They crouched beside it, Karen and Will wrapped around one another. Freezing air flowed in a steady stream through the wrecked windows. Stu jammed his hands under his armpits and thought of his wife and daughter. In his head, he told them he would see them soon, he'd be home before morning, he loved them.

Conversation came and went. They spoke of the moments before they'd come to this place, if anyone had seen them and what others might have made of it. Karen mentioned Andy and where he might be, and Mick changed the subject quickly.

Their voices faltered and fell silent. They shifted closer together, disturbing dust, eager to share body heat. Stu dozed. His thoughts blurred into a surreal mix of half-dreams, imagination and fear all bathed by the freezing air.

Then in the silence of the ruined pub, a shrill crash rang from below.

The tinkle of falling glass immediately followed it.

91

Twenty Five

'Shit,' Mick whispered and leaped upright. Stu followed him, his thin sleep forgotten. He reached for Will and Karen and the group raced towards the other side of the pub floor. Animal fear pushed Stu on past the broken tables and filled his head with images of hiding in a tiny room, hiding in the dark.

The outline of the bar rose ahead, more glass broke downstairs and a grunt joined the breaking glass. It was unmistakeably the sound of someone satisfied.

Stu halted the moment before he crashed into a doorway behind the bar. Will struck him; he overbalanced and Mick's hand yanked him upright. Stu stared at his friends, unable to speak. The moonlight showed their terror and he took that as silent agreement.

Stu entered the corridor beyond the doorway, felt the others come with him and slid against a wall until Mick whispered behind him.

'Go further.' Mick pointed.

More sounds rose from below and Stu couldn't be sure what they were. Holding his breath, he walked blindly, arms outstretched until he hit a wall and realised the corridor turned. A window at the far end let in enough moonlight to show the open door on his right. Stu paused and strained to hear. There was no way of being sure if he could hear footsteps out in the bar or if his imagination had made the sounds.

Will pushed him and gestured for him to move. Stu crossed to the door and peered inside.

The room wasn't large. From what he could see, two office chairs lay on the floor beside the remains of a table. What might have been a computer was on the table and a wrecked pot plant had clearly been smashed into a corner. The outline of a door directly opposite beckoned him. Pulling Will, who in turn held Karen with Mick behind her, Stu crossed the little office to the door and wanted to laugh despite his bitterness.

The room wasn't the same tiny cupboard he'd imagined but nor was it far off. Perhaps six feet across with what he guessed were shelves lining the walls, their safety came down to a room smaller than a prison cell.

Stu crouched and pulled Will with him. Wood grazed his neck and he shifted forwards. Their collective breathing seemed much too loud and he wanted to tell them to keep quiet. Instead of speaking he reached for their hands, hot and sweating despite the outside cold.

I could die here.

The thought didn't bring fear, only resignation. He understood it. There was no way out and if whoever had broken the window downstairs found them here, he and the others would fight and more than likely die.

He shifted position as slowly as he could. They were leaning against a wooden wall, not brick as he'd imagined. Freeing his hand from Will's, Stu ran his fingertips over the wall, felt the nicks and grooves in it and froze when his finger slid over a tiny hole. Keeping his finger there as a guide, he pressed his eye against it.

The view of the upper floor bar was close to non-existent. The odd broken table, shafts of moonlight coming in through smashed windows and casting odd shadows as they struck the furnishings—nothing was clear. Nothing but a new stink of dirt and sweat come to the chill air.

Movement.

Stu flinched but kept his eye fixed against the hole.

More movement. He took a guess that it was at the top of the steps, a low figure, maybe a crouching man.

The figure shuffled across the floor and Stu flinched again. A second figure had come from below, another crouching shape following the first.

Then a third and a fourth.

There'd been no time to focus upon his fear during their dash to this room. All that had been in his mind was getting away from whatever was below. As Stu watched the moving shapes, resignation vanished and fear of the dark and the unknown things that might be inside it took its place.

He swallowed, forced saliva into his mouth and glanced at the shape of the others.

'Don't make a sound,' he whispered and looked through the hole again.

The shapes were no more defined. Even so, he could see what they were doing.

Eating the body at the top of the stairs.

The greatest wave of terror he'd ever known crashed over him and he could do nothing but swallow his scream.

Twenty Six

Hours passed.

Mick knew he'd dozed as unbelievable as it seemed. Time didn't matter here, nor did the impossibility of their situation. All he had to think about was the bat in one of his hands, and Karen's hand in his other. Even the horrific sounds from the bar didn't matter when put against his bat and Karen beside him.

He dozed, he thought he dreamed and those silent hours trickled by. Mick's mind took him far away and he thought of little other than his bat and his friend.

Karen stirred beside him. Mick lifted his head, wincing as tendons in his neck cracked. The movement had started with Stu, Mick realised. Stu, then Will, then Karen and now him stirring in the dark.

'We can go,' Stu said in a low voice. The first complete sound in hours seemed too loud and Mick winced again.

'Up,' Stu muttered. 'We're getting out.'

'How do you know it's safe?' Mick said. A horrible taste of old beer and tiredness filled his mouth.

'They're gone. Went about an hour ago.'

Mick licked his teeth and banished the memory of the sounds from the bar: the tearing, the crunching, and what could only have been lips smacking together.

'What's the plan?' Mick said. He stood. Pins and needles stabbed his legs.

'Find Andy.'

Andy. Shit.

Shame burned Mick's face, reddening his cheeks. Andy hadn't been in his head for hours. But maybe that was a good thing. If the worry over his mate remained, so would the need to find out where he was. Andy hadn't been with them so wherever he was, he was safe from the people in the pub.

People. Right.

'I'll go first,' Will said and brushed past Mick.

No chance, Mick thought and realised he hadn't spoken the words. He pulled Will back from the door. 'No chance,' he said.

Will faltered. Mick eased his way past him to the door. In a close line, they moved to the doorway which led to the bar. Mick took a few breaths which did little to calm him and walked forward.

Dawn hadn't come. The pub was still illuminated by thin streams of moonlight. Mick's eyes travelled over the dust and pieces of wood, all a little more visible for some reason. They passed over lumps of cushions, reached the steps and shot back to the lumps which were body parts.

Horror rose in his throat and he hissed. Stu slid forward, slapped a hand over his mouth and swayed.

Wherever Mick looked, he saw what he'd mistaken for bits of cushions were bits of body. A foot, something long and sausage-like, and grey pieces of meat which could only be pieces of skin were dotted around the floor of the bar with no obvious care or pattern.

'It's a pantry, isn't it?' he whispered and the vomit rose before he could stop it.

He let it splatter beside him, felt someone's hands rubbing his back and thought of running past the body parts earlier.

He vomited again, closed his eyes and let it fall out of him.

'Finished?'

It was Will rubbing his back.

Mick tried to speak but nothing came apart from a weak croak. He wiped his mouth, stood straight and gazed at the horrors in the murky light.

'We're in a nest, aren't we? This is where they keep their food.'

'Who the fuck are they?' Will whispered.

'I don't care. Let's just go. Right now. okay?' Karen said.

They moved together and Mick realised the change in light was down to a simple lack of cloud. Through the long row of wrecked windows at the front of the building, the moon was clearly visible. Stars gleamed in a sky perfect for a winter night.

He hugged himself, shivering, and looked all around, eyes not resting on any one object. The ground floor appeared even more horrendous than it had before they'd run. The bar had been smashed apart at some point; the window behind the bar which showed a little of the kitchen was nothing but a hole of jagged glass, and stains covered the floor. Mick didn't want to look at the stains.

'Out,' he croaked. 'Outside.'

They crossed to the doors; Mick paused and thought of Andy.

You better be all right, Pateman, you fucker.

He opened the pub doors.

Twenty Seven

The phone rang.

Kirsty woke instantly, both hands gripping the arms of the chair. A thin slice of morning light broke through the gap between the curtains.

The phone was ringing.

Stu.

She lunged upright and crossed the floor to the sofa. The phone was on the arm as it had been since last night, sitting there, silent and mocking her.

She grabbed it, the ringing fell silent and she threw up a blurred image of a prayer that was simply her husband's name.

'Stu?' she said and her fingernails dug into her palms.

'No, sorry.' It was a man's voice but not Stu's. It was a million miles from Stu. 'My name's Phil. I was hoping to speak to Stuart Brennan.'

'I'm his wife,' Kirsty said. The reply was automatic. It was one she'd given countless times to the gas company or Sky or anyone else who phoned when Stu was out. The big difference, her mind said with horrible cheerfulness, was that all those times, she'd known where the hell Stu was.

'He's not in?'

She swallowed. Her throat clicked. 'No, not right now.'

'Do you know when he'll be home?'

Abrupt anger gave her strength. She pushed the anger back far enough so only the touch of it emerged in her voice. 'Sorry, who did you say you were?'

Another pause and when he replied, he sounded a little more formal.

'Phil Paulson. I'm sort of an old friend of Stuart's and I was hoping to speak to him.'

Kirsty's restless gaze fell on the clock. 'You always call your old friends at six in the morning?' she said.

'I ...'

'You're a liar.' She couldn't stop the tremor in her voice. 'Nobody who knows my husband calls him *Stuart.*'

Her fingers moved to disconnect the call and he spoke again in a different tone. She recognised the panic in his voice and responded to it with her own panic.

'Okay, I don't know Stu. Well, I did sort of years ago. He was friends with a couple of other people. Karen Miller. Andy something. And Mick Harris. They were friends with Stu. And another guy called Will ...something. I can't remember his last name.'

'Elton,' Kirsty said.

Much of the colour in the room had bled out of it. She sat, held the arm of the sofa with a fierce grip and wished for the rolling in her stomach to die.

'Will Elton, that's right. I knew them years ago. They were ...'

He sighed and tears filled the soft sound. All at once, Kirsty knew what was coming next. Her mind flashed back to the night before, Stu at the door, hands in his pocket and telling her something she couldn't believe because it had no part in their lives, of Lucy, work, their mates and anything real.

'They were friends with my sister,' Phil said. 'Geri Paulson.'

***

The clock again. Quarter past six. Lucy would wake up any minute. Then breakfast, coffee, a load of washing on while Stu got up, got ready for work and ...

And that wasn't how today was going to be.

'He's out. Has been since last night,' Kirsty said.

'You don't know where he is?'

'He went out to meet his friends. Karen, Will, Mick and Andy. He hasn't seen them in ages but they're all here so they went out for a drink.'

'Why haven't they seen each other in ages?'

The question she'd never put in such blunt words to her husband; the question she'd asked herself, always with the same answer.

Geri killed herself and she killed their friendship.

'They all moved away. It's been a long time.'

How thin that sounded. She almost laughed.

'Yeah, I know,' he said and some bitter note in his words froze her urge to laugh.

'So, what has this got to do with Stu?' she said.

'I'm not sure. Has he been normal lately?'

He said it as if he might have said *does he still work in that record shop?* Any horrible weight in the question was surely in her mind.

'What do you mean?'

'Sorry. Stupid way to put it. It's just ...well, I know how odd this will sound, believe me I know. You're probably the tenth or eleventh person I've phoned. Although you're the only one who hasn't hung up.'

He fell silent and she waited.

'My sister Geri, she's been dead for best part of ten years,' he said.

'I know. Stu told me about her.'

'Has he mentioned her lately?'

A burst of heat rose from her breasts just as cold flowed downwards. Her hand shook on the arm of the sofa. 'Why?' she murmured.

'Please. It's important.'

She couldn't lie. Not now. 'Yes,' she whispered.

'I really need to speak to Stu.'

The tears dropped without warning. She choked them back, furious with herself and spoke over him.

'You can't. He went out last night and I haven't heard anything from him. I can't get him on his phone, I can't get the others and I'm about three fucking seconds away from calling the police so you tell me what the fuck this is about.'

Her voice rose in the last few words; she slammed a hand over her mouth and waited for Lucy's cries. None came and she shut her eyes for a moment.

'You tell me what's going on,' she whispered.

He studied the ground, perhaps embarrassed by her shouting.

'I've seen her. I've seen Geri.'

Kirsty opened her mouth and discovered she had literally no idea what to say. She closed her mouth and waited.

'I know how it sounds. Either like I'm insane or taking the piss. I wish I was.' He sighed loud enough for her to wince and pull the phone away from her ear for a moment.

'She's been in my house, at work and anywhere else she wants to appear. She's just there like ...I don't know.' He sighed again but with barely any force. It was as if all his breath had escaped during the last few seconds. 'Do you believe me?' he asked.

'I don't know.'

'Would Stu believe me?'

Stu at the door last night, turning back to her and telling her he wouldn't be too late. Stu, smiling and telling her he loved her.

Kirsty placed a trembling hand over her eyes.

'Maybe,' she said.

Phil hesitated before speaking again. The moment span out and Kirsty heard nothing at all on the line.

'Stu's seen her as well, hasn't he?' Phil said.

Kirsty couldn't do anything but weep.

Twenty Eight

Karen stared at Bishop's Gate and all her words dried up.

The moonlight shone almost as brightly as sunshine to expose the road and buildings. Not one window on the other side of the road was whole. Not one door hung straight. Her mind cross referenced the street with images of New York in the minutes and hours after 9/11, the surreal sight of streets and roads choked with debris. Even as she made that connection, a shrill voice told her that didn't make sense. This was Dalry, for Christ's sake. Fucking Dalry. What the hell did explosions and broken windows have to do with Dalry?

'We should get off the street,' Will said.

'What?' Mick said. He sounded drugged.

'This is just about the roughest place I've ever seen.' Will spoke quickly as Karen knew he did when nervous or angry.

'Worse than Wolverhampton?' Stu muttered and Mick let out a girlish laugh.

'Andy,' Karen said in as much an effort to focus the others as to focus herself. The word helped to block out the sights of the damaged buildings, the sense of the pub looming over her and the mental pictures of the horror on the second floor.

'We have to find Andy,' she said. 'I don't care about anything else.'

'I've been thinking. He told us about that flat, remember? When we were in the pub, he ...'

Will stopped and let out a breath that shook with nerves and close tears.

'He told us about the flat he lived in as a kid, didn't he? It makes sense if he's there. I mean, we all woke up or appeared or whatever the hell it was in our homes. What were our homes, I mean.'

'I didn't,' Karen said and saw a look on Will's face. She recognised it: Will attempting to think his way around a problem rather than through it. The look had only come before during difficult work or with an approaching deadline.

'So, most of us did,' he said. 'I think Andy is in his old flat. St Mary's Court.'

'It's got to be a fifteen minute walk,' Mick said.

'We could get the bus,' Stu muttered and Karen wanted to shout at him, to hit him. What the hell place did jokes have here? She readied herself to speak and paused.

Stu was being Stu. There'd been no humour in any of his comments, just a weak confusion and a need to make sense of things. He glanced at her, and she didn't hide her appraisal.

'I don't think they're running today,' she whispered.

Will eyed Mick. 'How's your bat, fatboy?' he said.

Mick swung it without much enthusiasm and Karen immediately loathed the whisper it made in the air.

They moved together, heading down Bishop's Gate to where it met Long Gate. Karen attempted to look in all directions at once and although she saw no movement behind the broken windows and heard no voices in the chill air, she was utterly sure of one thing.

They weren't alone.

Twenty Nine

Keeping her grip on Lucy tight, Kirsty lifted her bag, mouth trembling with the effort, and rang the doorbell again.

The door opened a moment later and Rich reached for Lucy or the bag. She was too tired to decide which. She handed him the bag and he held it beside his leg.

'You okay?' he asked.

'I don't know,' she replied and entered their house. He let her pass and stood against the wall, awkwardly holding her bag. She briefly wondered what he made of her coming to their home at twenty past seven in the morning, of the mad conversation she'd had with Jo. Unreality touched her and she shook it off. There wasn't time to pretend this wasn't happening.

Jo appeared at the top of the stairs, holding Susan. She descended quickly, passed Susan to Rich and embraced Kirsty.

'Nothing?' she said and Kirsty shook her head, not trusting herself to speak.

They went through to the living room; Rich placed the babies in a playpen and Kirsty fell on to the sofa. She leaned forward, hugging herself.

'I keep thinking I should call the police,' she said. 'I mean, this is what you do, isn't it? When someone goes missing, you call the police.'

'He hasn't necessarily gone missing,' Rich muttered and Kirsty's anger rose fast.

'What the hell else would you call it?' she said and he held up a placating hand.

'I'm saying it's not like this is normal, is it? He's out with a load of mates and you can't get hold of them either. Then you get a call from some guy who's loosely connected to Stu and his mates' past. You tell the police all that and they aren't automatically going to be looking for Stu like they would for a missing person.'

Her anger fell away, leaving her nauseous and tired. 'I know.'

He squatted beside the playpen and slid his fingers through. The babies gripped them.

'I'm calling in sick so I can come with you,' he said.

She shook her head and Jo spoke.

'It's not a good idea to go alone. You don't know anything about this guy.'

'It's all right.' Kirsty watched her daughter hold Rich's fingers and pictured leaving her here. The idea was ghastly.

'I'm meeting him in Memorial Square so you couldn't come, anyway. It's too close to your shop. I told him I'd meet him there, talk to him about his sister and whatever the hell that means about Stu. Then I'm going to the police.'

'I still don't like it,' Jo said.

'It's broad daylight; the Square's about as public as you can get. Even if he is, you know, a nut, he can't do anything there.'

She watched her friends share a silent look. Agreement passed between them.

'Okay, but only as long as you phone me when you get there and when he turns up,' Jo said.

'I will.' Kirsty watched her daughter again. Both the girls were playing with a blanket, Rich's fingers forgotten.

'You think I should call the police, don't you?' she said and watched Rich and Jo share another glance.

'I don't know. I think someone has to be missing or whatever you want to call it for twenty-four hours. Plus they might just say he's out with his mates so they're going to be okay.' Jo watched the babies. 'Have you thought about calling Jodie?'

'Yeah, but I figured if she'd heard from Mick, he or she would have called me. I can't tell her I can't get hold of any of them. Not yet.' Kirsty rubbed at her eyes. They ached with tiredness. 'I told this Phil he's got a couple of minutes. If what he tells me doesn't make sense ...'

'Which it doesn't,' Rich said.

'I know, but I have to let him talk. I'll give him a couple of minutes and then call the police to report Stu missing.'

She hadn't known she was going to state it outright in such bald terms. The words were full of fear in her mouth.

She pulled a scrap of paper from a pocket.

'This is his number.' She handed the paper to Jo. 'I told him I'd be giving it to you so even if he is a weirdo, he knows you have his number.'

'Don't worry,' Rich said and smiled in an easy way. 'If he's a weirdo, me and Stu will just burn his house down.'

She wanted to return his smile but couldn't.

In the playpen, the babies gurgled at one another.

Thirty

Kirsty checked her watch. Twenty past eight. The Square wasn't as busy as she would have liked. Most of the shops around it wouldn't open for another forty minutes or so which meant a lack of the public. She counted ten people in the Square: two street cleaners, a couple of teenage kids, one guy and his dog and others passing through the Square. She stood in the shadow of NatWest, resting against the cool stone of the building. Directly opposite, Memorial Hall was empty. She could see into the open plan floor of the old building and wondered when she'd last really paid any attention to it or walked up the few steps to stand where people had stood a hundred and fifty years before. Easily fifteen years ago. Maybe more. A New Year's Eve, perhaps; the square full of celebrating people, of bitter cold and dirty snow.

She shook the thoughts off. She had to focus, keep her eyes open for Phil Paulson. A tall guy, he'd said. Blonde hair, going a bit thin. He'd be dressed in a black jacket and he'd carry a newspaper in his right hand so she could recognise him. He hadn't asked her what she looked like and he'd understand if she changed her mind, he was asking a lot, after all, but he hoped she'd be there and they could talk.

Nobody in the Hall. The shops were still shut. Kirsty studied the square for a moment and focused on a spot of ground between the edge of the Hall and the shopping centre. It was probably the only place she wouldn't be seen from the record shop. There was enough to think about without wondering if Stu's colleagues could see her with a man who wasn't Stu.

A few people exited the shopping centre. None wore a black jacket. Kirsty wanted to check her watch and resisted the urge to do so.

Talk to him for a few minutes, then call the police. Stu's missing. It doesn't matter what this guy says about his dead sister. Stu's missing. Give this guy five minutes and leave it at that.

Time passed in painfully slow trickles. She watched more people pass through the square and watched her shadow slide over the paving slabs when the sun drifted in and out of clouds.

'Nice day for it,' she whispered and hugged herself. August didn't seem that far behind despite the calendar. Edging to late October and still pretty mild.

She relented and checked her watch. Twenty to nine. He was ten minutes late. She leaned against the wall of the bank again and tried not to think of walking away, cutting through the shopping centre and getting back to the multi-storey, getting back to her car and phoning the police.

The sun broke free from the clouds and great shadows ran over the slabs in front of her. They span away as if pushed by the wind and she saw the man hurrying from Cross Street, aiming directly for the Hall. Black jacket. A big guy. Paper in his right hand.

'Phil Paulson. Five minutes,' Kirsty whispered.

She pushed herself from the wall and strode towards the square. She let Stu's face fill her mind as she walked and moved her feet faster.

Thirty One

Will kept Karen close to his side and kept his eyes away from the buildings.

Not looking didn't help. He was still aware of the damage that surrounded them. It was there in the smell of cold air, exposed brickwork and mould. It was there in the piles of rubble and broken glass they had to step over, and it was there in the occasional burned out car he saw from the corner of his eye. They'd come from Bishop's Gate to Long Gate via a couple of side streets. He'd led them, Karen at his back, their hands linked and when Mick suggested they cut through Memorial Square, Will said there was no way they were doing that. The area was too open and exposed. At least on the side streets they were covered by shadows.

They'd heard nothing, seen nobody. Dalry was beyond a ghost town. It reminded Will of a documentary he'd seen once. Somewhere in remote Russia, some town used for nuclear weapon testing. It had been abandoned fifty or sixty years ago and nobody had been back since. The cameras had shown streets full of crumbling buildings, of misshaped objects that had once been cars. Nothing lived there and hadn't done so in decades. That was what Dalry had become.

They drew level with the fire damaged museum, then older buildings used as restaurants, then the back of estate agents. All the windows were smashed and streaks of spray paint coated the frames and doors.

Will stopped and glanced at the others.

'Which way do we want to go?' he muttered.

'Straight on.' Stu pointed. 'Across the road, down Cathedral Precincts and then across the park. We'll come out at the back of St Mary's, but it's still the quickest way.'

Will pictured the park. Lush grass, a small play area, and healthy trees surrounding it. Overlooking it, St Mary's Court.

They moved on in the same line, passed the damaged buildings and holes in the road and moved through Cathedral Precincts. Will glanced at the cathedral as they walked and looked away fast.

Fire damage stained the old stone and marble. White beams of moonlight coated walls and brick scorched by flame, and Will found himself sniffing the winter air, searching for the scent of a fresh fire. He smelled nothing but his own sweat, cold on his skin.

They reached the edge of the park and Will pointed, fully aware he didn't need to but desperate to speak.

'St Mary's Court.'

Eight floors tall and as ugly here as he remembered it.

At least we only have to go up one floor.

'Flat nineteen, wasn't it?' Mick said.

Will nodded.

'Then let's go.'

They walked across the park and nobody commented on the crunch of grass crumbling below them. The park ended at a narrow path which in turn opened to the rear of the building. The road and paths that encircled the building were full of car wrecks and piles of broken glass. Mick kicked a loose pile of glass with the toe of his boot.

'All looks about the same,' he whispered and Stu giggled, the little laugh full of nerves.

'Call out *chav* and see if anyone appears,' he muttered.

Will glanced at them, silently telling them to shut up and fully aware their words and little jokes were nothing but a cover for their shared fear.

He tightened his hold on Karen's hand. The group stepped over the broken glass and stopped at the front doors.

The doors were nothing more than smashed wood, shoved open from the inside. The little moonlight that shone on the opening didn't extend far into the building.

'Flat nineteen,' Karen said and Will lurched forward a second before his wife could. They grouped in the entrance; Will gestured to the vague outline of the steps. In silence, they went up.

Thirty Two

Stu pressed his hand against the door; it opened without a sound and the smell struck them a moment before sight.

A rich, meaty smell that made him instinctively recoil, and a sight that sent cold creeping over his flesh.

The lower half of a man's legs were visible at the end of the hallway. And the stink had to be blood.

He glanced back at the others. The little streaks of daylight coming through the holes in the wood over the windows showed the fear on their faces.

Stu faced the interior of the flat again. 'Andy?' he whispered.

Nothing replied.

'Andy? You in there, dude?'

Nothing but his fear.

Stu pushed the door open fully. The aroma of blood grew stronger as did the smell of decay and dirt. Stu held a hand over his mouth with no self-consciousness. The others did the same and they entered the flat. After a few steps, the dead man in the living room was fully visible. Blood coated his face and chest. Behind Stu, Karen made an odd noise. Time slowed for Stu. He felt his body turning; the movement passing in stages. Legs, waist, chest, all moving as if through water as his mouth opened to ask what was wrong, and Mick's hand clamped down on his arm, a hiss of hurt blowing between Mick's lips.

Andy lay on the kitchen floor, hands on the knife jutting from his stomach.

'Andy?' Stu whispered.

Karen let out a scream and dashed to Andy's corpse. She fell at his side and her hands landed on his bloody stomach. She screamed again and the stink of blood crashed into Stu's nose. He gagged, coughed and managed not to vomit. For a few seconds, in which he felt removed from his body, he closed his eyes and tried to think past the bellow of outrage echoing in his head.

No thoughts managed to remain solid. Just a rolling wave of grief.

He slid down beside Karen; Mick and Will pulled Karen upright.

'Andy. Jesus Christ,' Stu whispered.

The tears wouldn't come. He felt them behind his eyes, it seemed, but they wouldn't come. He touched Andy's cheek with a fingertip and winced. The flesh of Andy's cheek went beyond cold. It was like touching the inside of a freezer.

Karen sobbed against Will, and Stu stood. A tremor ran up his legs and Mick took his arm, supporting him.

'We need a blanket or something,' Stu said. His words were thick, his tongue much too big.

Mick crossed to the curtains in the living room and yanked on one. It fell in a cloud of dust. Mick waved at it in front of his face and wordlessly offered an end of the curtain to Stu. Together, they placed it gently over Andy's body.

Sorry, mate.

The thought was nothing. Worse, it was all he had.

Close by, someone stepped softly, the movement sly in the gloom.

All conscious thought fell out of Stu's head. He yanked Mick's bat from his hand and ran to the hallway, then to the corridor, swinging the bat and raging.

Thirty Three

Kirsty stopped a few steps from him and kept her eyes on his.

'Thanks for coming,' he said.

His voice was soft, calm. He had the look of a manager about him, she decided. She could picture him as the sort of boss his staff liked and found him easy to talk to. His hair was thinning as he'd said and despite the paleness in his face and the slight bags under his eyes, he looked a few years younger than the mid-forties or so he had to be.

'Five minutes,' she replied, grateful her voice remained steady.

'What happens in five minutes?'

'That's how long you've got before I call the police to report my husband missing. No matter about your sister. I'm sorry, but I have to focus on my husband.'

'Of course.'

Kirsty gestured behind him. 'Over there,' she said and saw his question. She nodded towards to the record shop on the other side of the Square. 'Stu works there. I don't want anyone there to see me.'

'Of course,' he said again and walked towards the side of the Hall. Kirsty took a few deep breaths and followed. Once they were out of sight of the shop, she felt a little better. Not enough to move any closer to Phil, though.

'I really appreciate you coming,' he said and appeared to consider. 'Nobody else let me get as far as you did.'

She waited.

'Geri, she ...' He ran a hand through his hair. 'She was never happy, you know? Always something up. But we just took that as her being like some people are. Some people are always upbeat no matter what. She was the opposite. All the time. So when she ...when she ...'

'She killed herself,' Kirsty said. The words were ugly but she'd told him the truth: her focus had to be on Stu.

'Yes. She killed herself and my family sort of fell apart. My other sister, Leigh, she died years ago. A car crash. My parents couldn't handle living here after Geri died, as well. I moved away; my parents did the same and I've barely spoken to them in years. Then a couple of weeks ago, I saw her.'

'Geri?'

'Geri.' He seemed more relaxed and Kirsty wondered if that was down to talking about it or having someone to listen.

'I was at work. I'm a teacher. It was right at the end of the day. She was at the end of the corridor and at first, I thought she was just one of the students. She was too far away for me to see her face clearly, but then she started coming closer and I saw her. My dead sister.'

He laughed and ran his hand through his hair again.

'My dead sister. Bonkers. She came towards me and I couldn't speak. Couldn't make a sound. Couldn't even move.' He paused and glanced at a few women passing them. Kirsty let him wait. It was mad enough hearing this story in daylight only a few hundred feet from her husband's workplace. Nothing would be helped if she forced Phil to rush through his story.

'You see ghosts and stuff in films,' he said abruptly. 'And they have a message for people; they try to communicate. Geri didn't. She just kept coming towards me down that corridor.' Kirsty stared at his eyes. They were far away. She shivered and Phil went on with a flat finality.

'She vanished just before she reached me. Just disappeared. I've seen her four more times since then. She comes towards me and I can't move. The last time was two nights ago. I woke up in the middle of the night and she was in my bedroom.'

'Jesus,' Kirsty whispered and Phil's eyes focused on her.

'Can I ask what Stu told you about her last night?' he said and she struggled to marshal her thoughts.

'Not a lot to be honest. I don't think he knew what to say even if he'd had more to tell me. It was mainly that he'd heard her calling his name like she was shouting it. Then he phoned Will who had a drawing of her. Will's an illustrator. Kids' books. This drawing just appeared in his house. Karen saw her, too. Then it turned out Mick and Andy had their own things. They all went out last night to talk about it. And I haven't been able to get hold of Stu since.'

She rubbed at her eyes, angry with herself.

'All right,' Phil said. 'It's okay.'

She barked tired laughter. 'Is it?'

He managed a smile. 'Not really.' He slid his paper into a bin and stood with his arms loose by his sides, looking like an awkward teenager. 'Can I ask you to do one more thing for me? I know you want to call the police about Stu and that makes sense. I just want you to do one more thing. It'll take ten minutes. Fifteen at most.'

'What?' Kirsty said. She'd been seconds away from telling Phil she hoped whatever Geri wanted could be dealt with soon but she had to call the police. Maybe he'd seen that on her face.

'Come to the cemetery with me,' he said.

Seconds span out between them. More people passed and Kirsty shivered in the bite of cold to the wind.

Autumn's here, she thought and nausea rolled in her stomach.

'Her grave?' she said.

'Her grave,' Phil echoed. 'I know how it sounds, but it doesn't matter. I think we should go and see Geri.'

Thirty Four

Mick squatted in front of the girl and leaned in close to her face. She wouldn't look at him. He lifted his bat and jabbed it towards her.

'You best tell us what the fuck happened here,' he said.

She didn't move.

'*Tell us,*' Mick roared and hands gripped his shoulders, pulling him back. He overbalanced and his bat dropped. Will kicked it away and, at his back, Karen spun him around.

'Leave her alone. She's not to blame for this, Mick.'

He leaped to his feet.

'How the fuck do we know that?' he said and Will pushed himself between them. Beside the petrol stained wall and carpet, Stu pressed his head against the tattered wallpaper. He hadn't spoken in minutes. His scream from the corridor, the thud of his bat striking the wall and the girl's cries chased each other around Mick's head. And Andy lay on the floor in the kitchen, utterly dead.

'Does she look like she could have done it?' Karen said and Mick strode to the window. He faced the dirty glass and wished he still had his bat. How satisfying it would be to put it through the glass. Doing his best to calm himself, he faced Karen and Will. Stu didn't move.

'What happened here?' he said.

Karen moved closer to the girl and squatted. The girl pulled her knees up to her chest, shielding herself. Standing back a few feet from her, Mick knew Karen was right. Despite her ill-fitting clothes of dirty coat and torn jeans which made it difficult to be sure, but the girl was plainly no older than eighteen. Andy hadn't been a big bloke at all but he would have towered over her and outweighed her by a couple of stone. Unless she'd come at him in the dark and without making a sound, she hadn't stabbed him.

'What's your name?' Karen murmured.

Stu shuffled across the carpet to stand beside Mick. Will joined them, leaving only Karen close to the girl.

'It's all right. We're not going to hurt you. We just need to talk to you,' Karen said.

The only sound in the flat was the girl's breathing.

'I'm Karen. That's Will, Mick and Stu.'

Nothing.

'Can you tell us about our friend?' Karen's voice hitched but she kept speaking. 'His name was Andy.'

The girl's breathing changed. Mick strained to hear and realised it was a quickening to her breath.

'His name was Andy Pateman,' Karen said. 'He was our friend. We need to know what happened to him.'

The girl's eyes moved to land on Karen's and Mick forced himself to stay where he was, to not run across to the girl and scream at her to talk.

The girl whispered and the breath didn't reach Mick. He glanced at Will and Stu who both shook their heads. Karen leaned in closer to the girl.

'What was that?' she said and the girl answered.

'He saved me.'

Thirty Five

Karen drew back from the girl and watched her follow the movement. Hoping the others wouldn't speak and scare the girl back into silence, she said:

'He saved you from that man?' She pointed to the corpse with the broken face.

'Yes.'

'Can you tell us what happened after that?'

'There was another man. In the kitchen.'

The girl's whispers were barely audible. Grief, fear and a terrible anger swam inside Karen's stomach. There was nothing upon which she could focus her anger. Her hands clenched, relaxed and clenched again. Andy, dead; this girl whispering like a frightened child and horrible, filthy events here in Andy's flat. Her anger pulsed and she closed her eyes, struggling to think. Just as Andy had described, just as he'd seen. His old flat, a rapist, a girl and another guy in the kitchen.

'He was hiding in a cupboard. He had two knives.' The girl lifted a shaking hand and pointed at Andy. 'He stabbed him. The other man. But then he stabbed him back.'

'Motherfucker.' Mick kicked the wall. Plaster cracked and fell to the carpet with a sigh.

The girl flinched and tried to draw herself into a smaller ball.

'It's okay. He's just upset about our friend, not at you,' Karen said.

'Too fucking right I'm upset.'

Stu grabbed Mick. 'Quiet, man. This isn't the place.'

Karen watched the men, the murky light shining on them.

Mick spoke and Karen had never heard his tone before. It went beyond resigned. It was dead.

'I loved Geri but this is too much to ask. Andy's dead. We're stuck in the middle of a fucking nightmare and Andy's dead. It's too much to ask.'

'We'll make it right,' Stu said and Mick replied in the same dead way.

'How?'

Stu remained silent.

Eventually, Mick relaxed and Stu let him go. Karen faced the girl. She'd shifted position a little and some of the moonlight shone on her face. Karen frowned. The girl moved again and the brief impression Karen felt was gone.

'Can you tell me your name?' she said.

'I don't know.'

Karen spoke as carefully as she could. 'You don't know your name?'

The girl shook her head.

'Do you know how old you are?'

'Nineteen.' The reply was immediate.

'And do you know the name of this town?'

She shook her head.

'This building?'

'No.'

'The date?'

'No.'

She gave each negative reply in the same flat tone. There was no deceit in the answers. In her teaching career, Karen had heard kids lie for years. This wasn't the same.

'Do you live here in this building?'

'No.'

'Where do you live?'

The girl gestured vaguely to her left. Karen pictured the street outside, the road. If the girl did live in that direction, there were only a few square miles of streets that way before Dalry reached fields and farmland.

'What were you doing here last night?' Karen said. The girl shook but managed to speak.

'I was out. They found me. Took me here.' She pointed to the dead man. 'He hurt me. Said he'd burn my face if I didn't do what he wanted. Then the other man, your friend, he came in.'

'Jesus Christ,' Karen whispered. Exhaustion and grief made rational thought close to impossible. 'All right. You're safe with us.' She glanced at the stains on the girl's jeans. The girl saw her gaze and spoke with a terrible matter of fact tone that sent spasms of horror through Karen.

'It's all right. The bleeding's stopped now.'

Karen cleared her throat. It was too dry and the stale stink of blood and dirt in the flat had impressed itself deep into her nose and mouth.

'What happened after Andy came in? After you ...'

'I ran. The other man, he's in a flat down the end. I ran upstairs.'

'Is he dead?' Will said.

'Yes.'

'Then what? You heard us?' Mick said.

The girl flinched at the aggression in his voice.

'I was going to run downstairs. Had to come past here to get to the steps, but then you with the bat, you ...'

'It's okay. We didn't know who you were,' Karen said and the girl appeared to relax.

Karen cleared her throat again and wished for fresh air even if it was cold. 'Listen. I know this will sound weird but we don't know where we are. This town, we know it. It's called Dalry but we don't know it like this. It's not like this.'

'You're from the other place, aren't you?'

Cold horror touched the fine hairs on Karen's arms. 'What? Where?'

'Where the sun shines.'

A moment of silence filled the flat. Karen's anger had become a block of ice in her chest. Now coupled with her grief and exhaustion, fear closed in.

'Yeah,' Will said. 'I think we are.'

Thirty Six

'I'm at the cemetery off Gullymore Road,' Kirsty said and Jo's reply was immediate.

'What the hell are you doing there?'

Kirsty tightened her hold on her mobile as if afraid she might drop it. 'I know it's mad, but there's some weird stuff going on here. I just need to do this and I'll go to the police.'

'The cemetery. Jesus. I thought you were going to stay where other people could see you.'

'It's okay.' Kirsty studied the few headstones she could see. Phil had passed them a few minutes before and she hadn't seen anyone since. 'I'm still in my car. Phil had his. I followed him here and he's gone to his sister's grave. I'll wait in my car until he gets back, then I'm going to call the police about Stu.'

'Christ, Kirsty. Why did you need to go there in the first place? Why not just listen to him, *then* call the police?'

Kirsty rubbed her forehead. The desire was there; the words weren't. How to tell Jo something that didn't make sense was happening here; how to say she'd needed to do this. If Stu was simply missing, then that was one thing, but there was more going on here. If that meant ghosts and visitations, then that changed all this into something new and unknown. She knew her actions made no sense. Coming here with a man she didn't know to visit the grave of someone she'd never met was mad. And yet, here she was parked outside the cemetery on a Saturday morning while the rest of the world carried on as normal.

'This guy is okay. If he was a nut, I'd know it by now. He's just upset about seeing his sister or thinking he's seen her. I don't know.'

'Kirsty ...'

'If Stu went out last night without telling me what he did, I wouldn't be here. But this guy's sister and him seeing her as well has got to be something to do with Stu, right? Why else would Stu and his friends have seen her or heard from her or had drawings of her in their house?'

Jo spoke in a quieter voice. Kirsty could picture her using the same voice with difficult children. 'I just don't like you away from other people with some random guy.'

'It's fine. I'm in my car. The doors are all locked. As soon as he comes back, I'm starting the car.'

She heard crying children in the background, then Rich's voice. It sounded as if he was singing.

'Are they okay?' she said.

'Fine. Just a bit grumbly.'

Kirsty summoned Lucy's face to her mind. Picturing her daughter brought an easy smile to her face.

'Don't let Rich sing for too long to her. Don't want her to have nightmares.'

Jo laughed but it was a simple dutiful sound. 'Just be careful,' she said.

'I will. I'll call you as soon as I speak to the police.'

She let Jo speak for another minute, telling her to be careful, to not get too close to Phil. Kirsty agreed with the right words and eventually hung up.

She studied the entrance to the cemetery. Nothing moved there except the bushes that lined it. Phil had said Geri's grave was a few minutes from the entrance but he'd be quick. Kirsty checked her watch. It was twenty past nine. He'd been gone about fifteen minutes. She tapped on her mobile.

'Come on, Stu.'

She hadn't known she was going to speak. The undercurrent of panic in her voice scared her and she pocketed her phone.

Stu. What the hell is all this? Where are you?

Her mind repeated the moments before he'd left the night before, telling her about his dead friend and how people he'd lost touch with had seen her or heard her voice. Not believing him last night hadn't occurred to her. Even if it was a joke, it wasn't his style of humour at all, and he wouldn't make it up for no good reason.

Where are you?

She couldn't even take a guess. Just as it wasn't Stu's nature to make stuff up about ghosts and dead friends, it wasn't his nature to stay out literally all night and definitely not to do that without calling her.

She checked the mobile despite it remaining silent, and movement from directly in front caught her eye.

Kirsty's breath froze in her lungs. The steady beat of her heart became a terrible pounding in her ears and all the warmth inside the car vanished in an instant to be replaced by a burst of bitter cold.

A figure had come from the opening to the cemetery. They moved as fluidly as water from the gates to the edge of the pathway beside the road. Sunshine shone on their hair. The red glinted in the morning light. And that same light shone through their body.

Kirsty stared through the woman beside the road. She stared at a ghost.

A wordless shout began to form in her mind, bellowing at her that this couldn't be real; it was imagination; it was tiredness and stress and worry.

The ghost remained exactly where it was, facing the road, its face in profile to Kirsty. Daylight moved through her body, her body faint like steam. The white form of her body tapered down to nothing below the waist and ...

Not nothing, Kirsty saw. A pulsing redness shone below the figure's waist, roughly at her centre. Something red, breathing in and out.

Movement above the light as the ghost began to turn. Kirsty's breath refused to come and the thud of her heart drowned out all other sound. Some horrible force dragged her eyes upwards, passing over the ghost's mid-section, over the shape of her breasts and up to her face, to her eyes staring directly at Kirsty.

The roar of her heartbeat vanished. Everything around her vanished and there was nothing but the dead girl looking at her.

The ghost's face blazed with a shocking red light; Kirsty closed her eyes, tears leaking from the corners and sound returned: her panicked breaths, tight and painful in her chest. She rubbed at her eyes, managed to open them and stared ahead, vision still blurry with tears.

The ghost had gone.

No ghost. No ghost. Wasn't a ghost.

Yes, she was.

'Stu, what's going on? Where are you?'

The sound of her voice shocked her. It was the voice of a child, abandoned by a parent. She coughed and blew her nose and reached for her mobile.

Phil appeared at the cemetery entrance. He sprinted to her, eyes staring, mouth open.

Instinct awoke. Kirsty's hands dropped; she turned the key and checked the door lock at the same time. The car was secure.

Phil stopped close to her car, panting hard. She unwound her window down an inch.

'Are you all right?' she said, marvelling at the change in her voice from child back to adult.

His words were lost below the noise of the engine. Kirsty leaned close to her window.

'What?' she called.

He flapped at the hand towards the cemetery. 'I saw her. She was there at her grave.'

The daylight seemed to fade and Kirsty's mouth opened. She licked her teeth.

'What?' she said.

'At her grave,' he shouted. 'Jesus Christ. We have to go. We have to go.'

'Phil, calm down.'

'We have to go. My old house. It's just off Audley Road. We have to go there.'

He ran to his car; Kirsty unlocked her door, opened it and leaned out to call after him.

'Why?'

He glanced back as he opened his own door. 'She's taken them there. They're all in my old house.'

He threw himself into his car and started it. As he sped from the cemetery, Kirsty slammed her door closed and followed, not aware she was saying Stu's name over and over, thinking only of the ghost beside the cemetery gates.

Thirty Seven

Stu pressed his back against the window. Karen was still squatting beside the girl and as much as he wanted to join her, he knew he'd only scare the girl by moving closer.

'Are there others here like us?' he asked and the girl murmured a *no*. 'What about you? Do you live with anyone?'

She shook her head. 'There are people here. I see them sometimes,' she said.

'People like him?' Mick said and kicked the corpse.

'Yes. And others.'

'People like you, you mean? People that men like that hurt?' Karen said.

'Yes.' It was barely a whisper. 'More of them than us.'

'Shit,' Stu muttered. 'Where are they?'

'Around. They'll know you're here.'

'What?' Stu jerked forward and relented when Will put a warning hand on his arm.

'They'll have been watching you,' the girl said. 'Since you got here.'

'We haven't seen anyone,' Karen said and the girl shrugged.

Stu chewed his upper lip and asked a question to which he wasn't sure he wanted an answer. 'How long have you been here?'

'I don't know. A long time.'

'So you're not from here?'

'No. I'm lost. Like you.'

'Wait a second,' Will said. 'We're not lost. We're ...just ...we're in the wrong place. That's all.'

'So am I.'

Stu stared at Will, then Karen. They shared the same look and Stu knew it was on his face, too. He glanced at Mick and there it was—the realisation of their mad situation.

This wasn't Dalry. It was the lost side of Dalry. Something had brought them here and because they didn't know what it was, there was no obvious way of getting back to the real Dalry.

'We should go,' he said in a thick voice. 'How far away do you live?'

The girl considered. 'Not far. You can come with me.'

Stu strode towards the door; Will followed.

'Wait a second.' Mick pointed to Andy's prone shape. 'What about Andy?'

Stu struggled for the words and found none. Karen rose and spoke quietly.

'He has to stay here for now. When we can, we'll come back for him.'

'Jesus fucking Christ. This is a fucking nightmare. Andy, he didn't deserve this,' Mick said, voice thick with tears.

Nobody replied.

Crying, Mick stood close to Stu and Will at the doors; Karen extended a hand to the girl who eyed it, then stood without taking it.

'You'll take us to your home?' Karen said and the girl nodded eagerly.

They grouped at the door and the gloom in the corridor stretched to either end. Stu stepped out, paused and spoke without looking back.

'Wait,' he said and entered the kitchen.

The shape of Andy's body lay below the curtain. Stu held his breath and pulled the curtain away. Andy's head was facing the opposite wall.

'Andy,' Stu said. The others were behind him; he didn't turn around.

'Andy. Sorry, dude.'

Stu inhaled sharply, pulled Andy's sticky hand from the blade of the knife and moved before he could think about it.

Stu yanked the knife; the hard flesh around it parted and it slid free from Andy's stomach.

Mick let out a sob and that was all. Stu stared at the weapon, blade thick with his friend's blood. He pulled the curtain back over Andy and rose. The others looked back at him as he held the blade up.

'Good plan,' Will said.

They returned to the door, then the corridor. Will offered Mick the bat. Wordlessly, Mick shook his head, leaving Will to hold it awkwardly.

'We're going to your house, right?' Stu said to the girl.

'I have food,' she said and Stu forced a smile. God knows how long it had been since he'd eaten. Even so, eating was the last thing from his mind.

'What do you do for food here?' Will said. 'And water?'

'We find it.' The girl shrugged as if it was not a big deal and a brief urge to laugh madly struck Stu. It passed and he stepped into the corridor.

'Downstairs, out and to the left, all right?'

The others muttered their agreement. Stu looked at the girl.

'You okay to lead us?' he said.

She responded by walking a few paces ahead of him.

'Thanks,' Stu said.

Conversation stopped until they were outside. Karen and Will huddled together; the girl watched them and Stu wondered how long she'd been here. After a moment, he decided he didn't want to know.

'Which way?' he asked her.

'The river.'

She headed towards the field. Stu glanced back at the others.

'We don't have a choice,' he said.

'Suppose not,' Will replied.

They followed the girl, their grief and fear walking beside them.

Thirty Eight

'So, you really don't know how long you've been here?' Will said and wished he'd kept silent. The question tasted clumsy. Worse than that, it sounded patronising. It made him think of talking to an elderly relative, not a terrified girl who'd survived horrors he couldn't imagine.

'No,' she said without turning.

They left the grass of the park, found a pathway and followed it over cracks and shallow holes. Will felt Karen's eyes on him. He glanced at her and she nodded, encouraging him.

'You live alone?' he said.

'Yes.' Again, she spoke without facing him and without much emotion.

'I ...' Will began and the girl whirled around to stare at him.

'Too many questions. You need to look and listen and nothing else.'

Only a little of her face was visible: one eye, a cheek and half her mouth set in a firm line. As she stared at him, it was impossible for Will to believe she was no older than twenty. This was an old woman staring at him in the dark.

'We're scared,' he said, forcing the words out. 'We need to know what's going on.'

'You're lost.'

'We know that.'

'This is lost.'

The girl pointed to the ground and the nearby buildings that formed the rear of Cathedral Precincts.

'This is another version of Dalry, isn't it?' Stu said. 'Like in another world or dimension or ...'

'What? This isn't Doctor fucking Who,' Mick said.

'Doesn't matter. It's real,' Will muttered. 'She's lost. This park's lost. Andy's flat is lost. The whole city is lost and that makes us lost, too. It doesn't matter whether you call this another version of Dalry or another side, it comes down to us being lost.'

'Dalry has a lot of sides,' the girl whispered and a nameless fear crept up and down Will's back.

She moved and Will pulled Karen to jog after her before she had gone more than a few steps.

'Who are the people here? The people who want to kill us? The people we saw in the pub? They were eating dead bodies, for fuck's sake.'

'And who chased me near the school?' Stu said.

'Bad things,' the girl said to him. 'There are bad things everywhere.'

Stu shook his head, muttering. Will reached for the girl's arm and Karen blocked him before he reached her.

'Who are they? We need to know. Everyone here wants to kill us. Who are they?'

'They're not people. They're not ghosts. They're just bad.'

Mick laughed and the bitterness in the sound hung low around them.

'Bad? What are we talking about? Evil spirits? Demons? What?'

'Bad. Bad things,' the girl told him. 'They're not people. They're from outside.'

'Outside?' Will echoed.

'Yes. Where it's dark. They came here a long time ago. They've always been here.'

A voice spoke to Will. He wanted to believe it was Geri but it wasn't even close. There was a terrible age in the voice, age that went far beyond Geri.

Outside, Will. Outside love. They're forgotten by love and by everything inside. They live in the void. They hate the inside even though they'd do anything to get back to it. They don't know what being human is. They only know the outside of being human. They only know they're forgotten.

'They've always been here? Now what the shit does that mean?' Mick said and Karen waved a hand at him to quieten him.

The girl didn't appear to hear Mick. She stared at Will. 'They're not people. We are. They're outside us and they'll kill you if they can.'

'We've all gone fucking nuts,' Mick said and Karen whirled to face him, her hand spinning out of Will's grip.

'Is what happened to Andy nuts? You need to accept this, Mick. It's real and that means we're in trouble.'

Mick stared at her and Will discovered something horrible. Karen's outburst had robbed him of his voice. He looked from his wife, to his friend and back again and couldn't speak. His gaze moved to the girl who was watching them, face unreadable. Will stared at her, unable to blink.

He knew this girl. Her face. He knew it.

She turned from him and he caught a brief glimpse of her profile. Although quick, the sight was enough to convince him he'd been wrong. Although she was around the same age as he sometimes pictured Geri, this girl wasn't her.

'What's that?' Stu said, head cocked.

'Someone's coming. Quickly,' the girl said and ran for Cathedral Precincts. They sprinted after her, reached the road and dashed into a narrow passageway between buildings. Claustrophobia pressed in on them for a few horrible seconds. Then they were out to Bridge Street, completely exposed.

The girl ran to the other side of the road and vanished into a side street. Ignoring the pain in his side, Will tightened his hold on Karen's hand and followed the girl. She'd stopped beside a shop window. No glass remained in the frame and although it was narrow, it was still wide enough for a person to slide through.

The interior of the building stared at him. Will stared back. The runners were coming closer.

He pushed Karen behind him, Stu and Mick behind her, and followed the girl into the gloom of the building.

Thirty Nine

Mick slid down next to the girl and shifted position until he was as comfortable as he could be. His movement disturbed dust and he held his breath until the urge to sneeze passed.

'I'm sorry,' he whispered to the girl.

She gave no reaction and remained facing out of the window and Mick realised she wasn't snubbing him. She didn't care about his aggression or disbelief. Despite meaning his apology, Mick was too scared and too exhausted to press it. He studied the street below and saw no movement. At least twenty minutes had passed since the girl had brought them into this clothes shop and led them up here to a stockroom, but the running people, whoever they were, hadn't yet appeared.

Will joined him and crouched low against the wall below the dirty window.

'Anything?' he whispered.

'Nothing.'

He peered behind them and could just make out the shapes of Stu and Karen in between two piles of old boxes. Karen's head rested on Stu's shoulder. Mick studied Will for a moment, then faced outside again.

'Are you all right with this? I mean, with Geri?' he whispered.

'What the hell are you talking about? Of course I'm not. Are any of us?' Will kept his voice low. Even so, Mick hoped their conversation wouldn't carry across the little room. He paused, then continued as patiently as he could.

'No, Elton. I mean, *you* and Geri.'

Will stared at him and Mick wondered if now was as bad a time to mention it as any other time.

'Me and Geri? What the hell, man?'

'Don't give me that. I know how you felt about her and how it messed you up when it all went down the toilet.'

'Jesus.'

Will shook his head and Mick waited.

'Fine,' Will said. 'I admit, this is some shitty stuff. It's not every day you hear from your dead girlfriend, but all that matters is keeping Karen safe and getting out of here.'

'Good. Just remember that.'

'Why?'

Mick glanced back at Stu and Karen, their shapes almost indistinct in the shadows.

'I don't know. None of us have a clue what's going on; we've already lost Andy and I've got a bad feeling, all right?'

Will's smile was weak. 'I've had a bad feeling since I woke up in my old house and it was on fire.'

Mick allowed himself a soft laugh and thought of Andy laughing in the pub before everything changed.

'I'm sorry about before. In the flat. When I said it was too much to ask. Geri. She doesn't mean us any harm. I know that. I'm just scared out of my mind.'

Will's reply came in a rush.

'It's all right. Don't worry about it.'

Mick let a few moments of silence pass

'Who do you think was coming?' he said to the girl. His mind let go of Andy begrudgingly. He'd taken the bat from Will at some point without registering doing so. The chilly wood felt welcome in his hands.

'Don't know. The cannibal ones, maybe. This is their area,' she replied.

'Cannibals. Fuck me.'

'How long before we can move?' Will whispered.

'When it's safe.'

Mick rubbed the bridge of his nose, eyes closed. When he opened them, the shadows across the street moved.

'There,' he whispered.

'I know,' the girl said.

The figure, crouching low and scuttling like a spider, emerged from the shadows outside the flats of Cathedral Precincts. It was male although Mick couldn't think of it as a man. Its movement was exactly like a spider and an instinctive disgust filled him as they watched it. The figure ran to the building beside the clothes shop and returned a moment later with five others, all creeping out to the street and all dressed in the same torn rags. They huddled in the centre of the street, appearing to confer before running back to the buildings opposite. In seconds, they had vanished. The girl didn't move.

'Are they gone?' Mick whispered to Karen, and Stu slid over the dirty floor towards them.

'Maybe,' the girl said. She looked from the window for the first time since crouching there. 'They weren't the cannibals.'

'No?' Will muttered.

'No. The cannibals would have gone through every building, every room until they found us.'

She slid away from the window and stood.

'We should go before they come back.'

'Who the fuck were they?' Mick said.

'They don't have names. None of us do. Not anymore.'

They're from outside.

The girl's words echoed in Mick's head and he did his best to shake the memory of them off. It wouldn't go.

This is bollocks. This is all a load of shit, Mick thought.

He wanted to believe that, to believe the real world was right here with them and this was all a load of images somehow stuck in their heads.

Cannibals, for Christ's sake. Shadowy figures in dark streets, hunting for them. A teenage girl without a name, telling them the people outside weren't people; they were *things* from outside, whatever the hell that meant.

Outside the world. Outside anything that makes sense. Outside anything good and safe. This is real. You better accept that. Or those things, and that's what they are, those things will come for you and they'll tear you apart.

They followed her towards the stairs, Mick a step behind her. He pictured the route they'd taken across the shop floor—a mad dash through racks of jeans and shirts from the broken window.

Get back outside and get the hell out of here.

The girl moved with the curve of the steps. At the same time, a gunshot crashed out to echo around the stairway.

The girl smashed into Mick, knocking him into Stu. She managed to turn her face. Blood coated her neck and narrow chest. Her mouth opened and she dropped.

'Run,' Mick whispered.

He shoved Stu and heard screams. His own.

They ran back up and barrelled down the corridor towards the stockroom. Cheers and mad shouting followed them.

They were followed by the sound of people running up the stairs.

Forty

Seconds from the stockroom door, Mick shoved Will and Karen towards another door. Will smacked into it and ran inside a narrow kitchen, Karen a step behind.

'In there,' Mick yelled to Stu.

They crashed into the kitchen and Mick pointed to an open cupboard door.

'Mick ...' Will began.

'Do it.'

Will grabbed Karen, they ran to the cupboard, and Mick pushed Stu.

'Go,' Mick shouted and feet pounded through the corridor. Stu pushed him back and there was no time left to think. Mick ran to the far door, Stu behind him. They fell into a small staff room and bracketed either side of the doorway. The only illumination came from moonlight shining through a window in a far corner.

Someone opened the kitchen door. Panting breath followed a whisper. Then a giggle. Mick's skin grew cold.

'Hello?'

The voice was oddly gruff.

'You here?'

Another giggle.

Then a sliding step over the kitchen floor.

Mick stared at Stu who showed his hand, all his fingers splayed. Mick blinked sweat from his eyes.

Another sliding step.

Stu's fingers: four.

Another step.

Three.

Another step and another giggle.

Two.

The last step.

One.

Mick and Stu moved at the same time, both screaming. Mick swung his bat at the figure in the corridor; it caught him in the face. The man fell back, and Stu came low. His knife plunged into the man's side; it coughed blood over Stu's lower arm. Stu twisted the blade, ripping a great hole in the man's body. Blood gushed. Mick smashed into him; another gunshot crashed out, and Mick shoved the man backwards. The man's insides splattered on to his legs. The two figures behind him smacked into the wall in the corridor and both fell. Another gunshot roared and something buzzed past Mick's ear.

Bullet. That was a bullet.

He shoved the man down, swung his bat and hit another in the chest. As he dropped, Mick swung his bat again and caught the man in the neck. He fell, choking. Then cold metal dug deep into the exposed flesh of Mick's stomach and he realised his shirt had come untucked a moment before he realised the third man had a gun shoved into him.

'The woman,' the man with the gun said. 'Want the woman.'

'What?' Mick whispered and the man dug the gun in further to Mick's stomach and still his flesh was much too cold.

The man eased himself upright and stood with his back against the wall. He paid no attention to his friends, one dead and the other still choking. His face wasn't clear in the dim light; Mick could smell him, though. The stink came as mix of sweat, dirt and decay. In his torn clothes and in the muck covering him, he was a bag of filth.

'Woman. You killed the girl. You give me the woman.'

'The girl? We didn't kill her. *You* did.'

The man pulled a little of his scarf from his mouth. Mick held his scream inside.

The man's mouth was open in a grin. Animal teeth, each one a jagged fang, were visible. Most were stained red and the killer's breath reeked in ways Mick couldn't let himself think about.

'Should have been you. Was her. You killed her.'

Stu shifted and the man didn't look at him.

'Stay. Or he's dead.'

Stu froze. Mick risked a glance to his side and down. Stu was weaponless. The knife he'd taken from Andy's body jutted from the stomach of the first man, and even if he grabbed it, the guy with the gun would have plenty of time to move first.

'The woman.'

A tickle touched Mick's ear. He clenched his jaw and it came again. Scratching it would be suicide. Sweat fell into his eyes. The tickle touched him a third time and Mick realised what it was.

A breath.

His eyes darted to his right and the corridor was nothing but shadows.

A scent. Perfume. Something warm. Something clear. Then: *Mick it's all right, call her, it's all right Mick.*

Horror filled him just as joy did.

'The woman,' the man said, and Mick understood it was for the last time.

He looked towards Stu again but couldn't see his face.

You motherfucker, he thought at the man with the gun. *I'm going to fucking kill you.*

'Karen,' he shouted. 'Will. Come out.'

'Mick, what the fuck?' Stu whispered and the man laughed.

'Shut up,' he said.

A door opened somewhere behind, then Will spoke. 'Mick? Everything okay?'

A solid wall of self-loathing smacked into Mick as hard as it could.

Oh, you son of a bitch.

'Yeah.'

He couldn't stop the break in the word and he wondered dimly if the man would shoot him right now.

Soft steps approached from behind, just a few of them before a sharp intake of breath. Then Will yelling:

'You fucking ...'

The man was looking over Mick's shoulder, his grin widening into something horrible.

A savage burst of rage exploded inside Mick. His arm struck the man's wrist, he heard the gunshot but didn't feel it. And without having seemed to have moved, he was pressed against the man as if they were about to kiss. The man slammed against the wall and something cold and hard hit Mick's fingers.

Pressure slammed down on his forearm, his fingers registered the trigger a second before his brain did.

Then he fired the gun over and over, howling his fury as he did so.

Forty One

Karen stepped to Mick and placed a gentle hand on his arm. He whirled to her and there was a horrible moment during which she thought he would hit her.

'Karen?' he croaked.

'We're okay.'

He let go of the dead man who slid to the carpet. Karen deliberately didn't look at the great smears of blood coating the wall. The stink of it was bad enough.

The man fell to his side and she couldn't help but to look at the mass of gunshot wounds in his stomach.

She closed her eyes, took a breath and opened them again.

'Thank you,' she said.

Confusion filled Mick's face. 'For what?'

'For killing him.'

He gave her a shaking smile and glanced at his arm. Karen followed his gaze and hissed.

A bullet had grazed Mick's forearm. Blood rolled from the wound to drip onto the carpet.

'Just a flesh wound,' Mick whispered and held his hand over it. His mouth trembled and Karen kissed his cheek.

'We'll get something to cover it, okay?' she said and he nodded.

She glanced at Stu leaning against the opposite wall with his arms wrapped tight around himself.

'All right?' she said.

'Yeah,' he whispered and took a few deep breaths. Without speaking, he ran to the girl's body, kneeled and touched her face. He ran back to them, met Karen's eyes and shook his head.

I wish this hasn't happened to you, Karen said to the nameless girl but it didn't help.

Gripping the bat Mick had dropped, Will held it over the remaining man. He'd stopped choking and gazed upwards, hate on his face. Karen stood close to her husband and welcomed the anger filling her.

'What's your name?' she said.

He said nothing.

'I'll give you a choice. You talk to us or we'll beat the hell out of you.'

Mick let out a nervous laugh and she understood it. The words didn't belong to her any more than her anger did. She'd become someone else if only for a moment.

'I mean it,' she said to the man.

'Fuck.' He coughed. 'You.'

She moved a moment before she realised she was about to. One movement of snatching the bat from Will and bringing it down on the man's chest.

He doubled over, coughing, trying to breath, and Karen's rage sang in her blood.

'What's your fucking name?' she screamed and he carried on coughing. His saliva spattered on her leg and she hissed in disgust despite the spit only landing on her jeans.

'Karen,' Will said, reaching for the bat.

She moved it out of his reach and held it an inch over the man's forehead. Despite his struggling breaths, his eyes widened and she relished the fear in them.

'Why are you trying to kill us?' she whispered.

He coughed weakly. 'Don't belong here.'

He coughed again and blood flecked his chin.

'I know we don't belong here. We don't even know where here is or what we're supposed to do.' Karen closed her mouth and cocked her head.

'Karen?' Will said and she jerked a finger up to quieten him. The breath beside her came again. She stared at the man on the floor. Her rage, quiet for a moment, returned and keeping it inside took all of her willpower.

'Stu.'

He stared at her.

'Get the knife,' she said.

'Why?'

'We're going to need it.'

He slid past her, squatted beside the dead man and as soon as she sensed all eyes moving from her to Stu, she lifted the bat. The man on the floor opened his mouth, drawing breath.

Karen brought the bat down on his head as hard as she could.

Forty Two

Will couldn't stop his squeal as the man's head cracked. Blood flew in all directions and Will smacked against the wall, hand raised over his face to shield it from the blood. The man lifted a shaking hand; it dropped and his final breath joined the blood and teeth bubbling out of his broken mouth.

'What the hell?' Will screeched, hating the girlish pitch to his voice.

Karen lowered the bat to her legs and spoke without looking at him. 'Did you hear her?'

'Hear who?'

'Geri.'

Will struggled for a reply and gave up when none came.

'I did,' Mick said and flinched when Karen stepped close to him. 'A minute ago. When I ...him, down there. He had the gun on me and I heard her. She told me it was all right to call you like he said to, she said ...'

'It's okay. You did what you had to,' Karen said.

'It's not all right. I risked you getting hurt.'

'Yeah, but I'm fine.'

Karen squatted beside the wall and rested her hands on the handle of the bat. Will had to force himself to move close to his wife. He glanced at Mick, saw his desperate need to apologise for calling to them, and gave him a quick nod. He put a hand on Karen's shoulder and she leaned her head into him.

'What do you mean, you heard Geri?' he said.

'She was here. She told me about him.' She pointed at the man she'd killed. 'A rapist. A child rapist. I was probably too old for him.' She let out a sobbing laugh and gripped the bat again.

Stu kept his hand on the knife buried in the mess that had been the man's stomach.

'Can I be the first to say it?'

'Say what?' Mick said.

Stu wrapped both hands around the knife handle but didn't pull it.

141

'We're in another world.'

Mick remained silent. Stu faced him.

'We are, man. Look at all this. It's Dalry but it isn't. It's another world.'

Mick lifted his hand from the graze in his arm and Will winced. Blood had splattered on Mick's fingers and wrist.

'Say that's right, what's next?' Karen said and a memory bloomed in Will's mind. He pictured the house as it had been over fifteen years before: the wide driveway and pretty garden at the front of the house, kitchen window; her bedroom window above it, and the few stone slabs leading to the door at the side of the house.

'Number twelve Oakfield Walk,' he said and Karen lifted her head to stare at him.

'Geri's house?'

'Yeah.'

Stu pulled the knife free and he wiped his hands on his jeans.

'Sounds good. Only problem is that's got to be three miles away. Seems like it might be a long walk given how friendly the locals are.'

He stood straight and Will saw his own need to do something, to get moving, reflected on Stu's face. He pointed at the knife.

'We've got that, the bat and a gun,' he said.

'How many bullets?' Mick said and Will shrugged.

'Don't know. Can you check?'

Mick fiddled with the gun, his blood coating the barrel. After a moment, the cylinder opened. Mick let out a bitter laugh.

'None left. Son of a bitch.'

He closed the cylinder and looked at the others.

'Anyone we meet won't know how many bullets we have,' Will said.

Stu pursed his lips and a slow grin spread over his face.

'So we just wave the gun around and threaten them with it? A plan.'

'Either that or stay here until their friends turn up,' Will said and gestured to the bodies. Stu's grin died.

'Fuck that. Let's go.'

They moved back to the stairs, Will holding Karen's hand. The group shuffled past the girl's body. Nobody spoke. She lay facing the wall, a great deal of blood coating her chest. It had splashed up to her neck and more smeared over her cheeks.

It seemed grossly unfair to leave her body where she had fallen but there didn't seem to be any choice. Will squatted beside the girl, head bowed.

'Come on,' Karen murmured.

Will stood and they descended. He looked back once but the bodies of the killers had disappeared in the gloom. The body of the girl Andy had saved lay in a small lump.

Will held his wife and let her lead him downstairs.

Forty Three

Kirsty parked four spaces behind Phil, took out the keys and rested a hand on the door lock. Conflicting urges struck her: to open the door and run to the house Phil had parked outside, or to stay in the car with the door locked. On one hand, he'd brought her to a pleasant, residential side street from a long road lined with trees and full of expensive cars. It didn't seem too likely that if he was a nut, he'd try anything here. On the other hand, she didn't know him and Stu was still missing.

Her window was unwound an inch; she lowered it a little more and leaned her face to it, tasting the air. Phil slammed his door shut and jogged towards her. She withdrew, keeping a hand on the lock.

'You stay here and I'll go to the house,' he said.

'What the hell is going on? What did you mean, Geri's brought them here?'

He wiped at his mouth and she felt a moment's sympathy. His confusion and pain were clear, and while she couldn't trust him completely without knowing him, she could empathise with how he felt.

'Sorry. I should have explained it better at the cemetery.'

'It would have helped,' Kirsty said and smiled. He did the same.

'At her grave. I was there, talking to her. You know. And she was there, just a few steps away, watching me. It was like she was a picture but as real as we are. And I heard her speaking. She told me to come here, our old house. She's sent them here and she wants us to do something.'

'What?'

Goosebumps had risen on her arms as she'd pictured Phil in the cemetery talking to the ghost of his sister. Even the fresh, autumnal air couldn't warm her arms just as it couldn't take away the memory of the figure at the gates, turning towards her.

'She didn't say. Just that it'd be clear when we got here.'

He looked towards the rear of the house and sighed.

'Not been here in years. Didn't think I'd be back today. Christ.'
He gathered himself.

'Stay here, would you? It'd be better if I talk to the people who live here first. Tell them I used to live here. Probably better that than both of us knocking on the door and telling them about ghosts and all that.'

'Stu's not here now?' Kirsty said.

'She said they'd arrive soon after us.'

Doubts pressed against her but she kept them silent. 'Okay. Let me know when I can come in.'

He jogged to the rear of the house. Kirsty stared at him until he vanished from sight behind a high fence which presumably moved towards the building's front.

The silence brought back the memory of Phil's dead sister, Stu's dead friend, appearing out of nowhere.

'Go away,' she said and the harsh whisper of her own voice frightened her.

'Not as much as the ghost,' she whispered.

The drive to this house and focusing upon that had helped to keep her mind from what she had seen outside the cemetery, and what that might mean for Stu, as well as herself. Sitting silently now, though, a garbled run of thoughts filled her mind.

Geri. Ghosts. Stu. This man Phil. The police. She couldn't focus on any single one of them. She couldn't think past the faint figure at the cemetery gates turning towards her and being unable to hear anything other than the great thud of her heartbeat in her ears.

'Shit,' Kirsty muttered.

She took a few deep breaths and began to count. She kept her gaze on the pathway Phil had taken and counted.

Three hundred seconds. Five minutes. Sitting in her car while the world carried on as normal and her husband was missing had been close to impossible, but she'd made it through five minutes, counting silently and keeping her hands on the wheel while she waited for Phil to reappear and tell her what was going on with his dead sister and this house he hadn't seen the inside of for years, this house Stu hadn't been to for at least the last decade.

Kirsty pulled her mobile from her pocket and checked the time. Just gone quarter past ten. Her fingers tapped on the mobile, typing a text to Jo. She made it halfway through, realised she couldn't explain it all in text and deleted the message. But then how to say it over the phone? Either way was ridiculous.

She tapped her fingernails on the wheel and considered her options, bitterly amused to realise they came down to staying in her car or going up to the front door as Phil had done and knocking on it.

An elderly man appeared on the path beside the fence. He walked a further few steps, stopped and studied the cars. Kirsty lifted a hand in an unsure wave and he hurried to her, beckoning to her at the same time.

She unlocked the door, opened it and leaned out.

'Are you Kirsty?' the man called. He had a high, nervous voice that seemed odd when put against his bulky chest.

'Yes, that's me,' she said.

He stopped a few steps from her and swallowed a few times, his throat working mechanically. 'My name's Sam. I live at number twelve.'

He jerked a thumb at the house and swallowed again.

'Is Phil in there? Phil Paulson?' Kirsty asked.

Another swallow. 'Yes. He wants you to come in. He needs to talk to you about his sister.'

Moving slowly, Kirsty stepped out of her car and studied Sam. There wasn't anything remarkable about him: just an old guy in his trousers and cardigan, an old guy who'd probably go to the pub at lunchtime for a couple of pints with the other old guys, a man who'd welcome his grandchildren when they came to visit and be silently grateful when they left and took their noise with them. Nothing remarkable about him at all so why the hell was she uncomfortable?

'Everything all right?' she said.

'We have to go in,' he replied and looked at his watch.

'Why?'

'He said it's about his sister and your husband. He said it's about Stu.'

He searched her face and despite her tiredness and worry, she saw his fear. Not of her, though. Something else.

'Are you sure we have to go in?' she said quietly and he checked his watch again.

'Yes, now. Come with me, please.'

Kirsty locked the car door and slid a hand into her jacket pocket. Her hand found her mobile.

'After you,' she said.

Kirsty shifted her hand around her mobile and rested her thumb on the nine as Sam walked in front. Her other hand stole into her jeans pocket and gripped her keys as tightly as she could. The sharp tip of one jutted from between her knuckles.

Forty Four

They moved through the cathedral grounds in a line, Stu leading. Their shoes crunched on pebbles and debris, making more noise than Stu liked. He comforted himself with knowing their route either had to be this way or right through the centre of the city which would take them in full view of hundreds of windows all acting as eyes. At least through the grounds of the burned cathedral, they had passageways and shadows.

He stopped at a corner, leaned around it, saw nothing moving and crept further. He glanced back when Mick hissed; he had caught his wounded arm on the wall. Fresh blood pattered on to Mick's legs and he clamped his hand over the wound.

'You okay?' Stu said.

'Hurts like a shitter,' Mick said and squeezed his arm as if that would pull the pain out.

'You ponce,' Stu whispered and Mick wheezed a laugh.

'We need to keep moving. What's the quickest way?' Will said.

Stu thought through his exhaustion. If they followed their current path, they'd hit a passageway which would take them out of the cathedral grounds to a narrow road. It ran behind most of the shops on Bridge Street. At the end, they'd need to follow the road into the car park at Tesco. Then from there to alongside the river for a couple of miles.

Simple.

He wondered if he'd ever been so tired.

'We need to get to the river. Follow that,' he said and studied Mick. 'You sure your arm is all right?'

'I'll survive.'

Mick flicked blood at the pavement and attempted a grin. It made his face look sickly.

'Seems pretty exposed going that way,' Karen said.

'Either that or straight over Thorpe Road bridge,' Will said.

'I think it'll be all right once we get closer to the river. If it comes to it, there are plenty of trees and bushes to hide in,' Stu said.

'I'm too old for climbing trees,' Mick muttered.

'And too fat,' Stu said and Mick punched his arm.

'Let's go,' Will said.

'Wait a second.' Mick coughed, clearly struggling for his words. They waited and he whispered towards the ground.

'I'm sorry about before. In the shop. Those men. I shouldn't have called for you, said you could come out, I ...'

'It's all right.' Karen sounded near tears.

'No, it's not.'

'Yes, it is. You did the right thing. If you hadn't, I'd bet we'd all be dead.' Karen touched his shoulder gently. 'It's okay,' she whispered and Mick managed to nod once.

They moved in the same line as before; Stu took them through the passageway and wished they hadn't stopped for as long as they had. The cold had turned his sweat into an unpleasant sheen on his body and he prayed for the early autumn mildness of the day and night before to return.

Hold that thought, he told himself and halted when the passageway opened to the road. He counted four wrecked cars, all burned out. The road itself was black in places: scorch and skid marks staining it. Once again, Stu wondered just where the hell they were.

Geri, you better start explaining things soon.

They moved on in a tight line and ran alongside the rear of the buildings. Broken glass littered the pavement in places and more stains coated the slabs. They reached the halfway point and a scream rang out all around them.

'Christ,' Stu hissed and froze. Mick fell on him and he only vaguely caught Mick's grunt of pain. The noise ran on, the sex of the screamer impossible to guess, the terrible sound a mix of pain and fear that fell silent either because the person had run out of breath or been silenced.

'What the hell was that?' Stu whispered.

'Was it a woman?' Karen said and Will leaned in closer to her.

'No,' he said. 'That was a bloke.'

Stu saw the command to agree on Will's face. He nodded. So did Mick. Karen didn't relax.

'We keep going,' Stu whispered and moved on again in a bent run, eyes straining in all directions.

They ran past old railings which met a narrow passage, and stopped again. The end of the road wasn't far ahead. Stu estimated they could be beyond it, over the road and into the car park at the Tesco car park within five minutes. First, though, they had to get beyond this passage which would expose them to Bridge Street.

'Stay low,' he whispered to Mick who said the same to Karen and Will. Stu pressed himself against the railings, leaned forward and peered around the edge into the passage.

His breath stuck in his throat and his heart gave a horrible skip. A cough rose from his chest and he desperately swallowed it back.

A body lay on the road in the middle of Bridge Street. Short, narrow poles jutted from it and streams of blood ran in all directions.

Not poles. Arrows.

With faraway horror, Stu realised what the strange, whispery sounds had been.

The body moved.

An arm rose and fell against the road, the fingers dug into cracks and it began to pull itself along. Sickened but unable to not look, Stu watched the body move a couple of feet, arrows jutting from it in at least five places. Its long hair coated the face and with the hunched body, there was no way of knowing if it was male or female.

Its hand lay splayed on the road, still for a moment, and Stu only registered the hissed whisper in the air a second after the arrow hit the hand.

The body howled, the head jerked up and the hair fell away from the face. One eye, full of hellish awareness, stared straight at Stu.

It was a woman.

He jerked back and swallowed cold air several times, afraid he would vomit.

'What is it?' Karen whispered and leaned towards him, head moving to the corner.

Stu shoved her back. 'Don't. Just don't.'

'What the hell is it?' she said too loudly and he raised a hand towards her mouth. Will pulled her close.

'It's a woman. She's been shot. With arrows,' Stu said. The beat of his heart hurt in his chest and the sour taste in his mouth suggested vomiting might still be close.

'We have to help her,' Karen said and Stu shook his head.

'She's still being shot. Someone's in one of the buildings, shooting at her.'

'Fucking hell,' Mick said. 'They're playing with her?' His voice rose, heavy with horror and incredulity.

'Looks that way,' Stu said.

Karen wept and her voice trembled, anger radiating out of her in waves. 'We can't leave her there. Jesus Christ, what the hell is going on here?'

Another sharp whisper hissed. A pained cry followed it straightaway and Karen slapped a hand over her mouth.

'Where are they shooting from?' Will said.

'Quiet,' Stu whispered. He listened and heard nothing.

Moving inch by slow inch, he eased his head around the edge of the building and peered to Bridge Street. The woman remained on the ground, arrows still jutting from her. Swallowing repeatedly and aware it wasn't helping to lose the sour taste of his spit, Stu scanned the little he could see of the windows opposite. Movement on the second floor caught his eye. He held his breath and prayed none of the others would speak or move.

The movement was definitely a figure, someone leaning through the broken window.

'Nobody move,' Stu breathed and sensed the others freeze beside him.

Something else moved behind the indistinct shape in the window. Stu could only take a guess as to how many people were in the room two floors up. At least three.

Three people shooting arrows into a dying woman.

Geri, what is this? What the hell are we supposed to do here?

Cloud covering the moon shifted and Stu had a glimpse, no longer than a second, of the figures in the window before the moonlight left the building in darkness again.

Instinctively, he threw himself towards Mick who caught him with his uninjured arm and pulled him against the rear of the building. Karen's arms embraced him and he shook.

'What is it?' Will whispered.

In the window. In the window. Jesus Christ.

'*Stu,*' Will hissed and Stu stared at his friends.

'People. The people shooting. They don't have any faces.'

He trembled in Karen's arms and wished he hadn't looked, wished he had suggested a different route, wished Geri hadn't brought them here.

And for a ghastly moment, he wished he had never known Geri Paulson.

'We have to go,' he said and the words tasted horrible. Strangely, they brought a thin slice of focus back to him. 'We can't help her without getting killed. We just have to hope that she ...' He choked and forced out the rest of his sentence. 'That she's killed quick.'

'Jesus,' Karen said dully.

Mick stood; Stu did the same and Will pulled Karen upright. Mick gestured to the road in front. The gap of the passageway at their side was just a couple of feet.

'On three,' Stu whispered. 'Just don't look.' He inhaled and let out it out with his words. 'One, two, three.'

They dashed across the gap and Stu couldn't help himself when he heard the sly hiss of a loosed arrow. He looked.

The woman on the road lay still. A new arrow rose from the exact centre of her back.

Got her spine, Stu thought. He crashed into the next building and vomited as quietly as he could.

Forty Five

They reached the car park at Tesco around five minutes later. Nobody spoke as they slipped between wrecked cars and kept as close together as possible. Will's fear had grown into a form of terror he'd never known and it was easy to believe he wouldn't have been anywhere as near to this level of fear if he'd been alone.

Karen. It was all about her. Keep her safe. Keep her in one piece. Keep her safe.

The thoughts filled his head to the point of knocking anything else out of the way. He saw the cars and the damaged buildings, but they were off to the side of his attention. Karen was what mattered. Nothing else.

They reached the pavement beside the car park, followed it and grouped beside a smashed wooden fence that blocked the pathway from the flats on the other side. Will glanced around. If he remembered correctly, the road on the other side of the fence was Magnolia Drive which in turn met Thorpe Road.

He poked the fence and wiped his finger on his jeans. The fence was real. No doubt of it. But he didn't want the feel of it on his skin.

'Two or three minutes down here. We'll be at the river in five,' Mick said.

'And probably another ten minutes to Geri's house,' Stu said.

They followed the path and stayed close to the low fence. It came to an end where it met hedges. Without debate, they walked away from the hedges and nobody commented upon the rotten stink coming from the greenery.

The path met a cycleway lined with patchy grass. Ahead, it curved into Magnolia Drive. Stunted trees lined the path. The branches were bare and Will wondered if this was a good idea. There'd be few places to hide out here. Maybe behind tree trunks but without any thick branches or lush hedgerows, they'd be exposed.

Mick led them to the path and towards the river. Colder air rose from the water to meet them. Will shivered and Karen held him tight.

The cycleway levelled into a straight line. Tired looking trees ran alongside it and the cold from the water grew the further they walked. Will placed a hand on his stomach. If they didn't find food soon, they wouldn't have the strength to walk much let alone run.

A sound caught his attention. He jerked his head to the right. Wind pushed through grass in a secret whisper. Opposite to the bare trees, the grass grew thick and wild; the wind blowing through it made the blades and nettles rub together and created a secret whispering.

He glanced behind; they'd come a fair way. The end of the cycleway and the road which would eventually take them to Geri's house had to be less than a mile beyond. He watched the waving grass as they walked. Several minutes passed; he didn't look away. Pressure built in his chest and despite their relatively fast pace, things around him felt too slow.

Geri. Where are you?

They walked, Will's eyes moving from waving grass to bare tree to the path beyond and back to the grass. He forced himself to relax as much as possible and kept his eyes on the back of Mick's head. His breath frosted in front of his mouth with each exhalation; the tips of his fingers burned owing to the ugly cold biting into his exposed flesh. He flexed his free hand repeatedly and relished the hold of Karen's fingers embracing his other hand. He studied her face, wishing he could see her clearly. He saw enough to know she was smiling at him and that was something wonderful in a horrible place.

Abruptly, his mind threw up the image of the girl from Andy's flat, her face superimposed over Karen's.

He jerked away from her, nausea rolling inside him.

'What?' she whispered.

He shook his head and breathed slowly. 'Nothing. Just imagination.'

She gave him a reassuring smile and he drew her close.

'The girl in the flat,' he whispered.

'Yeah?'

'Did she look like anyone to you?'

The question sounded stupid. And it felt stupid.

'I don't know.' Karen frowned. 'Maybe. It's hard to say.'

Mick and Stu glanced at her; Stu met Will's eyes, his eyebrows raised.

'What's up?' he said.

Will spoke as quickly as he could, describing the idea he'd known the girl from somewhere. Karen nodded when he finished speaking.

'I hate to say this, but she looked a bit like Geri. Not a spitting image. Maybe a cousin.'

'Sort of the idea I had, too,' Will muttered.

'What are you saying?' Mick said.

'I have no idea. It's just odd, is all.'

'We can deal with that when we get to Geri's house. For now, come on,' Stu said.

Will held Karen as they walked, one arm around her waist, his fingers touching a tiny patch of exposed skin and relishing the feel. He refocused his attention on Stu and Mick a step ahead and the sound of their shoes and boots on the path.

Something flickered to the side of his vision. He stopped walking and gazed to the field off to his right.

Through the thin trees, lights advanced.

They came from nowhere, it seemed. Six flaming torches, all on the far side of the field, the vague shapes holding them not hurrying but all coming towards the river as if they had all the time in the world to get there.

Will's hand clamped hard on Karen's and she drew in a pained breath.

'Will, Christ, that hurt.'

'Oh, shit,' Mick whispered.

Stu and Karen followed his gaze. Stu swore and lifted his blood-stained knife.

'What do we do?' Will said. The pressure in his chest, which had faded for a moment, returned, growing with each passing second.

The blazing lights changed direction. All of them began to move in a straight line across the river, heading for the pathway.

'Run,' Will said, pulling Karen.

They sprinted, their makeshift weapons swinging beside their legs. A shout rose from the field and Will knew without looking the others had given chase.

He didn't think. He ran with Karen's hand in his; the group covered a hundred yards of path and Mick dropped to the long grass growing on the riverbank.

Stu halted and Will came within a foot of crashing into his friend. Stu grabbed Mick's hand.

'Get up, you shit,' Stu said, panting.

Mick rolled over, eyes much too wide. *'Got me, it's fucking got me.'*

A pallid hand jerked out of the grass, dirt and earth ingrained in the pale flesh. Will screamed as a pale forearm shot from the grass. The hand raced up Mick's leg, reached his thigh and pulled. Mick slid a few inches, bellowing. The long grass parted around him and a second hand, as white as a fish, pulled at his other leg.

The second hand had eight fingers. It splayed over Mick's leg like a pale spider.

Will lunged at Mick's other hand; he and Stu pulled hard. Mick came with them. The hands in the grass pulled in return and Mick went with them. The shouts from the field came again and Karen grabbed Will's bat. He saw her movement with stupid wonder.

I don't even remember dropping it, he thought.

She swung it at one of the hands on Mick's leg. It jerked away at the last second and she struck Mick's thigh.

He howled.

The hand shot back to its place on Mick's leg and both pulled. Karen swung the bat at the grass, aiming for the body of whatever held Mick. The bat hit something solid, the hands pulled and the people, if they were people, shouted again from the grass. They were closer now, much too close.

Karen.

She stared at him and Will realised he'd spoken aloud.

'Fucking pull him,' Stu yelled and Will realised a second thing: Mick hadn't stopped screaming since he'd fallen.

Will's grip faltered just for a second. The hands pulled Mick and he broke free from Stu's hold.

He slid into the grass and vanished.

'Mick.' Stu ran into the grass. At the same time, a ghastly splash rang out and a huge explosion of blood coughed out of the river.

It pattered down on to the greenery and back into the water. Karen shrieked, a broken shriek of rage and hurt. Stu lunged forward again. Will grabbed him and they both whirled. *They're coming. Run,'* Will shouted.

The hollers behind had become whoops of savage joy. Will pulled Stu again who stumbled back to the cycleway.

'Mick, Jesus ...' he said, sobbing.

They ran, made it fifty yards and the sound of those behind changed. They'd reached the cycleway.

Will ran faster than he thought possible, Karen and Stu beside him. No solid thought existed in his head, only the need to run. They reached the end of the cycleway, shot on to the road and crashed through an overgrown garden. Pain had bloomed in Will's side a moment before and the stitch stabbed him eagerly as they ran.

They dashed over another garden, crossed the pavement and sprinted in the middle of Audley Road. And there it was—the sign on the side of the road for Oakfield Walk.

Speech wasn't possible. Will pulled Karen onwards, heard people shouting from behind and understood the bellow of hate and rage following them.

They skidded over black grass, mud licking the legs of their jeans, and ran into the Walk.

All the houses apart from one were as damaged as all the others they had passed.

Number twelve stood untouched. The front door was open, beckoning them.

Will looked back. The six figures from the field were seconds behind them, hoods and rags covering their faces.

Will, Karen and Stu reached the front garden of number twelve, sprinted to the front door and a strange whisper stung the air right behind Will.

His mind shrieked one word

—*arrow*—

and then nothing.

Forty Six

The front door wasn't locked. Kirsty stayed a few steps behind Sam as he pushed the handle down and opened the door to a hallway, walls lined with photos, stairs off to the right.

'We're here,' Sam shouted and Kirsty didn't miss the trembling in his voice. She remained still even when he gestured for her to follow.

'Where's Phil?' she said.

'In the living room. It's at the back. Just down here.'

A tiny voice whispered in Kirsty's mind, telling her to phone Jo and let her know what was going on. More importantly, where she was.

'Come, quick,' Sam said.

His mouth trembled.

This is wrong. This is all wrong.

'Come on,' he shouted.

'No. Tell me what's going on.'

He flinched and said the rest in a low voice. 'It's her. His sister. She's here.'

Cold terror crept up and down Kirsty's arms. Her light jacket did nothing to warm her. Her mind attempted to flash back to the figure outside the cemetery. She wouldn't let it.

'Geri?' she said, feeling stupid. 'Here? Now?'

'Yes.'

'Alive?'

His eyes remained nailed to hers.

Confusion and panic stopped her thoughts making sense. Geri. It was all about Geri, and she was here now.

Which meant Stu must be on his way.

The logic of the thought didn't matter. She jogged forward, hands still on her phone and keys, and passed Sam. He closed the door gently and pointed to a door at the end of the hall.

'In there,' he said.

'After you.'

He grimaced; Kirsty wrapped her hand around her car keys, satisfied with the way the metal jutted from between her index and middle fingers. She glanced up the stairs as they passed. Nothing there but more photos on the wall. Nothing on the other side but the open kitchen door.

Sam pushed open the living room door and Kirsty heard him speak. 'We're here.'

Nothing replied to him.

Kirsty crept forward and realised she was sweating as if she'd sprinted here.

Sam was facing what looked to be a sofa; Kirsty could only see the arm of it and a patch of the blue carpet.

'We're here,' he said again and a woman's voice, faint and weak, came in a reply Kirsty didn't catch.

'Stu?' she called.

Kirsty rushed forward, shoved the door open and faced the living room. There was nobody on the sofa, nobody beside her but an old man.

Something cold pressed against the back of her neck and Phil murmured behind her.

'Don't move, Kirsty.'

She couldn't breathe. The movement of her thumb seemed to be happening to another person. That other person pressed the nine on her mobile three times.

'I'm really sorry about all this, Kirsty. I really am.'

He pushed with his other hand and an old lady fell past Kirsty. She hit the carpet and rolled, crying and holding her wrist. Sam ran to her, also crying, and tried to pull her upright. He glared past Kirsty and shouted:

'You bastard. Get out of my house.'

'I need your mobile, Kirsty,' he said. Tears filled his voice. She wanted to turn, to see him, but didn't dare move.

'Mobile?'

'Give it to me. Please, Kirsty.'

He pressed the knife a little harder into the back of her neck; a tremor ran from his wrist to his fingers and into the blade. Kirsty fished around in her pocket as if having trouble pulling it free. There was no way the operator could have heard everything; they'd probably hung up when she hadn't told them she wanted the ...

'Police.' She threw the phone towards a chair. 'Twelve ...'

Phil's boot smashed down on the phone. It snapped and he leaped back to her. His movement to the phone had been so fast, she'd barely felt the lack of metal on her skin. He lifted it to her face and leaned towards her.

'We have to talk,' he said. 'You and me.'

He was crying and the kitchen knife shook inches from her face.

'Phil, please.'

He shook his head and wiped at his nose and eyes like a child.

Kirsty couldn't speak. A dream-like terror had come, banishing all thoughts apart from of her daughter. Even Stu was out of her head for the first time since the night before.

'We're going to talk about my sister,' Phil said. His breath tickled her lips and she struggled to think past the fear. The first conscious thought that came was an image of Phil in Memorial Square, covering his mouth as he fought tears and she'd thought him good-looking in an odd way.

Horror rose into her mouth and she said the name. 'Geri.'

Phil sighed and all the weariness she'd ever heard was a weight in the sound. 'Geri,' he whispered.

Tears ran down his cheeks.

Forty Seven

Stu hit the bannister, his forearm struck the wall and he bellowed his pain. The crash of the slamming door filled the hallway and Karen, holding Will, dropped to the carpet. Stu struggled upright and fought for words, any words.

Will fell out of Karen's grip.

'Am I alive?' he said and Karen pressed her face to his, lips to lips.

'Mick,' Stu croaked and staggered past Karen and Will. He gripped the handle and saw the splinter in the wood of the door level with his head.

'Arrow,' Will said and Stu stared at him. 'Bows and fucking arrows.'

Stu touched the splintered wood, cold. If they'd been a second slower, the arrow wouldn't have hit the door. It would have hit Will.

'Mick,' he said again.

'He's gone,' Karen whispered.

Stu screamed once. It hurt his throat and he didn't care. Andy, now Mick. Not Mick. It couldn't be true.

'Those bastards. I'm going to fucking kill ...kill ...'

His words fell apart and wept hot tears. He tried to choke them back and they fell anyway, bitter in his eyes and on his cheeks. He punched the door, relished the pain and did it again. A hand took his and held it. Karen.

'It's all right,' she whispered.

'It's not fucking all right,' Stu yelled and she didn't flinch or let go.

'No. It's not,' Will whispered.

'Will,' Karen said.

'It's my fault,' Will said and Stu stared at him through the blur of his tears. Will's shape wavered; Stu blinked his tears away and Will returned to focus.

'It's my fault,' Will said again.

'How do you work that one out?' Stu whispered.

'I let him go.'

'It doesn't matter. If we hadn't run, we'd all be dead,' Karen said and Stu attempted to summon anger just as he pictured himself punching Will in the face.

'I can't do this. It's too fucking much. Geri, she's dead. She's dead and they're killing us.' Stu's voice rose into a scream. 'We're dying here and I can't do this.'

He drew his foot back and smashed it into the front door. It shook and a small piece of wood broke from the impact of his foot. He kicked again and again and only stopped when Karen pulled him back.

'Stu, stop. Stop it. Please.'

Stu shook and held a hand a hand over his mouth.

'Geri's dead, Karen. She's dead and we can't help her. Mick's dead. Andy's dead. Who's next? Huh? We can't help her. She's dead and we're dead if we stay here.'

'I know, Stu. I know.' Karen's voice sounded as if it was coming from faraway. Stu took a few breaths and did his best to focus. 'I know she's dead and I know we're hurt, but we can get through this, okay? We'll be all right.'

'How?' Stu croaked.

'I don't know. But we have to keep ourselves together. We have to keep in one piece otherwise we've got no chance.'

Stu's rage faded away to leave him feeling sick and cold. Anger made no difference, though. His grief didn't change Karen being right.

'Christ on a bike,' he whispered.

He crossed to a window which overlooked the front garden and stared outside. Grass, flowerbeds, the path leading to the walk which in turn led back to Audley Road. Nothing moved.

'Where the hell are they?' he whispered.

'Keep your head down,' Karen said. 'They could be hiding but able to see us.'

'They're not there. Nobody's there.'

Stu strode through the hallway to the kitchen. A few paces inside the room and the reality of their situation hammered into him.

Geri's house.

He leaned against the fridge and stared as Karen and Will followed him.

It'd been over ten years since he'd last set foot in Geri's house. Nothing, in this world at least, had changed. Everything from the spacious kitchen which opened to another room was the same. The same washing machine, the same table in the centre of the next room, the same patio doors letting in the moonlight. It was like standing in a photo.

'Are we here?' he whispered.

'Yeah, I think so,' Karen said and touched the wall. She stared at it, then at the table. Stu watched her cross to it while Will stayed at the door. Karen ran her fingertips over the table surface and laughed.

'This is unbelievable,' she said.

'Why is this place normal and nowhere else is?' Stu replied.

'This is Geri's house,' Will murmured. He stared at Stu. 'This is her world, isn't it?'

'How the hell does that work?' Stu shouted.

'Think about it. Her house is okay and everywhere else is a wreck. Just about everyone we've seen has tried to kill us and this is the one place we're safe. She probably wanted us to come here to begin with.'

'Geri's dead,' Stu said and knew that didn't change anything. Mick and Andy also being dead changed nothing as well and that was as horrible as things could get.

'Does that matter?' Will said and stepped towards the hall.

'Where are you going?' Karen asked.

'Upstairs.'

He headed to the stairs and Karen stood. Stu shook his head. She sat back down and rested her hands on the table. Stu fell beside her and tried to think of anything other than his dead friends.

Forty Eight

'Twelve steps,' Will whispered and gazed upwards.

How many times had he walked up these steps all that time before? How many times full of nerves and excitement? How many times with Geri in front of him, looking back, taking his hand and smiling?

He climbed the first two steps and a memory came fast and hard.

Walking behind her, her hand in his with the house silent and empty this lunch time, with his shoes on the floor beside the front door, and the winter sunlight striking the white of Geri's legs below her knees as they ascend. She sees his gaze on her shins and calves and she laughs and she lifts her skirt to flash her thighs at him and she laughs again. There's a glimpse of her underwear and every thought is shot out of his mind at the sight of her thighs and the white cotton. And it's November and he's twenty and she's holding his hand as they go upstairs and there are another four months of this, of being happy, before it all goes bad, before he can't cope with Geri, anymore.

The memory fell off him in small degrees. Will took a few deep breaths, glad to lose the picture of all those years ago. Moving with slow, deliberate care, he reached the second floor, gazed at the closed bedroom doors and wondered if going back in time would feel anything like this.

Back in time. Save her. Save Andy. Save Mick.

'Mick. I'm sorry.'

He barely heard the sound of his voice. Everything of the last few hours was far away.

Will crossed to the nearest door.

Opening it was easy.

Stepping into Geri's bedroom was impossible.

Will gazed at the bed, unmade as always, at the posters of bands long since disbanded, singers long since out of the music industry, and at the piles of clothes on the floor.

This is exactly what going back in time would feel like.

It was all as it had been almost twenty years before. His life of university, jobs, drawing and Karen hadn't happened in this room. Here, everything was stuck in the seven months he and Geri had been a couple.

You weren't a couple. You let her down. You let her go.

'Fuck you,' Will whispered and entered Geri's room.

At once, the cold from outside which had pressed into the house vanished. Warmth replaced it. More than warmth. This was the gentle burst of heat that rose early in the morning on good days which would grow hot.

'Geri?'

Will moved a few steps further into the bedroom, vaguely glad the door didn't close behind him.

'Geri. Geri.'

Saying her name brought some small sense of calm. He gazed at her desk and pictured her sitting at it, studying, revising. The memory of his last two years at school and the time after drew in close around him and he welcomed it. In a mad way, it was like going home, going back to the days when everything had been okay and it didn't matter that it hadn't been, really. They'd been together, they'd been friends; Andy and Mick had still been with them, and most of all, things made sense.

'I miss you,' Will said and let out a little laugh. 'How about that?'

He traced his fingers over a poster of Oasis, then another of Blur.

'Why all this, Geri? Why this place? Why is your house not the same as the others?' He paused and gazed at posters of Britpop bands. 'Why *this* time?'

He couldn't take a guess. If the house was a sort of memory of Geri's life, then why fill it with a time ten or so years before she died?

Will eased himself down on to the bed and fought the strong urge to lay back. Do that and he knew he'd never want to get up.

'Andy, Geri. Mick, too. They're gone.'

Those horrible seconds on the cycleway returned: the feel of Mick's sweat soaked hand in his, the shouts of the killers who'd chased them, and thinking of Karen the second before Mick's hand fell from his.

He closed his eyes and didn't open them.

Even when the lips kissed his.

Forty Nine

Karen balanced the plates of sandwiches; Stu held the glasses and the carton of milk. Together, they went to the stairs and up. Will lay on Geri's bed, arms by his side and he didn't move when they approached the door.

'Sarnie?' Stu said.

Will rolled over and sat upright.

'Food?' he said as if the concept was foreign. Karen answered, mostly in an effort to not focus on her husband on his ex-girlfriend's bed. She knew it was stupid given the situation but that didn't change the bizarre note of jealousy she felt.

'Kitchen's full of it. The fridge works, the cupboards have got a lot of stuff. It's like someone stocked up for us.'

She and Stu entered the bedroom and placed the food and milk on Geri's desk. Karen eyed the food. She wasn't hungry and didn't think Stu was either. Thinking of Andy and now Mick taken from them had stolen her appetite. Even so, she knew they needed to eat. God knows where or when they'd next find food if they had to leave Geri's house.

She offered the plate to Will. He took a sandwich and nibbled at it without enthusiasm. Karen did the same and rested beside him. Stu sat at the desk and they ate in silence for a moment.

'I felt her,' Will said around his sandwich. 'She was here.'

'You saw Geri?' Stu said.

'No. I felt her. Just for a minute when I came in. I think she always wanted us here.'

Karen gazed around the room, struggling with vertigo. Being in Geri's bedroom with it looking exactly as it had when they'd all been sixteen or seventeen was too surreal for her to get a grip on.

'Anyone got a plan?' she muttered.

'Sort of,' Stu replied. He chewed the last of his sandwich. 'This is all about Geri, right? It's her house; she came to us before all this. She's dead and I'm guessing she wants to either tell us something or wants us to do something.'

'Suggestions?' Will muttered around his sandwich.

Stu waved a loose hand at the clothes on the floor and by the wardrobe.

'There's got to be something here that will mean something, right?'

Karen eyed the wardrobe. It was easy to picture the messy clothes inside it just as it was easy to see her friend in her short skirts, in that black wrap she'd loved so much. Those clothes would be in the wardrobe and below them would be Geri's shoes and boots, and in the cabinet beside the desk, there'd be a load of her tapes and CDs.

The past was in the wardrobe and in the cabinet. It was all around them, breathing their air.

'Who wants to look?' Will said and put his plate on the bed. Karen glanced at him. He had his hands linked on his knees and his head hung limp. Pity came instead of jealousy, followed by a fierce wish Geri had left them alone, had stayed dead.

'I'll do it,' she said and crossed to the wardrobe.

It opened easily and inside was just as she'd imagined it. Skirts and tops hung together on the rack, and piles of more skirts and jeans lay at the bottom of the wardrobe beside shoes and boots. Karen squeezed one of the skirts between her fingers and thought of Geri as she liked to remember her: seventeen and laughing.

I miss you, you bitch, she thought and blinked back tears.

'Anything?' Stu asked.

'Give me a minute.'

She touched more clothes and ran her fingers over a pair of boots she hadn't seen in years. Geri's favourites. Black, two inch heels, and a silver pattern in the stitching up the side.

Karen opened the second half of the wardrobe. Four built-in shelves were piled high with CDs and paperbacks. Two photo albums jutted out beside the books and Karen didn't have to try hard to resist opening the albums.

Not ready for that. No way.

A small cabinet with three drawers was below the bottom shelf. Karen squatted and opened the top drawer. Jewellery. In the second, everything from pens to cassette tapes, and in the bottom, a mix of underwear and colourful bras. Karen touched them and there was no surprise when she felt the shape of a book below the bras.

She pulled the book free. A simple notepad with the cover torn off and the first page full of tidy handwriting in a steady blue. Karen read the first line. For the third time, she fought back tears. When Will placed his hand on her shoulder, she gave up and wept over her friend's diary.

Fifty

'I'm sorry.'

Kirsty tried to think. Was it the fourth time the old guy had apologised or the fifth? Fear made it impossible to be sure.

'Don't worry about it,' she replied and did her best to give Sam a reassuring smile. He and Charlotte were on the bed, his arms wrapped around her while she quietly wept against him. Kirsty pressed herself against the wall below the window and eased her legs flat. At the bedroom door and holding the blade close to his side, Phil watched her. She risked staring at him for a moment and again wondered how fast he could move.

'I'm not a bad guy,' he said. She hadn't been expecting him to talk and did a good job of keeping herself still.

'Okay,' she said.

'It's just that the last few days, they've been difficult. I've had to think on my feet a bit.'

He smiled. He actually smiled. That was somehow worse than his tears.

You fucking bastard.

Kirsty kept her face blank.

'I didn't know what I was going to do until we were halfway here. Of course, it depended who lived here now. This used to be my parents room.'

'Did it?'

The window was only a foot or so above her head. How fast could she stand, open it and scream? How fast could be move across the floor and stab her with that knife? The bigger question was one she had no answer for.

Would he?

'Yes,' he said.

He glanced at Sam and Charlotte. 'Good thing for me it was you two here,' Phil said.

'Get out of my house, you bastard,' Sam roared.

Phil flinched but that was all. 'Please keep your voice down, Sam. I don't like this any more than you do, but it's a strange business. I'm doing the best I can to keep this all together so please keep your voice down.'

Sam subsided and pulled his weeping wife against his chest.

'I gave him to the count of two hundred to get you from your car,' Phil said to Kirsty and she nodded although he'd already told her this. That had been just before Sam's first apology. 'He did a good job. One hundred and seventy.'

Sam shook and Kirsty mentally willed him to keep quiet.

'When are you going to tell me what this has got to do with me?' she said.

'It's not to do with you. Not really. I tell you, I knew it would create problems when I got you instead of your husband or Will or Karen or anyone else. Getting them would have made it a lot easier.'

'To do what?'

'To get to my sister.'

Kirsty paused, unsure of what to say next. He watched her; she watched his face and watched it change. All the life fell out of it, leaving him standing at the door like a corpse.

'You need help.'

They were the first words Charlotte had spoken. She'd lifted herself from Sam and faced Phil. 'You need help,' she said again.

Light and life returned to Phil's face as if trickling into it.

'I do,' Phil agreed. 'But probably not the same sort of help you're thinking of.' He pointed a stiff finger at Kirsty. 'I need *her* help. More importantly, I need help from her husband.'

'I want to help you. We all do, but you have to tell me what this is about,' Kirsty said and prayed he'd believe her.

'It's about my sister,' Phil replied as if it should have been obvious. 'I told you. I'm not a bad guy. I don't want to hurt anyone here and if there was any other way of doing this, believe me, I'd be doing it. You wouldn't have heard from me; you wouldn't be here, I ...'

He broke off and placed a trembling hand over his eyes, then lowered it to cover his mouth.

'She wouldn't be haunting me,' he whispered and the words were close to being lost below his hand.

'Let me help you. Please,' Kirsty said and risked a glance to Sam and Charlotte. He was watching her, unblinking and unable to keep his face clear of the obvious wish she could find a way out of this.

'Tell me about Geri. I know you saw her at the cemetery.'

Kirsty wished for more saliva in her mouth and on her tongue. It felt like a piece of dead meat in her mouth. 'I saw her, too.'

Phil stared at her and she had no idea what to make of the look on his face.

'At the cemetery?' she said.

'Did she speak to you?'

'No. She was by the gates when I was in my car. She was facing the road. She started to turn towards me and vanished.'

Describing in such matter of fact terms robbed it of any power, of the fear that had made her deaf. At the same time, it helped to bring it into the real world. She could deal with it a little more by stating it in a basic way.

'How did you know it was her? You never met.'

Kirsty surprised herself by laughing. 'Who else would it have been? I don't make a habit of seeing ghosts.'

Phil let out a noise halfway between a laugh and a snort. He eyed her. 'You want to help me, don't you?'

'Yes.'

She didn't hesitate in her reply. A little hope bloomed. She could talk him out of this, get herself and the old couple out of the house and get the police here. Then get Stu back from wherever he was.

'Then we need to find your husband.'

Kirsty's hope wilted. 'Why? What's this got to do with Stu?' she cried.

'He was her friend,' Phil said as if that explained everything.

Staring at him, Kirsty realised that to Phil that was exactly what it explained.

Fifty One

Stu took the diary from Karen's hand. She'd been holding it towards him for at least thirty seconds with no sign she'd sit down. Will wouldn't take it. Not that he could be expected to, Stu thought. And Karen had done enough with going through Geri's stuff. Stu had seen the photo albums and an urge to grab those albums and look at pictures of the past had come and gone quickly. Even just thinking about doing so was enough to make his stomach threaten to reject its little meal.

Karen joined Will on the bed, their legs touching. Stu moved to the window, then decided being in full view of anyone outside was a bad idea. He crouched and gazed at the diary without reading it.

'Should we really read this?' he said.

'Yes,' Karen said.

'Jesus.'

Marvelling at the feel of the little book, Stu ran his fingers all over it. It felt as real as his own skin or the dirt and sweat covering him, and yet his rational mind told him it couldn't be. Geri was gone. Her home was gone. And this diary was just dead paper.

'I keep thinking we've gone back in time,' he said without taking his eyes from the diary.

'Read it,' Will muttered.

'Or we're inside Geri's head, maybe. She created all this and we're stuck inside something she imagined. Maybe none of this is real and we're just somewhere Geri made up.'

'Stu,' Karen said.

'Yeah. All right.'

He couldn't get away from it, no matter how much he rambled or voiced his fears.

Stu focused on the neat handwriting and said the first word on the page.

'I ...'

Everything went black.

Fifty Two

Light first. Then heat. Will, Stu and Karen exist in the heat and light, exist as one. Their eyes are blind, their skin bakes. And when the light roars down on them, their eyes are opened.

Colours and space; gaps and light. Red sits below their skin and swallows them and digests them. They drop into the gaps, they swim in the red down there and in that bleeding light, in that horror and in that hope, everything shrinks in an instant to an infinitesimal dot. They live inside it, still bathed in red, still lit by that light, dancing there on the last day of summer, on the first of day of winter and all the days in between when life makes sense, when the city and its streets and grasses and secrets are theirs. They love there; they live there and it's the most wonderful place in the world. More than that, it's all theirs, every dark inch, every lit corner, and they exist as one; their friendship will never be brighter or louder and how they shine right now, how they glow in the red. This is the centre of their town, the middle of their youth and they love here, they live for each other here and now.

Vision comes. Scenes flipping from one to another on all sides.

A razor touching a forearm, a line of blood welling from white flesh. Children playing football and the lush green of the grass below their feet. A glimmer of a flickering light in a bathroom and a girl leaning over the toilet, vomiting. Night on a suburban street, teenage boys and girls in a rambling line and small drifts of snow cover gardens. The razor again, and a long sleeve sliding over the arm to cover it. A school desk, glowing yellow light bouncing on to it from the window behind, the timeless yellow light of a thousand schooldays that all last forever.

Vision goes.

The centre of the tiny dot explodes; they race with the growing dot, pushed out to the edge, growing with that edge and falling away from the centre as fast as it wants to push them away. Still lit by the red and the horror and light, they streak through time, racing from the dead days of childhood at the centre of the dot, racing from what is theirs, expanding always, always further out to later years, teenage years and those years burn in space; they burn with each other through their time of love and grief and doing all they can to forget that grief even if it costs them their time and all the love inside it.

Now their thoughts each belong to the others, their shame and their hurt all race with the speeding growth and come crashing into the end of everything, crashing as they reach the end of their time.

Within the swirling red and its love, they see the end of everything. A howling void. There is nothing but one forever scream in the dark, no light or love or red. And somewhere beyond that endless scream is home.

The life in the red buries them alive and brings all its horror and all its hope for love to them in one crushing instant and it brings a name with that horror and all that hope.

A name spoken from the other side of the scream.

A name in the dark.

Red.

The red.

Oh god the red, the red between ...

Fifty Three

The diary fell from Stu's hands, hit the carpet and Stu collapsed. He lay sprawled on the carpet, staring at the ceiling. Will watched him with an odd detachment. It was a little like being drunk or lightly stoned and that was fine. That meant he could handle what had just happened.

'Were you?' Karen whispered.

Speaking was an effort but he managed it. 'Was I what?'

'Glad it finished.'

He stared at her. Her face, so familiar and so lovely for the best part of twenty-five years now belonged to a stranger judging him.

'What?' he said.

'We know,' Stu said. He pulled himself against the desk but didn't rise any further. 'We know how you felt which means you know how I feel.'

Karen didn't drop her gaze from Will.

'Sort of,' he said and his cheeks flamed.

'Sort of?' Karen echoed.

'Okay, a lot. Christ, what do you expect me to say? It fucked up with Geri and *that* fucked me up, but it was still a relief. She was hard work, more hard work than I wanted. For Christ's sake, I was twenty. What twenty-year-old wants a manic depressive girlfriend?'

He fell silent, face still red, and stared at his hands.

'I didn't want her to sleep with a load of other blokes and I didn't want her miserable but I couldn't change what she did or how she was. So when it ended, I ...' He managed to look Karen in the eye. 'I was probably more messed up because of knowing it was a weird relief than because it ended. Does that make sense?'

'Yes,' she said, her voice sluggish. 'I always wondered how you really felt about her and what that made me. If it made me second choice.'

'You've never been second choice. You're my wife.'

Karen made no attempt to wipe her wet eyes. 'You know what I felt,' she said.

'Yeah. And there's no need for it. Geri, she's gone. I want her to be happy or at peace or whatever but that doesn't change anything between us.'

He took her hand and offered silent thanks when Karen kissed him. He glanced at Stu as Karen pulled away.

'You really think any of this was your fault?'

Stu studied his hands and took his time before replying. 'I'm the one who stayed here. And I always felt like I could have kept us together after Geri died. Probably bollocks but it's how I felt. Like I could have done more.'

'It's not bollocks,' Karen said and Stu gave her a weak smile. 'You were always a good bloke.'

Stu's smile grew stronger even though he looked away from her.

'Thanks,' he murmured and gestured to the diary. 'Want me to have another look? We still need some answers.'

'As long as we don't see all that stuff again,' Will said and attempted to picture all the red and the light, the images of the past, of Geri cutting herself, of the howling in the void beyond.

'She was there, wasn't she?' Stu said.

'I think that might have been her ...soul or spirit or whatever. We were inside her. We saw her, didn't we? Cutting herself. At school. With us, walking home from somewhere. We were all there,' Karen said.

Stu picked up the diary and opened it at a random page. He scanned the page and the colour bled out of his face.

'What?' Karen said.

Stu looked up and his eyes met Will's. 'Dude, this is ...it's like a letter to you.'

'Read it,' Will said and wished his heartbeat would slow to a normal rate.

'Sure?'

'Read it.'

Stu licked his lips, dropped his gaze to the little notepad and went on without a pause and without looking back to Will.

'Will, I am sorry, there, I said it finally. Only took me far too long. I am sorry, I am sorry. I can say it as long as you like or as long as I can keep saying it. I am so fucking sorry, this is not what

I wanted. This is all the way from anything I wanted to happen or for you to feel this way. I am sorry. Is it okay now? No, of course it isn't. I'm not that stupid even though everything I've done has been stupid lately. Not that I'm making excuses, I know I can't. I wouldn't try to even if I had any. This is as bad as it can get, isn't it? I think that and hope sort of I'm right because I don't want anything worse than this. But there's always worse things like how I can make myself feel, how I can fuck myself. There. Said it. I didn't know if I would till I did. I can fuck myself and the worst part is what I think of. Because I don't think of you. I don't. I'm sorry. I fuck myself and I think of the worst thing to happen to me. Sounds small doesn't it? The worst thing to happen to me. The worst thing to happen to you and I'm part of both, I was there for both, I was involved in both. I'm sorry. I'm sorry. I'm sorry. I'm sorry. I'm sorry. I'm sorry. I'm sorry. I'm sorry. I'm sorry. Jesus Christ God I am sorry. How many times do I have to say it? Will. Will. Will. Will. Will. Will. I can keep saying that. I really can. I really can. I really can. I really can. I know you won't ever see this. I know you never will but I still had to tell you I am sorry. I didn't want to do this to you or for you to feel like this I really didn't. Sorry Will, so sorry always. Geri.'

Silence.

Will inhaled once, twice, and the tears broke out of him as if eager to taste the air. Karen took him and he wept against his wife. He wept for dead love.

Fifty Four

Kirsty eased her arm down towards her knees and moved her wrist in slow circles on the pretence of fighting its stiffness. Phil watched her, unspeaking. She massaged the flesh, waited until his gaze moved from her and snatched a glance at her watch.

3:42.

As bizarre as it seemed, she'd been sitting here, trapped with an old couple and a man driven crazy with grief and confusion for easily five hours. Jo would have called the police hours before; they'd be looking for her at the cemetery and they'd be calling her friends and family to see if she'd been in touch with any of them.

What they wouldn't be doing was searching an address that had nothing to do with her. And that meant they probably had no chance of finding her.

Her stomach rumbled and the sound almost made her laugh with the ridiculousness of it. Her body didn't care about being trapped with a dangerous man or the threat of ghosts. It cared about food.

Despite her growing hunger, she didn't vocalise it. Phil had taken the three of them to the bathroom an hour before and although he hadn't put his knife to any one of them while the others used the toilet, it had been raised to his waist and the threat of it was clear. Kirsty hadn't dared to try anything, to call for help or even open the bathroom window during her minute in there. So what if she could open it without him hearing? There was no way she could call for help and have any of the neighbours see her before he could open the door and silence either with his fist or his knife.

But would he, her mind asked? Was he dangerous because of aggression or was he just a man confused and still grieving for his dead sister, and made dangerous because of that grief? Would he really wound or kill any of them if they made a move?

Her stomach rumbled and Phil glanced at her. 'Hungry?' he said.

'No.' She knew how pointless it was to lie. Even so, she couldn't bring herself to admit it. Admitting her hunger would give him another edge over her.

Another edge? He's got a knife. What more does he need?

'Yeah. okay. I am.'

'So are we,' Sam said. He still had his arms around Charlotte. Neither of them had spoken in hours and Kirsty had discovered she was madly envious of them. They weren't facing this alone. They had each other. She had a missing husband and a daughter she might never see again.

Exhausted tears threatened and she kept them inside. Phil appraised her, then Sam and Charlotte. He swapped the knife between his hands and flexed his fingers. The white tips bloomed with red as he wiggled them.

'I should have thought. Sorry.' He stood and pointed at Kirsty. 'Best way to do this is if you go downstairs and make us something to eat. Some sandwiches or something.'

'All right.'

Kirsty spoke as calmly as she could while her mind raced through options. Get downstairs, run to the door and run outside. A neighbour's house or the road? Shout for help as soon as she was outside or leg it to a front door and scream through a letterbox?

'I'll have to trust you, Kirsty. I know you want to get out of here. I do, too. But we have to wait a bit longer.'

'How much longer, Phil?'

'Until it gets dark. Shouldn't be long.' He checked his watch. 'Just another couple of hours. Then I'm gone, but until then, I have to trust you to just get some food and nothing else.'

'Yeah.'

She stood, the curtains heavy against her back and neck. With a tremendous will, she kept her gaze from Sam and Charlotte, desperate to not see their hope and trust that she could somehow get help.

How can I? He's got a fucking knife. What the hell can I do?

The answer was as simple as it was obvious.

Get your own knife.

'Sandwiches,' she said.

'Yes.'

'Give me a few minutes.'

He opened the bedroom door and stood to the side. Kirsty took slow steps towards him and the door, her eyes staring ahead to the hallway. As she drew level with him, he placed a gentle hand on her wrist.

'I'm trusting you, Kirsty. And you have to trust me. I don't want to hurt anyone, but unless all you do is get some food ...'

The threat hung between them. All at once, she knew it didn't matter why he was dangerous. Grief or not, Phil was dangerous. All she could do was hope she could somehow get through to him.

'Just food. That's all,' she said.

He opened the door fully. She left the room and started down towards the kitchen.

Fifty Five

Karen finished speaking when the words ran out on the page in her hands. The last word—*school*—brought a range of emotions and memories. Greatest of all those emotions was fear, and the strongest memory was a pained one: the last day of school, a hot day with all the time in the world stretching away from it. Despite the hurt inside the memory, she did her best to hold on to it. There was sense and logic inside it. She knew it.

'Girl's got issues,' Stu muttered and Karen let go of the picture of the long dead day.

'We still don't know why,' Karen replied and tapped the page. Despite the room temperature, the page was cold.

'Does it matter?' Will said. They were the first words he'd spoken since Stu finished reading Geri's letter. He answered his own question in the same flat tone. 'It does, doesn't it? Otherwise we don't know what to do.'

'We've got an idea from that,' Stu said and pointed to the diary. 'We need to go to school.'

'How the hell can we do that? We go outside and we're dead. Jesus, you saw what happened to Mick,' Karen shouted.

'So, we just stay here?'

'Yes,' she yelled and took a breath to calm herself. 'At least for now.'

'We can't,' Will said and she stared at him. 'We can't stay here forever and we have to help Geri. That means leaving.'

She wanted to hit him, to scream at his face that Geri was dead and they would be too if they left. His mild eyes looked back at her; she squeezed the bedcovers between her fingers and took another calming breath.

'Okay, say we do go. How do we do it without getting hurt? For all we know, those mad bastards are right outside now.'

Stu stood and walked to the window. He ducked below the ledge, then rose an inch so his eyes were level with the bottom of the pane. 'I've been thinking about this. This is different to everywhere else here, right? I don't think Geri's house is part of the rest of the town otherwise why haven't the people outside tried to get in? If they could, I think it's safe to say they'd have broken down the door the second after we got here.'

'Fine. Which means?' Karen said.

'Which means this place is like a protection for us.' Stu splayed his fingers over a section of the wall between two posters. 'We really should have come here first. We would have been safe.'

He left the rest unsaid. Even so, Karen heard it.

And Mick and Andy would still be alive.

'If this house is our protection, our safety, we need to keep it with us,' Stu said and took his hand from the wall.

'How? We can't take the whole house with us if we leave,' Will said.

'I know, but I think if can keep part of it with me, I'll be okay.'

'You?'

Stu glanced at Will. 'Yeah. I can run faster than you.'

'What are you talking about?' Karen said. She knew, though. It was all over Stu's face.

'I'll go to the school. I'll go and see what Geri's doing.'

'No way,' Karen said immediately.

'You've got a better idea?'

'Yeah. We stay here and work out what the fuck's going on.'

'There's nothing we can do here.' Stu faced the window. 'I think if I take Geri's diary with me, I'll be okay.'

'You *think?*' Karen whispered.

'Yeah.'

'Christ.' Karen laughed. 'We're making this up as we go along, aren't we?'

Stu gazed at her and Karen saw the sweet boy she'd known twenty years before.

'Yeah,' he said and his face split into a sunny smile.

He stood and extended his hand to her. She gazed at it and handed him the diary without speaking. The last few words in the diary played over in her head—

he did it again and I couldn't stop him and I want them to hurt like me, all of them at school—

'Wait a second,' Karen said and crossed to the wardrobe. Steeling herself, she rummaged through the messy piles of clothes and shoes and closed a hand over one of the photo albums.

'What are you doing?' Will said.

'Getting more protection.'

She pulled the album free and let it fall open to a double page spread of pictures. At once, grief filled her just as joy did.

'Geri,' she whispered and traced her fingertip over Geri's smile and her face. The shot was from a night in a pub, probably around the time she and Andy had left for university. In the photo, Geri was smiling and lifting a drink to her mouth, Mick beside her with two fingers held up to the camera and his tongue sticking out. In the photo beside it, Mick had lowered his hand, Geri's drink was at her mouth and not quite obscuring her smile as Mick kissed her cheek.

Karen's tears pattered on the picture and she let them fall, smiling as she studied the other photos. They didn't appear to be in any order. Shots of their late teen years mixed with older shots of Geri and her family when she'd been twelve or so, then shots from university life. Karen turned the page to photos of childhood pets: a large black and white cat, one ear tucked under his head and a paw reaching towards the camera; a border collie pup chasing a ball in the garden. She turned the page again and her gaze immediately fell on a photo in the top right.

It was all of them. She sat beside Geri on a school table. Stu was on Geri's other side, Mick beside him, and Will in front of Geri, her hand on his shoulder with Andy squeezing into frame beside Will.

Others had crammed into the shot and while she could name all of them, she knew they weren't part of the photo in the same way she, Geri and the boys were. Maybe they knew it, too. A few were smiling, but most were looking out of shot or at each other. She touched Geri's hand on Will's shoulder and there was no jealousy. Seeing them together in such a perfect moment was exactly as it should be.

'Christ, look how much hair I've got,' Stu said.

She hadn't heard them come to her and that was all right. She reached for Will without turning and he was there.

'Let me see that,' Stu said.

Karen handed him the album. He traced two fingers over the photos and eased the group shot from the page.

'I remember this. We were seventeen. About a week before the Christmas holiday.' He laughed. 'Look how fat Mick is.'

Karen smiled although it hurt to think of Mick just as it hurt to think of Andy.

'Wasn't that the time he said he'd lose two stone for a new year resolution?' she said.

'Yeah. And he did it, too. The fat bastard,' Will replied.

Stu gently placed the album on a shelf in the wardrobe and looked at both of them.

'When?' Will said.

Stu held the diary in one hand and the photo in another. Karen watched his throat work as he swallowed twice.

'Now.'

Fifty Six

They stood beside the bannister, Stu a little way from Karen and Will. He kept his eyes on the front door and his hands on the diary and the photo.

'I figure it's ten minutes to the school, I spend no more than twenty minutes there, and ten minutes back,' he said.

'What if you don't find anything?' Will said and Stu shrugged.

'Then we're back to square one.'

Silently, Karen offered the baseball bat and knife to Stu. He glanced at both and took the knife.

'Sure?' Karen said.

He nodded once, eyes back on the front door. He'd seen that door countless times but never like this, never when things were so wrong. Mick and Andy both gone, and how the fuck could that be? The rest of them haunted by their dead friend who'd never done anyone any harm if she could help it, and how the fuck could that be, and here he was about to go outside by himself, go back to their school and how the fuck could that be?

He crossed to the door.

'You shut this the second I'm out,' he said.

'Stu,' Will said weakly. 'The diary, man. The picture. What if they don't work?'

'Then I'm fucked.'

Will rubbed at his mouth and spoke, eyes on the floor. 'I've been thinking about that girl in Andy's flat and how she ...I don't think she looked like Geri, exactly. I think she was a version of her.'

'What makes you say that?' Karen said.

'No one thing. There was just something in her face that looked a bit familiar. And that makes me wonder if ...shit, this will sound mad. It makes me wonder if there's anyone else here like us, like that girl or if everyone else is just another version of Geri.'

Stu managed a smile that actually appeared real. 'You're right. That does sound mad.'

'Think about it. We haven't seen anyone else human like us. Everywhere but Geri's house is a threat. This is her world. This is like being in her head. I think that girl ...' He hissed and said the rest in a pained rush. 'I think that girl was meant to die so we'd come here. I think Geri wanted to send us here.'

Stu considered. 'Yeah. You're nuts. But you're probably right.'

Karen pushed past Will and embraced Stu. Her breath was hot and quick on his ear.

'Come back,' she whispered.

'Of course.'

He let her go, eyed Will and gripped the diary, photo and knife in one hand. With his other hand, he gave Will a weak shove on the shoulder.

'See you, Elton,' he said.

Will wiped his mouth with a shaking hand and didn't speak.

Stu faced the door again. He kissed the front of the diary, did the same to the picture and jammed both into his jeans pocket. They made a comforting bulge. He gripped the knife handle, counted to three and opened the door.

He was outside and the door shut behind him before the urge to look back overran him.

The arrow they'd fired at Will grew from the door. Stu didn't touch it. He faced the silent road and the silent houses and pressed a hand against Geri's diary and the photo. A queer sensation rolled in Stu's stomach. He knew the door, house and his friends were behind him but even so, his surroundings seemed vague. He concentrated on the pathway, the hedges and other houses. All felt to be mere impressions of solid objects. It was like looking at a drawing and the thought of Will and Karen in Geri's house was a loose, baggy image. A step from the front door and he was in another country.

Forget it. Just move.

Stu slid one foot over the paving, then his other. Standing still, he heard nothing at all.

He wasn't alone, though.

Stu scanned the still trees and hedges. No twigs or leaves moved. The only sound was his breath. He could have been the only person in the world.

I'm not. They're watching me.

No interior argument replied. The people who'd chased them here, who'd killed Mick and Andy and the girl, were watching him, unable to get to him. They were in the leaves and grass, in the cracks in the pavement and in the broken windows of the houses all around him. While they couldn't touch him, they wanted him to hear their breath, to smell the rotten stink of their dirt. They wanted their hands around his neck and they'd be with him every step of the way.

Geri, this had better work.

He ran and the night swallowed him.

Fifty Seven

Will stared at the little pane of glass in the centre of the door as if expecting to be able to see Stu. All he could see was a square of darkness. Staring at it made his stomach tight and hot; he sat on the bottom stair, rested the bat against the wall and leaned into Karen when she joined him.

'He'll be all right, won't he?' she said.

'Sure.'

The reply was nothing more than automatic. He wished for more words to add to it, for a way of giving it strength the way Stu would have done.

'He'll be back in less than an hour.'

The words felt weak, stupid. Karen reached for him and Will spoke before he realised he was going to.

'What happened upstairs. Me and Geri. You need to know all that is old shit now. I wish she'd been okay and I wish things hadn't happened like this, but it's still old stuff. I don't want you thinking it's anything other than that.'

'You don't need to explain it.'

He pushed her away so he could see her face. 'Of course I do. You're my wife.'

'And she was your girlfriend.'

'She was my friend.'

Neither broke eye contact.

'Listen to me,' Will said and realised with bitter humour he had no idea what came next.

'It doesn't matter,' Karen muttered.

'It does.'

She shook her head. 'No, it doesn't. You're right. I'm your wife and I'm scared. Mick, Andy. Stu's gone. I'm so scared, Will.'

She'd dropped her head as she spoke; her hands twisted restlessly in her lap, and Will thought of a day a couple of years previously. They'd been driving home on a Saturday night after visiting friends and a car had come from nowhere, shooting out of a side street as they drew level with it. It had missed them by a few feet.

That's the last time she was this scared.

She lifted her head to his and her tears wet his cheeks. She kissed him hard and he shifted to face her fully, mouths open, her tears meeting his.

They became limbs and undone clothes and kisses and tears and then they were on the floor of the hallway, somewhere between the foot of the stairs and the front door of Geri's house, of their friend's home. They were a little light in the dark. And the moment before he entered his wife, Will closed his eyes and pictured all of them together, all laughing, all together as they had been in the photo from Geri's album. He held the thought of them as tightly as he could, tracing the December light around them and listening to Mick's big laugh as Karen's legs were around his hips and he buried himself inside her. She cried out into his mouth and the picture of his friends all together soared above his own cries.

Fifty Eight

Kirsty hunted through the cupboards and fridge until she found bread, various cheeses and sliced chicken. Although she ensured she faced her hands and the food, her eyes kept moving to the drawer beside the sink. She'd taken a dinner knife from that drawer and pretended not to notice the three large knives before closing it. On all rational levels, she knew Phil couldn't see what she was doing or know she had seen the knives, but she couldn't stop herself pretending to be focusing on nothing but the sandwiches. Her stomach growled as she moved and she had to eat a slice of the chicken in an effort to quieten it. The taste of the meat filled her mouth and she quickly ate another slice.

Get the knife.

She placed a pile of sandwiches on a plate and began making more. Phil would surely not give her more than another couple of minutes before expecting her back. Time enough to make a second pile of sandwiches, time enough to take a knife from the drawer. But where the hell to hide it? Up her sleeve? Wedged between her arm and side? Both too risky and dangerous to her. It'd be a big joke if she managed to stab herself with her own defensive weapon.

Feeling the time slipping away from her, Kirsty scanned the kitchen. Three tea towels hung on a rail near the fridge. She paused.

A knife hidden in tea towels? Her mind raced through a possible reason to take the towels—a lack of napkins, the need to wipe their hands and look here Phil, a great big fucking knife at your throat.

Before she could talk herself out of it, Kirsty grabbed all three tea towels, dumped them beside the plates and finished making the sandwiches.

'Let's do it,' she whispered.

Lucy's face filled her head. She had never in the child's short, sweet life wanted to see her daughter as much as she did at that moment.

Kirsty slid the drawer open, took one of the knives and wrapped it in the tea towels. They didn't provide a great deal of camouflage for it but with the plates against the towels, she was pretty sure she could keep up the pretence for the few seconds she'd need. A jab to his leg, a non-lethal wounding and hopefully Sam and Charlotte would already be running for the door and with her right behind them.

'Let's do it,' she whispered again and picked up the plates and towels.

A few steps took her back to the hallway and to Phil crouched beside the bannister, staring at her.

Fifty Nine

Stu rested against a low wall which ran alongside houses. He'd run for the last five minutes, seeing and hearing nothing but feeling eyes all over him. As he leaned on the wall, he studied the pools of shadows in gardens and at the sides of houses. It wasn't simply that they were empty, he knew. They were void. He wasn't exactly in the nightmare version of Dalry they'd come to. This was somewhere else, and while it might be safer without people trying to kill him, it was also worse.

This version of Dalry was like a drawing the second before it was tossed into a bin. If Geri's diary was acting as a sort of protection, it had done so by keeping him outside the place in which he'd left Will and Karen.

'And that means you're even further away from home,' he whispered. Even further away from home, from Kirsty and Lucy. Stuck outside everywhere, stuck in the deadest of dead places.

'Bollocks,' Stu said and felt a little better.

He inhaled deep lungfuls of cold air and faced the path ahead. The moon illuminated ahead for a little way and that was all.

'What are you worried about?'

Speaking aloud didn't help. His voice sounded too flat. Stu tried to shake off his nerves and jogged down the pathway beside the houses. The memory of running earlier returned, running and chased by things he couldn't see. And what would have happened if he hadn't made it to the shelter of the school and Karen? What about *that*?

'Bollocks,' Stu said again. He jogged for another few moments, doing his best to think of nothing. His trainers pounding on the road created hollow slaps; he tried to count his paces and gave up when the seemingly empty houses looked as if they were mocking him.

He emerged on Cromwell Road, not far from where he had been earlier. The road looked the same; the damaged houses looked the same. Nothing was the same.

Stu halted and did his best to control his fast breathing. Behind, the road stretched off into darkness. No sounds came from that way but Stu didn't relax. The fact that he couldn't hear anyone made no difference.

He was being watched.

Stu stared at the few whole windows and saw nothing. It was the same in the thin hedges. There was nobody anywhere near him but he was still being watched.

He pressed his fingers against the shape of the notepad in his pocket and tried not to think what would happen if he lost the diary or the photo.

'At least it's working for now,' he told himself and wished he hadn't spoken. Too much like tempting fate.

Stu jogged in the middle of the road, passed houses and a few smashed cars and stopped at the road which led into the school car park. Sweat coated his forehead, neck and back. It cooled as he remained still, leaving his skin clammy.

'Geri. Where are you?'

He walked into the school grounds, crossed the car park to the main building and tested the first set of doors he came to. They were locked. Stu moved alongside the building and reached the side of the English block. He paused, thinking. Unless the school was different here, following the path would take him into an open space surrounded on all sides by the separate blocks. It would also give him a perfect view of the library and the floor above it.

'The steps. Don't forget the steps,' he whispered.

He hadn't thought of them in years, a set of faded yellow steps built in metal railings which led up to the fire exit of the sixth form room. He and the others had used those steps almost every day for two years, the thud of their shoes on the metal sending out a high ringing as they descended.

'Block.'

Naming the sixth form room delighted him. He hadn't really thought of it in years, let alone said its name. Giving it some slight degree of flesh here brought a sense of control if only briefly.

Climbing those steps now, though, that couldn't be done. No way.

'Screw that,' Stu whispered. It was one thing to be here on the ground where he could run in any direction he liked. It'd be another to climb those steps and see the door swing open as he reached the top, see the emptiness inside the room.

He kicked at the earth below the hedges with the toe of his trainer. Mud crumbled. Sticking close to the hedges, Stu followed the path in a straight line, counting his steps as he moved. Twenty steps took him to the open space he'd pictured, the languages block to his right, science beyond languages, maths off to the side and the school library a little way ahead. And there were the steps just as he'd last seen them. He scanned them, tilting his head as they rose. There was the fire exit, a faint grey rectangle in the middle of the brickwork. There was the long window that overlooked the cafeteria. Stu stared at the building, aware he was trying to work out how long it had been since he'd stood here; aware but not truly focusing on it. He couldn't focus on it, not with the school formed from solid brick and glass and right in front of him as if nothing had changed since he'd been eighteen.

'Goddamn.'

He glanced at the imposing bulk of the other blocks, then back the way he'd walked. In the movement of turning to face the library and Block again, a shifting rolled in his centre. His free hand rose, pushing into the air, coming to touch his stomach. The shifting moved, rising into his chest, neck, face and eyes.

It's a building, something tall, and the temperature has dropped. This is deep winter, the air a bitter tang in his nostrils, the threat of ugly snow heavy over him and Stu knows what this is. More than that, he knows where it is.

He draws breath to scream Geri's name and sees her as he does so. She stands twenty or thirty feet from him, facing away. She stares towards the dark sky and the ground gleaming with Christmas lights, and that ground is much too far below.

The scream of her name breaks out of his mouth and she doesn't turn. He's not here for her and it doesn't matter to the world that the reverse isn't true. She's as here for him as the mid-December cold and the knowledge of a street filled with Christmas shoppers moves below, none of those shoppers knowing what's about to happen up here on this car park. And why should they? This isn't their world. It's his. It's Geri's.

Move, he bawls at his legs and feet and wonder of wonders, they do. He runs across the car park, trainers kicking up loose snow and splashing through puddles of icy water. This isn't a nightmare with salvation out of reach: Geri's coming closer, a little of her hair visible despite her long coat and thick scarf. His feet break through dirty ice; he skids but manages to stay upright and shrieks her name a third and final time.

Nothing changes. He's close enough to reach for her, fingers straining for her coat, her body and what happened happens again.

Geri throws herself from the car park ledge, the air brings her down to the Christmas shoppers and Stu lets loose a terrible scream.

Abruptly, the shifting sensation dropped out of his eyes, his face and neck. It trickled out of him like water down a plughole and he collapsed to hold his stomach and wonder if he was going to vomit.

The nausea faded moment by moment. He stood as straight as he could and took several breaths.

'Geri,' he whispered. 'I didn't need to see that. I'm sorry. I'm so fucking sorry, but I didn't need to see that.'

Stu opened his eyes and the figure in the window aimed their gun down at him.

He tried to scream but nothing emerged other than a weak exhalation of air. His legs wouldn't move; his chest wouldn't rise and fall.

The gun looked at him, the barrel a long line with one dead eye. He stared back, thought of Kirsty holding Lucy, both smiling at him, and his cry shot around the school grounds, his horror and fear hitting the benches, the walls and windows.

From roughly the other end of the world, he saw the shape lean forward, the face and body rippling as if under water

The figure moved a fraction and Stu had time for one word.

Something smacked into him. He flew to the concrete beside the hedge and the gunshot chased the echo of his cry.

The crash of his fall and the gunshot vanished. Stu scrambled to his feet and stared upwards.

The window was sealed.

He rubbed his arm and shoulder, still feeling the impact on his body, and tried to look in all directions at once.

He was utterly alone.

A laugh rang around the school grounds, childish and excited. Stu's breath jammed inside his lungs; his throat was a pin hole. The laugh tapered off into a soft giggle. Then silence.

Stu's breath rushed out of him. He whirled, attempting to look everywhere at once, and couldn't focus on anything.

Something rustled.

The squat bushes outside the maths department moved, tattered leaves shifting, twigs breaking. Fifteen feet from where Stu stood, something was coming through the greenery.

He backed up two steps, then a third, eyes unblinking and stuck to the bushes. Leaves parted. A pale hand, small and horribly white, jerked outwards. A second one followed it. Both twisted, revealing bloody scratches ingrained with mud on the palms.

The thing in the bushes laughed again, a child's mocking giggle.

Stu backed up again and tried to fight the ghastly cold that had encased his flesh. The hands in the bushes pulled the green apart and two wide eyes glared at Stu.

A final mocking laugh stung his ears.

Stu ran.

Sixty

A second of silence passed between them, surely no longer. Even so, Kirsty felt as if she had been standing in the kitchen doorway, balancing her plates and knives wrapped in the tea towels, for days, weeks, years. The handles of the knives pressed into her fingers, the smell of the sandwiches rose to her nostrils and she thought as clearly as she had thought anything in her life:

If you don't speak right now, he'll know.

'What are you doing?' she said and it had to be a miracle that her voice didn't crack.

Phil gazed at her for another few moments, then stood. 'Thought you might need a hand.' He extended one of his as if to take a plate from her.

'No, it's all right. I can manage.'

'Sure?'

'Yes.'

He lowered his hands, stood awkwardly and then slid them into his jeans pockets.

Where the hell is his knife?

'Kirsty, listen. I don't want this. I don't want any of it.'

'I know.'

He stared at her. 'Do you?' he said and answered his own question. 'Yeah. You do. And you believe me, don't you? I know you do. It's just ...well, it's not like this sort of thing happens all the time.' He laughed. 'If I had any other way of sorting this and getting to Geri without involving you or your husband or your mates, I'd do it in a second.'

'You don't have to do it like this,' Kirsty whispered and he grimaced.

'I wish that was true. Either way, it'll be over soon. I can leave as soon as it gets dark.'

A childish sense of dread trickled through her. To be here in daylight with this man was one thing. After dark was another.

Anything can happen when it gets dark.

'Upstairs, then?' he said and stood as if to let her pass.

Kirsty kept her eyes focused on his and didn't think of her next words or what they meant—

—the biggest lie you've ever told—

She said: 'I believe you. You want to help your sister. I can understand that. I want to help my husband so we want the same thing. More or less. If I can help you, I will. If you can help me, will you?'

He nodded immediately and a smile bloomed on his face, turning him into something that went beyond handsome.

'Definitely.'

'Good. Then lead the way.'

Still smiling, Phil began moving up. Kirsty took four fast steps to the bottom of the stairs, dropped the plates and flung the tea towels off the knives. Phil turned as she did so, alerted by the smack of crockery into the carpet. He stood halfway up, colour bleeding out of his face.

'Kirsty?'

'I'm going. You won't stop me, understand? I'm getting out of here and you won't stop me.'

He began to cry. Kirsty welcomed her anger like an old friend.

'We're going to the bedroom. We're both going up there. You're going to sit on the bed and me, Sam and Charlotte are leaving, all right?'

He wept.

'Turn around and don't do anything I ...' She coughed, voice catching in her throat.

Don't do anything I wouldn't like? Christ. Is this really happening?

'Just go up slowly,' she said and moved towards him. He took each step with deliberate care and halted at the top.

'To the bedroom,' Kirsty said.

She saw him in profile, wiping his eyes and sniffing. Pity, laced with a heavy weight of disgust struck her. This was like threatening a child.

'Bedroom,' she said.

He shuffled over the carpet towards the door. Kirsty followed and swallowed the thick taste of adrenalin. He'd closed the bedroom door before coming down and as he reached for the handle, something kicked into life inside Kirsty: an instinctive warning, an alert from somewhere deep and secret.

Phil pushed the handle down, the door swung open and he raced into the bedroom, a man-shape blurring with movement. She dashed forward, but too slowly. Phil yanked his knife off the dresser and shoved it towards Charlotte's throat, missing her flesh by less than an inch.

Kirsty stared at the scene, seeing it with another's eyes.

Sam and Charlotte were tied together with a bedsheet; balls of underwear jutted from their mouths. They wept. Urine had spread from Charlotte's crotch to stain the mattress. Sam struggled beside his wife, unintelligible noises of rage coming from behind the makeshift gag.

He knew the whole time.

'Drop that fucking knife or I kill this old cunt right now.'

Phil's tears had ceased. He smiled at her. Spit coated his teeth.

Kirsty's fingers relaxed and the knife hit the carpet with a gentle thump.

'Inside. Shut the door.'

It was all over. She'd tried. She'd believed him. She'd been wrong to do both.

Lucy. My baby.

Kirsty entered the bedroom and closed the door. Phil placed his weapon on a bookshelf and smiled at her again. It didn't hold the slightest warmth.

Then while Charlotte sobbed behind her gag and Kirsty jammed a hand over her mouth to keep her own screams inside, Phil beat Sam into unconsciousness.

Sixty One

Karen heard the movement outside before Will, simply because she stood closer to the door.

'Will'.

She didn't care if whoever was outside heard her raised voice. This was Geri's house and they were safe. Even so, goosebumps rose on her arms as the movement came again. Will ran from the kitchen, bat in hand, and Karen pointed to the door.

'Someone outside,' she whispered.

'Stu?'

'I don't know.'

They stood motionless, both staring at the door and listening for footsteps. Will lifted his bat and his arm jerked when the knock struck from the other side of the door. A tired voice followed it.

'It's me.'

'Stu?' Will said and ran to the door.

'Wait,' Karen shouted and Will froze with his hand on the lock.

'What?'

'How do we know it's him?'

'It's me, for Christ's sake,' Stu said, still with the same tired voice. 'Stu Brennan. Thirty-six. Married to Kirsty and my daughter is Lucy. Now open the door.'

Will hesitated, then said: 'Suck my fat one.'

'Whoever told you you had a fat one, LaChance?'

Laughing and crying, Karen ran to Will's side and shoved the lock down before he could. The door opened and Stu was there, pale and looking weak, but there and back with them and her heart was happy if only for a moment.

He entered in a stumbling walk and Karen let him fall against her. For a glorious moment, all her fear vanished. Then Stu muttered against her neck.

'This is bad.'

Sixty Two

They sat at the kitchen table with all the lights on. Stu shifted aside the small pile of gloves and woolly hats Will had placed on the table a few minutes before. Karen kept her hand on Will's while Stu told them what he'd realised about being outside the world with Geri's diary and the photo shielding him, about being watched by the things who couldn't get to him and the darkness in the school grounds.

'It was Geri with a gun. Above the library. A big gun. A rifle, I think. One of those guns with a sight on it like a sniper would use.' He held the cup of coffee Will had made, both hands tight on the mug. 'She shot and I don't know if it was real or what. I didn't hear the bullet hit anything and it definitely didn't hit me.' He laughed. There was a wild note to it that Karen didn't like. 'Someone else was there. They bashed into me, knocked me over. That's how I got these.' He pointed at the grazes on his forehead and his arm. 'Obviously I got up pretty fucking quick. There was nobody around me, no way they could have got away without me seeing, and there was nobody at the window. In any case, it was closed. If someone had been up there, I would have heard the window close; I'd have seen something.'

His hands shook and spilled coffee. He didn't seem to register the hot liquid on his skin.

'That's not the only thing. In the bushes. Christ.' He sipped his coffee and gazed at the cup. 'I heard a laugh. A kid's laugh. Then in the bushes. They didn't come out. I didn't give them time.'

'What the hell are you talking about?' Will said.

'In the bushes. A kid, I think. They laughed at me. I saw their hands, all scratched and dirty. Then they were looking at me through the bushes and I legged it.'

'Jesus.' Karen looked at both men. 'So the photo and diary didn't protect you?'

'They did. Whatever it was, *whoever* it was, it was just there to scare me. They couldn't get to me which is why they didn't follow me back here. I think it was like a picture, maybe. A film. Something frightening but not real.'

'You sure about that?' Will said.

'Not in the fucking slightest.'

'It was definitely Geri with the gun?' Karen said. To think of Geri in such a way hurt in some deep way of which she couldn't get hold.

'I saw her. Only for a second, but it was her.'

Karen opened to ask how Geri would get a gun. She closed her mouth, the question unsaid. *How* wasn't the issue. What came next was.

'So who knocked you over?' Will said.

'No idea. The thing is, they came at me from my right, knocked me over so unless they fell with me when I fell or they jumped back the other way, they would have been exactly where I was when Geri fired.'

'It doesn't make sense. Why would Geri want to shoot anyone let alone you?' Karen said.

Stu tapped the diary.

'You read it. *I want to hurt people. I want them to feel how I felt. I know that's wrong but it's still true.*'

'Geri wasn't like that.'

'Maybe she is now,' Stu muttered.

'I can't believe that.'

'It doesn't matter what we believe,' Will said. 'It's what we do next. Any ideas?'

Karen and Stu looked at him and nobody spoke.

Two heavy blows hit the front door.

Sixty Three

Show them.

Take them.

Lead them.

The thoughts. In a circle. Around my head. Nothing else there.

My feet on. The ground. Solid. Walking. Taking me. Path. Grass. The houses. I know. I know. This is. The street.

Geri's house.

Geri. Geri.

House. Her house. Right there. Lights on. In the windows. I'm walking. To. The door. The door. Hand up. Knocking. Once. Twice. Knock knock. Who's there? Me.

I'm. Walking back to. Back to the path. And. And looking at the. House.

The window. In the window by. The door.

Face.

Two.

Three.

Them. Staring at me. Big faces. Mouths open. I know. Them.

Their names. Elton. Elton. Will. Karen. Stu. Watching me. Running. We ran. We were. Running. Water. Water around me.

I'm here. I'm walking.

With my friends.

Friends.

Take them.

Lead.

Take them.

Sixty Four

Will yanked the door open, saw the figure on the path at end of the garden and all the air fell out of him. He fell back against Karen, deflated. She pushed him up and spoke in a little, hurt voice.

'Mick?'

Will gazed at the shape on the grass. It had Mick's face, his body and it wasn't him. It was like an idea of him, a life-like drawing created by someone who'd had Mick described to them.

'Mick,' Stu shouted and the figure lifted a slow hand. Splayed fingers. Waved.

'Jesus fucking Christ.' Stu stepped outside. Will grabbed his arm.

'It's not him,' Will said.

Stu shook Will off and took a few small steps on to the grass. Mick, or whatever he was, didn't move.

'He's dead. We saw him die,' Will said.

'It's Mick,' Karen whispered and Will stared at her.

'How do you know?'

She smiled despite her tears. 'I just do.'

Before Will could react, she ran from the front door, brushed past Stu who immediately followed, and ran to Mick.

'*Karen.*' Will ran after them, leaving the light and safety of Geri's house.

Sixty Five

Take them.
  Water.
  To the hole. The space.
  Gap. Between.
  The gap between.
  Dalry.
  Home.

Sixty Six

Charlotte eased the blood-stained pillow case from Sam's head, dropped it to the floor and replaced it with a fresh one. Sam's head rested against her legs; he made soft noises that may have been words. Kirsty didn't know and couldn't look at the old man. She couldn't look at Charlotte either. The fear and anger on her face were too much to take in.

That left Phil to study and that was somehow worse than watching Charlotte. His tears, if they'd ever been real, were long gone. Smiles hadn't replaced them. Instead, he studied the unconscious Sam with a frowning curiosity, a look that suggested he couldn't quite work out what was wrong with the old man.

'He needs a hospital,' Charlotte said and dabbed at a fresh line of blood oozing from Sam's nose.

'He can wait.'

'He needs help. He's bleeding. Can't you see that?'

'Shut up.'

Phil ran a finger over the blade of his knife and Kirsty prayed Charlotte would stay quiet. There wasn't any reasoning here, and no hope of connection. She'd been an idiot to think there might have been. All they could do was keep quiet and hope for an opportunity.

Charlotte closed her mouth and Sam made no sound beside her.

'Girls,' Phil muttered and shifted position. Kirsty had spent half an hour seeing him in profile. With his movement, his face brightened by the orange illumination from a streetlight. Dusk had fallen minutes before and the orange light turned Phil's face into a sickly mask, the face of an ill man. His eyes were worse than the rest of his face. They were dead.

Girls? What the hell does that mean?

His eyes landed on hers and a panicked shriek inside her head told her he'd heard her thought.

'Your daughter. How old is she?'

Kirsty's fear reached a level she'd never known. 'None of your fucking business.'

He blinked as if she'd moved to slap him and life returned to his eyes and face.

'Probably not, but in my defence it's been a difficult few days. Not often you see your dead sister, is it?'

She didn't answer. She couldn't.

Phil stood, stretched his legs and back, and grunted with pleasure.

'Getting a bit stiff.'

His eyes landed on hers for a second too long and her stomach clenched. He pulled the curtain back a fraction and peered outside. Kirsty's eyes flicked from the knife in his hand to the back of his head. She didn't move. Not enough time.

'Always depressing when it starts getting dark so early. I hate it when the clocks change,' he said and let the curtain fall back into place. Sam snorted and groaned. Fresh blood pooled out of his nose. Phil paid him no attention and Kirsty wondered if Sam and Charlotte still existed for Phil. Or if everything for him came down to her because of who she was.

The wife of his sister's friend.

A new target for her hate came. Geri. So what if they'd never met? This was her fault, the whole fucked up business. If she had stayed dead, if she had left them alone, then Stu wouldn't be missing, their lives wouldn't have been torn in half by whatever the hell all this was about.

Geri. All her fault. All of this down to her.

'It's time,' Phil said.

He looked at Kirsty and only Kirsty.

'Get up,' he said and her fear, buried in resignation for hours, returned.

Moving with exaggerated care, she stood, back against the door.

'What about them?' she said and gestured to Sam and Charlotte.

'They're staying here.'

'You can't leave them like this, for Christ's sake.'

'Why not?'

It was like arguing with a child.

'He needs help,' Kirsty shouted and Phil shrugged.

'I don't care.'

He moved with the same horrible speed he'd shown as they'd come into the bedroom, striding to Sam and Charlotte, shoving Sam from Charlotte's lap despite her pleas, and tying both of them together with bedsheets. Kirsty watched, impotent with fear, cursing herself, Phil and Geri.

Phil stood and faced the couple. 'We're going. The police will rescue you soon, I imagine. Just sit tight.'

He laughed at his own joke, pushed Kirsty to one side and opened the door.

'After you,' he said.

For a mad few seconds, she pictured herself sprinting past him and crashing through the front door. The idea died. She'd never get past him and even if she did, the front door was locked. And God knows what he'd do to Sam and Charlotte if she tried anything.

'You'll be safe,' she said to Sam and Charlotte. They stared at her with wide eyes and as much as she wanted to give words that would be more comforting, she couldn't think of any.

'Come on,' Phil said.

She walked to him, arms and legs tense. As soon as she was a step past him, he grabbed her arm, slammed the door shut behind himself and marched her to the top of the stairs.

'I know you'll be thinking of running or calling for help, but don't. Remember my knife?'

'Yes,' she whispered.

'I'm fast, so even if you do shout anything, I'll cut you a second later.'

There were no tears. She had that much to be grateful for.

He took her to the back door. The outside light had come on; it showed most of the garden and the fence encircling it.

'Your car or mine?' he said.

She didn't answer.

'Yours in that case.'

He unlocked the door and opened it. The temperature had dropped considerably since the morning and Kirsty wrapped her arms around her breasts to hug herself.

'What are you going to do with your car?' she said.

'Don't worry about it. Come on.'

He pushed her outside, pulled the door closed and it was right then that she thought about running straight out of the garden to the path and road beyond. He took her by the shoulder but with a gentleness.

'Don't,' he said softly.

They walked to the gate and out to the little road. The cars were exactly where they'd left them. Seeing her car in this part of town she didn't know and didn't belong to was somehow worse than the threat of Phil's knife, and it was so hard to think of the car outside her house where it belonged.

Desperately, she tried to look around without moving her head. It didn't make any difference. People were in their homes, not out on the street. Even if they were, they'd think nothing of a man and woman walking so closely together.

Phil led her to her car and told her to unlock it. She reached for the keys and one loud thought clamoured at her.

You get in the car with him and you're dead. You'll never get away.

I don't get in the car and I'm dead, she replied to herself and pulled her keys free.

'Good girl,' Phil said against her ear.

She unlocked the door and moved to slide inside.

'You're driving. I'm in the back,' he said.

She unlocked the car and they entered at the same time. The sound of the two closing doors made her want to weep.

'Start the car,' Phil said.

'Where are we going?'

She started the engine and looked at him in the rear-view mirror. He'd tilted his head and stared past her to the little road. The angle of his head was unmistakable.

What's he listening for?

Another question followed that one immediately and Kirsty bit back a hiss of fear.

Who's he listening to?

'To see my sister,' Phil replied.

'She's dead.'

The words were out before she could stop them.

He smiled, exposing perfect teeth.

'I know.'

Sixty Seven

They raced across the garden, Stu and Karen ahead of Will. He put on a burst of speed and caught hold of Karen.

'What are you doing?' he shouted.

'It's Mick.'

'He's dead.'

Stu stared at both of them and it hit Will how exposed they were, how open the road was. He looked behind. The lights were still on in Geri's house, the front door still open. Whatever kind of protective bubble covered the house, they were outside of it now and had been since leaving the diary and photo on the kitchen table. Even though he held a knife from the kitchen and Stu had grabbed the bat before sprinting outside, the weapons felt like no real protection.

'We should go back,' he said.

'Not until we speak to Mick,' Karen said and shook off his hold.

Will gazed at the figure at the corner of the road, somehow dozens of steps from the house despite knocking on the door just seconds before. It looked like Mick, no question, but it couldn't be him. Mick was gone just like Andy.

He ran a hand through his hair and fought tears of grief and exhaustion.

'Mick?' he called. 'Come here.'

Mick remained still.

'He's a ghost, isn't he?' Stu murmured.

Mick was too far away to hear Stu's low voice. Even so, he nodded. The movement was awkward as if he wasn't quite sure of it but there was no mistaking it.

'God,' Will whispered. 'What do we do?'

Stu took a few steps towards Mick, then looked back at the house.

'Wait here,' he said and sprinted to the house. Karen and Will stood as closely together as they could, Will looking from Mick's shape to Geri's front door.

'It can't be Mick,' he whispered.

'It is.'

Will trembled. Mick was dead. There was no getting away from that. And the shape who'd waved at them, while looking like him, resembled a picture, *had* to resemble a picture or a suggestion of Mick.

It couldn't be him.

Running steps made him look back to the house. Stu ran to them, holding the diary and photo. He slid both into his jeans pockets.

'We're okay as long as we've got these. Let's go.'

'What about what you saw at school?' Will said.

Stu replied as if Will hadn't spoken.

'We're safe. Let's go.'

He set out ahead of them. Will resisted when Karen took his hand; she pulled and he relented.

The three walked towards Mick, the houses of Oakfield Walk watching them.

Sixty Eight

Coming to me.
  Walking to me. They are here. I am here.
  Mick. They call. Me Mick.
  My name. Remember me. I am Mick.
  Coming to me. Lead them.
  The water. To the water.
  I am here.

Sixty Nine

'Jesus,' Will whispered.

Mick, or whatever he was now, stood a few steps from them. On the surface, he appeared normal. It was only when the moonlight caught the angle of his jaw in a particular way or when he didn't focus on any one aspect of him that the truth was clear.

Mick was dead.

There were no visible wounds, no tears to his clothing. But he was dead. In his face, his eyes, in his mouth, he was dead.

'Mick? Can you hear me?' Karen said.

He nodded, the movement still awkward. It was like watching someone too drunk to speak attempt to communicate.

'Mick? Fat Mick?' Stu whispered and Mick nodded a third time. 'Good to have you back.'

Will wept. Karen took his hand and he was unable to speak.

'Come back to us, man. We're here. Come back,' Stu said.

Slowly, oh so slowly, Mick shook his head. He lifted an arm, extended a finger and pointed down the still street.

'What's down there?' Stu whispered.

In reply, Mick began walking. He moved as if his legs didn't work properly, making lurching steps in the road.

'Is it safe, Mick?' Will said and Mick didn't stop.

It's safe. This is Mick. It's safe.

Any lack of logic in the thought wasn't important. Will had to believe it. They walked together, a step behind Stu.

Mick led them and a minute passed before anyone spoke.

'Mick?' Stu whispered.

Mick gave no reaction.

'Can you hear me?'

Mick kept walking with his lurching steps and it hurt Will to see his friend this way. He focused on the road stretching ahead and tried to keep his eyes on it when Stu spoke.

'Come on, Mick. Talk to me.'

'Leave him alone,' Karen said and Stu glanced at her, his mouth a tight line in his face.

'He's not here like we are,' Karen whispered and Stu pointed at Mick.

'So what is he then?'

'She's right. Mick's a ghost, aren't you, Mick?' Will said.

Mick's head turned even while he kept on with his strange, sad walk. His dead eyes watched them and while there was no anger in his expression, there was also no light.

He faced ahead again.

'We can still talk to you, right, Mick?' Stu asked, sounding like a little boy. He looked at Will and Karen as if asking for permission.

'I think we can,' Karen said.

Stu appeared to consider his next words. They passed two small side roads and their path veered slightly to the right. Will estimated there was only another few hundred yards before the road curved towards Bradwell Road. If that was Mick's route, he'd take them to the school in no more than five minutes.

'I'm sorry you died,' Stu said abruptly. It sounded like he was coughing up hard words. 'I miss you, you fat bastard.'

'Me, too,' Karen said and freed her hand from Will's to rub her eyes.

'Yeah,' Will said. Guilt stabbed him. He'd let Mick's hand go by the river. What had happened was down to him.

Mick looked at them again and Will wondered if he'd imagined the slight grin on his dead friend's face.

'We'll get out of here. We'll get out and whatever killed you, we're going to fuck it right up, all right?' Stu said.

Will found his voice. 'Wait a second. Mick, you're back with us, yeah? You're here.' He was babbling and couldn't stop it, couldn't look away from Mick even though he knew Stu and Karen were staring at him. 'Geri's come back, right?' He finally took his gaze off Mick and glanced at Karen. 'Maybe Mick and Andy can come back.' His voice fell apart and he coughed back a sob.

'I don't think it works like that. I don't think they get any say when they come back. Maybe things, maybe they just have to be in the right place,' Karen whispered.

'Jesus. Mick.' Will couldn't say anything else. He let Karen take his hand and he could no longer look Mick in the eye.

They walked on, Stu talking in a low voice, telling Mick he missed him and he was sorry and they'd make sure Jodie knew Mick was a good bloke who'd helped them like this and Will let Stu's words fall over him. He didn't want to think about Mick being dead or this horrible road or whatever might be watching them, eager to get to Karen, to hurt her while he could do nothing to stop it. Best to not think of any of that, better to keep walking, one foot in front of the other in the constant night of this hideous place.

They reached Bradwell Road as Will had imagined. Mick stopped in front of Stu who came close to walking into Mick's back.

'Mick?' Stu said.

Mick lifted his arm again and pointed. Bradwell Road curved at the corner and moved into Cromwell Road. With no surprise, Will saw Mick pointing at the school. He stared at it, seeing it as Stu had described it earlier. Too big, too quiet, and too fucking dark. Anything could be in there. Things in the shadows. Geri with a gun. And whoever had knocked Stu out of the way of her bullet.

'Mick. Was it you? Did you knock Stu over in there?' he said.

Mick shook his head in a slow movement.

'Do you know who it was?'

Mick spoke.

The word didn't come from his mouth and he didn't move. Will heard him though and, judging by Karen's hurt gasp and Stu stepping backwards as if Mick had swung a punch at him, they'd heard him as well.

School.

He resumed his awkward steps, crossing to the pavement, then heading to the main entrance.

'Do we follow him?' Will said.

'What else can we do?' Stu said.

'But Geri, the gun.'

'What else can we do?' Stu said again and ran after Mick.

Karen pulled Will; he resisted and pulled her right against him.

'Stay close to me,' he said and wished as fiercely as he could that she wouldn't argue.

They ran after Mick and Stu, followed them on the pavement into the car park and Will had time to wonder at his old school as it hadn't looked in years. None of the newer buildings, none of the remodelled swimming pool and none of the new sixth form block on the grass at the side of the building remained. The whole school looked exactly as it had on the day he'd left it.

What? What the hell does that mean?

He didn't have time to answer himself.

Daylight exploded into life all around them.

Seventy

At first, it was a simple white, dazzling in their eyes. Then it eased to simple daylight, leaving a painful afterglow. Karen blinked until her vision steadied, felt Will's hand still on hers and her mouth dropped open.

They were on the pavement, still close to each other. The school hadn't changed. What had changed was the time.

Some indefinable thing in the air and in the ground of the car park had altered; they'd moved with it. Maybe it was the smell of the air, fresher and lighter than usual; maybe it was the light and maybe it was neither. Maybe it was just how things were here. Here in their past.

The word was alien. She spoke to make it feel human and almost succeeded.

'This is the past, isn't it?' she whispered. All at once, her stomach was a hot, loose muscle. She breathed deeply a few times until the sensation passed.

'Yeah. This is school how it was.' Will whispered.

He stared at Mick who hadn't reacted at all to the change.

'When is this?' Stu shouted. He ran to Mick, close to grabbing him. He halted at the last moment and instead leaned into Mick's face.

'When is this, Mick?' he whispered.

The voice came out of Mick again. Not speech. Not a thought. It was in their heads like background noise.

Last. Day.

Stu stepped back from Mick, eyes too wide.

'What last day?' Karen demanded. 'Our last day? Do we die here?' She froze, realisation flowing into her.

'What?' Will yelled.

'It's our last day. Of school. We're back here.'

Mick began walking again, moving into the car park, not looking back.

217

'Wait.' Karen ran after him, Will and Stu behind her. Mick took them over the car park, passed the main entrance and onto the path Stu had followed. Stu spoke.

'Mick, wait. I came this way. Geri, she was here. With a gun. She shot at me. We can't go any further.'

Mick carried on walking and Stu shouted after him, telling him to stop and his words faded when the sound of voices, many different voices, came.

'What the hell is this?' Will whispered.

The three of them stood in a tight group, Mick still walking away and the first of the students appearing.

They bloomed into existence as if born of light, kids all around, some running, some talking to their friends, others moving alone. Four stood not far from Stu's side; another five walked past the three. Karen tried to look everywhere at once, unable to speak. More students came into view, all kids between twelve and eighteen, some with their bags, some eating chips, a few of the older ones hiding cigarettes in their hands, and there were some of the teachers crossing the car park; men and women she hadn't seen in years and not one of them a day older than they had been on this day, the last day of school.

'Mr Barnes,' she whispered.

The science teacher reached the pavement and headed to the school entrance, long shadow walking with him. And coming behind him, Miss Jenkins and Mrs Nasreen.

'We're seeing this, aren't we?' Stu said.

'Yeah. We're here,' Will whispered.

Here. In the past. Watching a long dead day unfold and play around them. Karen wanted to laugh at the idea and couldn't. This was as real as Will's hand in hers.

Mick was almost level with the cafeteria entrance, moving with his ungainly steps. Stu pointed at him.

'That's where I was when Geri shot at me.'

The words were like a spell. A change shifted over them and over the ground. It was like a silent tremor. She studied the building, the paving and children. All appeared normal. Fear crept up her spine. It was much too easy to picture the children with gunshot wounds, blood staining the white paving slabs, sunlight shining on screaming mouths.

'Christ,' she said and shook the images away.

'She can't do it,' Will said desperately. He pointed at the children. 'This is how it was, right? So how the hell can she change that? She can't go back in time; she can't kill people. We were there.' His voice rose with outrage. 'We were fucking there and this was our fucking time and she can't change that.'

He shook, looking as if he might vomit.

'She can't do it,' he whispered.

The tremor shook again in the ground and air. Stu and Will felt it just as she did.

'Quick,' Karen said and the word was too slow, too heavy.

She took hold of Stu, kept her grip on Will and they ran after Mick, passing children who didn't react to them, passing benches and the silent tremor rocked through her again.

No, Geri. Please, no.

A second of rational thought tried to speak to her, to ask where the hell Geri would get a gun just as it repeated Will's point. This was the past, this was their time and Geri couldn't change that.

A single gunshot cracked through the air. Screams followed it immediately.

A second shot roared.

Will tried to pull Karen down into the bushes growing alongside the school; she yanked her hand from his and sprinted towards Mick. He faced the library, head tilted up to a second floor window. All around her, students ran, maddened by terror, in every direction. More gunfire cracked, and Will screamed at her, screamed her name as her feet bashed against the concrete. She sprinted towards Mick, her head tilting like his and there was Geri at the window, gun jutting from it, firing shot after shot at the running children.

'Geri.'

Karen howled her friend's name and fire burned through her throat. She crashed into Mick, saw the barrel of the gun swinging around to stare at her. She shouted Geri's name again.

Will and Stu smacked into her and Mick and for a solitary beat, her skin touched Mick's, life touching death.

Night swallowed daylight and the horror went with it.

Seventy One

'How long have you two been married?' Phil asked.

The question came from nowhere. Neither of them had spoken since driving from Oakfield Walk and now here they were seemingly driving in circles and he was asking about her personal life.

'Seven years. Where are we going?'

'Just keep going down here. Were you together long before that?'

Kirsty focused on the road—Northfield Avenue—searching desperately for anyone in sight she could maybe signal or other cars who'd pass her and see the man in the back.

'Were you?' he said again and she spoke quickly.

'What's it matter to you? And when the hell are you going to tell me where we're going because all we're doing is going in a circle.'

He laughed. His breath was hot on her neck and ear. She grimaced and hoped he hadn't noticed.

'Go left at the end of the road.'

'Then straight on until we get to Midland Avenue, then up there to Sovereign Street, then over the bridge to Thorpe Road. We've done this six times. What the fuck are we doing?'

He gave her the same small laugh as if amused by her close tears. 'Were you?' he said.

'Was I what?'

'Were you together long before you got married?'

'Two years,' she said, jaw clenched tight enough to hurt.

'And your daughter is your only child?'

'Yes.'

'How old is she?'

'Fuck you.'

He roared laughter. Kirsty jerked forward, grimacing again. The feel of his breath on her skin, the bellow of his laughter in hear ear and his horrible questions were all too much. She couldn't take much more.

Yes, you can. You have to. For Lucy. For Stu.

She glanced at him in the mirror. His laughter cut off and he pressed cold metal against the back of her neck.

'Don't get the idea you're in charge, Kirsty,' he whispered.

'I'm not.'

'I have to disagree.'

He leaned close to her. His breath tickled her neck and her imagination provided a gloriously savage picture of her index finger driving into his eye, her nail stabbing through the ball and sinking deep into his head. How he would scream if she could do that. She'd relish those screams.

'I know you're thinking about getting away from me. Why wouldn't you? Your friends will have reported you missing hours ago; your husband is God knows where and you're stuck with some mad guy with a knife. That's the truth of it. You're not in charge of anything.'

He whispered against her ear.

'We're driving around like this to give my sister a chance.'

'I don't know what you're talking about.'

'She's got her chance to do something now. She won't, though. She never took chances.'

A queer silence fell over him. Kirsty waited, her chest and throat tight.

'She was never brave. Never in charge.' Phil's voice had dropped to a whisper. 'I was in charge of her. Always. She knew that. That's why it went on for so long. Because I was in charge.' He made a noise somewhere between a giggle and a sigh. 'And because she wanted it to. Can't forget that.'

Say nothing. Don't even breathe.

Kirsty listened to the interior voice and kept her eyes aimed directly ahead to the empty road.

'She's got her chance right now. She can save you. She can stop me. She won't. I know she won't.'

She could barely hear him.

'This is my time right now. This is my town. Dalry. Good old Dalry. I'll miss this place.'

Her fear shifted focus as she realised this seemingly pointless drive was for Phil to look at the buildings and roads of his hometown and to say goodbye to them.

They reached Midland Avenue and drove in silence. As they neared the end of the road and Kirsty signalled, Phil leaned close again.

'No. We're going the other way this time.'

Kirsty indicated right. There were no other drivers on the road. The night seemed darker than usual. A few of the streetlights were out and her headlights didn't illuminate enough as they drove.

'Your daughter,' Phil said and there was something horrible in his voice. She couldn't look at him, not while he was talking about Lucy.

Metal dug into the skin of her neck and she hissed.

'Eight months,' she whispered.

'Really?'

Jesus Christ, why does he sound disappointed?

'Yes,' she said and pictured driving her car into another vehicle. Just smashing straight into one and who gave a shit if she was killed? At least it would stop his fucking awful questions.

'Eight months,' he said and there was no mistaking the fact that he was musing on the figure.

Kirsty swallowed until the taste of vomit faded from her throat. They passed houses that appeared empty. The occasional street light was lit. Even so, the city seemed to be empty apart from her and Phil.

'I lied, you know,' he said abruptly.

Kirsty's exhausted mind did its best to cross reference the sudden statement with anything that made sense.

'About the first time. It wasn't in my school although that did happen. Just a couple of days ago.'

Phil fell silent and Kirsty realised what he was talking about: his first vision of Geri's ghost. In his school, he'd said. She'd come towards him and vanished at the last second. He'd told her that this morning and that was roughly a million years ago.

'The first time she came, it was in my bedroom.'

Phil paused; she saw his eyes in the rear-view mirror and understood. He'd made a joke. She didn't get it, didn't want to get it, but it was still a joke to him.

He bellowed laughter and she flinched away from him. He giggled and cleared his throat as if forcing himself to remain in control.

'Came in the middle of the night. I tell you what, that's enough to shit anyone up.'

He fell silent and Kirsty wished for him to stay that way.

'It's because of the girl.'

Kirsty gripped the wheel tighter. This was a nightmare. She was stuck inside it, stuck with Phil and his horrible words and there was no way out.

'The girl. At school. I'm a teacher. I didn't tell you that, did I? No. I didn't.'

Although his eyes were on her, he wasn't speaking to her, not directly in any case. Nor was he speaking to himself. This was something else.

'Best part of six years I've been doing this. It's not too bad. Fun, actually. But, this girl. Christ. First time I saw her, I thought I was seeing a ghost. Which is quite ironic, I suppose.'

He let out a soft laugh and his breath tickled her.

'Absolute spitting image of my sister. I couldn't believe it. Same face, same hair, same everything. And I can't just stand by and do nothing when this happens, can I?'

With a ghastly speed, he leaned much closer to her and bellowed into her ear.

'*Can I?*'

Kirsty shrieked and tried to pull away. 'Please. I don't know. I don't know.'

She loathed the voice of a terrified child coming out of her mouth and loathed Phil for causing it. He appraised her for a moment, then relaxed a little.

'I can't just stand by and do nothing. I knew what I had to do. Not done it yet, though.' He smiled and it may have been the first genuine one she'd seen on his face. 'I'll get to it when I'm ready, know what I mean?'

'I don't have any fucking idea what you mean.'

He laughed again, but didn't reply.

Kirsty swallowed her fear as best as she could and concentrated on driving into Dalry's suburbs.

Seventy Two

Silence lived and breathed around them. The brief warmth of that day in an early summer had been replaced by the chill of the last several hours. Moonlight had returned with the biting air.

Stu caught Karen as she collapsed. Will took hold of her gently. Mick watched them.

'Mick. What's happening here? Talk to us, dude,' Stu whispered.

Mick's face remained motionless and savage frustration filled Stu. He wanted to punch Mick, to punish him for dying, for coming back and for being part of whatever this fucking world was.

'Mick, we need to know what to do.' He sobbed as he spoke and reached for Mick's big arms, not caring in the slightest about his tears. He twisted his friend's jacket between his fingers and wept. Mick gave no reaction. A hand brushed Stu's shoulder. It was Karen. He let go of Mick and faced the sixth form block. All the windows were shut but what did that matter? Geri was here or at least in another version of this place; she was here with her gun and her rage.

'We need to stop Geri,' Karen said.

'Stop her from what? Shooting people?' Stu shouted and Karen nodded.

'But we know that didn't happen,' Will said and looked at Mick. 'Right? That was the last day of school. Jesus, that was pushing twenty years ago and it didn't happen. She didn't kill anyone.'

'I don't think that matters,' Stu said dully. 'Something's changed. If she wants it to happen then, then it will. We have to stop her.'

'How the fuck do we do that?' Will screamed. 'She's fucking dead and we're stuck in this fucking ...'

Come.

Mick's word was as solid as a crypt door. It silenced Will; he covered his mouth and shook just as he had earlier.

'Where are we going?' Karen whispered.

Mick's response was simply to turn away and walk back to the school car park. They followed, not talking, Will walking with his head down. They returned to Bradwell Road and followed a few side roads for several minutes, crossing over patchy grass, passing stunted trees. The breezed played between the leaves and when they stepped from the grass to a cycleway, Stu realised where Mick was taking them.

To the river.

Will lifted his head and frowned, slow realisation coming to his pale face.

The cycleway ran between trees for the next quarter of a mile before opening to a wide stretch of grass and a creek. The river was just ahead of the grass.

Monk's Cave was between them and the river.

Seventy Three

'What are we doing here?' Karen whispered. The idea of speaking at any louder volume was terrifying. It was far too easy to think of her voice carrying into the spaces between the trees and bushes just as it was easy to wonder if following a ghost far from the safety of Geri's house was a good idea.

'It's all right. Mick's here,' Stu replied and she wanted to ask him if he really believed that. She didn't dare.

Mick took them along the cycleway, the wind blowing over leaves and the moonlight a white beam tracking them. Karen gripped Stu's hand in her left and Will in her right. The thought came that they could be three friends walking home after the pub and it almost made her laugh.

'He's taking us to Monk's Cave,' Will said.

'Why would he do that?' Stu replied.

'No clue. I just know it's a bad idea.'

'It kept you safe from those kids who burned your house down,' Stu whispered.

'I don't care. This is still a bad idea.'

They passed below the overhanging trees. The moonlight vanished and left them almost completely blind. Karen forced one foot forward, then the next. A primal terror of the unknown had come; her imagination told her anything could be in the woods on either side, coming with them, matching them step by step and making its move any second: a rustle of leaves, a snap of twigs and that was all they'd get before whatever was hunting them came, screeching as it fell on them with its claws and teeth.

She listened to the wind and the rustling in the undergrowth and despite what Stu had said about being safe with Mick and Geri's diary and photo, she knew they weren't alone. Looking past Stu, she peered into the black beyond and imagined eyes low down and staring straight back at her. At once, the rustling stopped; she clenched her fingers on Stu and Will's hands, heard them both hiss their pain and her words were stuck in her mouth.

In the bushes, it's in the bushes.

The thing Stu had told them about, the thing watching him. It was here.

Karen stared into the trees and bushes. Something stared back at her. She knew it.

What the hell are you? What do you want?

Inside her head, something laughed without any joy or humour. Something wanted her scared, wanted her weakened by her fear.

Try harder. Try fucking harder, you understand?

It laughed again, amused by her rage and her fright.

'You all right?' Will said.

'In the bushes,' she whispered as they moved beyond the overhanging trees and the only noise around them was the wind blowing over leaves.

'Nothing there,' Will said and he didn't sound convinced by his own words.

They left the path and walked over damp earth. Karen looked back but could see nothing in the bushes and trees. Even so, eyes stared at her, wanting her to leave Stu and Will and come into the dark spaces between the trees.

It wanted her in there, wanted to touch her down there.

'That's where I hid,' Will said and pointed to a growth of rocks. Karen forced her eyes to move from the trees and path behind and followed the direction Will pointed. She could just make out the pool and entrance to the cave beyond.

'They came from that pathway, went over the grass and a couple came towards me. Then they joined the others at the water. That's when something took them.'

Will said this as flatly as he might have relayed a boring story. Even so, Karen heard the fear in his words. It was a little thing far below.

'It's okay,' she said automatically.

'Did you see anything?' Stu said.

'Nothing. I just heard something laugh in the water and across the other side.'

'Christ.'

Karen inhaled as deeply as she could. Fierce cold filled her lungs and she searched for the good memories of Monk's Cave. Warm days. Fresh grass and flowers. The sound of wind blowing through the trees. The trickles of sweat on her skin. The wild

227

smells coming from the water that were full of nature, the smell of the water and the greenery all together, all around her.

She couldn't get a firm hold on the mental pictures. All too long ago. All too cold and dark now.

Mick was a fading shape ahead of them; they'd stopped while talking and Karen called his name. The volume of her shout made her wince. It worked, though. Mick turned around and she could just make out his face.

'We're not safe here, Mick,' she called and Stu waved at Mick, gesturing for him to return to them.

'Come back,' he said.

Mick didn't react at all.

'What do we do?' Will whispered.

'We trust him,' Stu said immediately.

'What?'

'We trust him.' Stu looked at Will, then Karen. In spite of however much time they'd spent in this horrible world and in spite of all that happened, Karen knew she was seeing Stu at his most terrified. She thought of Stu's daughter Lucy, of the day she'd been born. Was that what Stu was thinking of now?

Of course it is.

And how much worse would the thought be for him than her? A billion times? A world beyond it? She couldn't measure it and didn't want to.

Stu spoke with forced calm. Despite his best efforts, his voice still shook.

'What choice do we have? Stay here and do what? Hide in Geri's house until whatever the fuck is out there works out a way of getting in? Or go with Mick? Trust our friend?'

His rapid speech made tiny puffs of vapour in the air. The temperature was dropping. Unbelievably, this place had found a way to be even more horrible.

'There's a third choice,' Will said and grinned for the first time in what might have been days. Karen's love for her husband was at once a simple and powerful song in her chest.

'Yeah?' Stu said.

'We could shit ourselves.'

Stu was silent for a beat, then cackled a great volley of laughter into the sky. The joke wasn't a big one, Karen knew, but its simple existence here in this terrible place was a miracle.

'Come on, ladies,' Stu said and took their hands.

They walked over the grass to Mick who'd remained motionless during their conversation. He watched them come and how it hurt Karen to see her friend dead but still with them.

I wish you were here, Mick. I really do.

His eyes moved to hers for a second, then somehow looked at all of them at the same time.

In the dark, they waited for Mick to tell them what to do.

Seventy Four

Them here. With me, them my. Friends.
Here. Dark here. I am here. They. With me I. I miss. Them.
Wish. I wish this wasn't. Me but no way. Back now.
Outside. Outside them. Will get them. Home.
Send them back. Miss them. Love. You. Love you.
Who's. There. Who's that here.
You. You. Miss you. Miss you too. Always loved. You.
Take them. Home.
Send them. Water.
To the water. To. The. Home.
Love. Miss you. Love you. Love you all.

Seventy Five

'Hear that?' Will whispered.

He tilted his head, listening, then moved in a slow circle.

'I heard something,' Stu said.

'Me, too,' Karen whispered.

They stood in complete silence for a minute. Even the wind had ceased and the smell of the river had come in its place. Wickedly cold air brought goosebumps to Will's exposed flesh.

'Was it a voice?' Will said and wished the brief burst of laughter he'd made from his little joke a minute before would return in place of this shitty, miserable fear.

'Relax,' Stu said. 'Big Mickey's here.'

Will didn't smile; the words hurt too much. It must have been ten years since anyone had called Mick *Big Mickey*. Hearing it, even out here, made him feel young if only for a few seconds.

'All right, Mick. What's the plan?'

For the last time, Mick lifted his arm. He pointed to the water.

'The river? What about it?' Will said. A horrible fear crept into his head.

No way. No fucking way could Mick mean that.

'Mick, dude. There's something in the water. I heard it earlier. I was here; I told you about it, remember? Something's in there.'

Mick hadn't lowered his arm. He pointed to the water. The wind played over the surface of it.

'We can't do this,' Will whispered.

'I don't think there's much choice,' Karen said and Will whirled to face her.

'You're suggesting we go swimming, *here*? After what I heard?'

'Think about it. Why would Mick take us here if it wasn't to help us?' Stu said.

'I don't care,' Will said and Karen grabbed both his arms and cried into his face.

'You need to care. This isn't just about us. Andy's dead; Mick's dead and he's here. He came back to help us so you better fucking care.'

She let go of him and shook, her anger still palpable. Voice lower, she went on without lifting her head.

'Geri's dead and she's in trouble. *We're* in trouble, Will. And this might be the only way to help Geri and help ourselves. It might be the only thing left to do.'

She lifted her head. There were no tears and Will wondered if they were beyond tears now. The thought sent his fear away. Simple exhaustion filled his blood and muscles.

He took her hand.

'Okay. If you say so, then okay.'

Mick faced the water again. He seemed to have turned without moving.

'Lead on, Mick,' Stu said.

Mick did so, his slow steps on the grass taking them to the water's edge. Will stared at the surface just beyond the little slope and the rocks and the long grass.

'I left my trunks at home,' he muttered.

'Have to do it in your vest and pants,' Stu said and Will managed a giggle.

Stu moved a few steps closer to the water and squatted to touch the grass. He jerked his hand back a second later and shook it.

'Cold. Too cold.'

'Probably warmer than the water,' Will said and studied the surface again. The moonlight did little to illuminate it or the opposite bank. The tall trees there and long bushes could be concealing anything.

'Will,' Karen whispered.

Turning, Will saw the expression on her face and whirled back to the water to see Stu rising, mouth open in horror. On the river's surface, a great line had formed, cutting through the water from bank to bank as it split the surface in two.

Below the surface was nothing. It went on forever.

A nothing of darkness. A darkness of the end of all things.

Karen took Will's hand. Then Stu was beside her, his hand in hers.

Will understood.

In those last few seconds, he had no hearing, no sense of smell and no awareness of the cold or the grass and trees around them. The darkness was all there was for them.

It spread on to the rocks and grass, creeping towards them, a hole coming for them.

Something lifted Will's head and his eyes met Mick's and Mick's voice was in his head for one last time.

Do it, Elton, you bender. This is the way out. Just don't let go.

Will stared down to the space where the water had been. It wasn't a simple void now. Movement lived far below: streaking things made of lights, made of all the colours in the world, made of eyes and mouths. The eyes stared upwards to see him and only him, marking him and knowing his name.

They know my name. Oh my God. They know my name.

Mouths down there in the dark were smiling as they opened wider and wider, coming to eat this patch of stunted grass, coming for this world, and Will understood.

The hole before them wasn't a door between worlds or a door from one to the other. It was the sleeping space of their past.

They stood on the gap between their lives now and the people they had been.

Karen took a step forward, Stu did the same and Will couldn't help but to move with them. Every muscle in his body protested, every urge told him to run. Geri, Mick and Andy didn't matter. Nothing mattered but the black below coming to eat him. He had to run, he had to go now, run away from Monk's Cave and leg it back to the house.

Geri's face came to him as clearly as if she was with them in the flesh. She was smiling and her hair shone.

Will clamped his hand down on Karen's and jumped. Karen and Stu fell with him, the hole below the water swallowed them and Will spun around as they fell and the wide mouths of colour below opened for them. He stared back up to Mick's fading shape and he didn't let go.

Seventy Six

Miss you. Love you.
  Bye.

Seventy Seven

The woman, Kirsty, was talking, asking him again where they were going. Phil let her speak. Her words weren't important. Neither was the hate she felt for him. He listened to the other voice, the one he'd always loved, as it told him it would be okay if he kept to his plan, they'd be together again if he kept to the plan.

He asked her if she was sure and she said she was. He asked her where to go exactly and she told him. She'd be in the big room above the library, she said. Block. He remembered it, didn't he? Of course he did. Never *the* Block. Always just *Block*. He'd been there a few years before her, making his mark on the school, leaving an impression that had stayed with people after all this time and why wouldn't it? If he remembered that and stuck to the plan, everything would be fine. And they could have some fun again.

Her voice faded, Phil strained to catch the rest but it was gone. No matter. She often came and went. Always had.

He glanced out of the window beside him, then ahead. Everything had worked out perfectly so far. The old people hadn't presented any problems; taking control of them and their house had been a piece of piss. Okay, having to wait a few hours for dark and spending all that time pretending to Kirsty that he was grief-stricken and panicked had been a pain in the arse. She'd helped him out of that, though, whether she knew it or not. Going for the blade in the kitchen, Christ, that had been obvious. It couldn't have worked out better if he'd handed her the weapon himself. No need for that, though. She'd tried her luck just as he'd known she would and he'd been free to reveal himself, to stop pretending all that tiresome crap.

Since then, luck had still been on his side. Very little traffic on the roads, nobody to see him in the back seat, leaning into Kirsty's neck. Things couldn't have been going better.

Phil allowed himself a smile, fully aware he couldn't get cocky or complacent. This wasn't over yet. It wouldn't be until they were together again just like the old days. And that would happen just as he'd planned unless this silly bitch tried anything.

'Next left. Go to the end of the road and turn left again,' he said and watched her stare at him in the mirror.

'The school? We're going to the school?' she said.

'What makes you say that?'

'There's nothing else there.'

'True.' He grinned again. 'Yes, the school. Go to the car park and stop there.'

'What happens then?'

'Then it's almost over.'

Kirsty indicated left and turned. They passed a few cars going the other way and she made no move to signal them. She'd been thinking about it, especially earlier. He liked knowing she'd given up on the idea. It made everything a little easier.

'What does that mean?' she whispered.

'It means whatever the fuck I want it to,' he screamed. Christ, her constant questions were annoying. Couldn't just drive and keep quiet, could she? Had to open her mouth all the fucking time.

Phil squeezed his long fingers into his thigh. The discomfort brought focus ...and something else.

A memory.

Of course. She'd done the same. All those times before. All those wonderful times.

Kirsty was staring at him again, a few tears rolling down her cheeks. He quite liked that. It meant he was in control.

Phil shifted in his seat, Kirsty made the final turn and he pictured the car park as it'd be tonight. Empty, silent.

He had to shift in his seat again.

They drove down Cromwell Road, passing parked cars and houses full of bright windows, and reached the main entrance. A locked gate blocked it from the road.

'Shit.' Phil thought quickly. Sweat dripped into his eyes, stinging them. He blinked it away. 'The other entrance. By the swimming pool.'

Kirsty drove to the end of the road, reached Bradwell Road and then the entrance which ran beside the swimming pool. Lights shone in the building and a few vehicles were parked around the car park. Not perfect, but close.

'Park right at the end,' Phil said and pointed straight ahead.

Kirsty drove slowly to the edge of the car park. Ahead of them, the school came into view. Phil stared at it, amazed to see how much it had changed since he'd left. Blocks had been developed, there was a large open area in the middle of the grounds and a load more greenery lined pathways.

'They spent some money on this place,' he said.

The block containing the main doors and reception area looked more or less the same which was a comfort. It helped to imagine going through those doors, seeing the same long sofas and photos of each Year on the wall, and the open plan reception off to his side.

The memory felt like the old days and that could only be a good thing.

Phil stared at the school and listened.

Go in, she said. Go through the little corridor that connects the cafeteria to the languages block.

Of course. The best place, wasn't it? Go in there and there'd only be a little bit further to the doors, the steps, and there they'd be above the library. There she'd be in Block.

Waiting for him.

Doubt pressed in.

Are you sure? I mean, going in those doors. That's going to make a lot of noise. No way can I get away from that.

Easy, she said. Hide. Hide on the second floor. I'll show you where.

Phil considered it. Hiding. Then simply waiting until the police left. No problem. Waiting was fine. He'd waited for her already, hadn't he? A long time.

'Best part of fifteen years. Long time.'

'What?' Kirsty said and he didn't care for her tone.

'Nothing. Shut up.'

Phil listened.

It was all right, she said. Soon.

Phil listened.

Seventy Eight

With one blink, the black of the land around Monk's Cave was replaced with a white void. Stu stared into it, attempting to focus on something, *anything*. The void ate into his eyes; he shut them, holding on to his scream, and heat ate his skin.

His eyes opened. The white void had gone. So had Monk's Cave.

They were back at the school, back how things had been during that vision or whatever the hell it was.

It's the last day.

The thought made it all solid. The grass he stood upon, the July light, the bricks and windows of the school were all utterly real.

A hand hit his shoulder and he whirled, fists up. Will backed away. Karen gazed at the blue sky as if she had never seen it before.

'Easy, tiger,' Will murmured and Stu felt a grin, too large and too out of control, split his face in half.

'Just thrilled to be alive,' he said.

'We're here, aren't we?' Karen said.

Stu gazed at the school. It held an indefinable something in its bricks and windows, something that said this was different to the vision Mick had taken them to. Compared to this, that had been like being inside a film or hearing a story told by someone who might have been making it all up.

'Mick,' he said and stared at the others. Will shook his head.

'I saw him when we left the grass. He was fine.' Will studied the grass and didn't appear to be able to elaborate. Stu had to look away from him. Mick, gone. Andy, gone. With Mick, it was somehow worse if that was possible. He'd come back, he'd been with them and now he wasn't.

What the hell do we tell Jodie? Mick, man. The babies. Bleeding Christ.

'Shit,' Stu whispered. 'What now?'

238

It seemed horribly unfair to jettison all thoughts of Mick, but they couldn't afford grief. Stu dug his nails into his palms and welcomed the sharp pain.

'She's here somewhere,' Karen said.

'Above the library,' Will said.

'Geri,' Stu whispered and a shiver ran through him. It dropped out of his feet and spread through the grass. A moment later, the first high voice of a child came. Others followed it. A dozen children, twenty, more: all laughing, talking, shouting; all moving around them on the lush grass. The air remained perfectly still, the sun beat on them and it was a gorgeous school day in a way that hurt Stu. It was a day a million miles from all the grief and trouble of adulthood.

The school bell rang, a sudden burst of a shrill noise, and the children's voices gained a focus, a direction.

'What's going on?' Will said.

Stu listened. The children's laughter and voices had definitely changed direction. They moved in one mass, heading across the grass to the school. It didn't take much effort to picture all the children moving towards the doors of the different blocks.

'Registration,' Stu said and let out a big laugh. 'Fuck me.'

He couldn't have said why the idea of registration filled him with such delight, only that it brought up images of early mornings and seeing friends. He laughed again and the second bell rang.

'The late bell,' Karen said and let out a nervous giggle as if they were the ones who were late for school.

The sound of the children rapidly decreased. Despite the lack of movement anywhere, Stu saw them all with his mind's eye. Dozens of kids were cramming in the doors, pushing, shoving, bags and jackets in their arms while they prepared for the last day of school.

Kids.

The last of Stu's exhausted laughter dried up. They were in the school and so were a load of children. So, they hadn't seen them; they'd heard them. They were here, and so was Geri with her gun.

'We need to get them out of here,' he said and tried to think of a plan that made sense.

'She won't shoot anyone. Come on. We're talking about Geri, for fuck's sake.'

Will did believe that, Stu knew. More than that, he wanted to believe that. He stayed silent although the urge to move was rapidly developing into panic.

'You don't think she would, do you?' Will asked both of them.

Karen struggled with her words but eventually spoke.

'A week ago, I'd have said no chance, but we've all seen it. And we've read her diary. You know what she said about here, about wanting to hurt other people. This is wrong, Will. I love Geri. Always did, but we have to stop her.'

'Jesus,' Will said and the corners of his mouth trembled. 'All right. Christ. All right. We know where she's going to be. I'll go there and if she's there, I'll talk to her.'

'No way are you going alone. Not when she's got a gun,' Karen shouted.

'It's Geri. She won't shoot me.'

'She shot at me,' Stu muttered and Will's anger faded from his face, leaving it sickly and frightened.

'Either way, we need to get the kids out of here. I'll go with you.' Stu gazed at Karen. 'You go to the reception and tell them what's happening.'

'You think they'll believe me?'

'Hit the fire alarm if you have to. Just get everyone out of here.'

Karen nodded. 'As soon as I'm done there, I'll come after you. If she's there, just keep her talking.'

'I can't believe we're doing this,' Will whispered. He rubbed at his mouth and kissed Karen. He let her go unwillingly and Stu watched a silent conversation pass between them: Will, telling Karen he loved her; Karen, telling him to be careful and she loved him. The words weren't there. Not aloud, anyway.

He and Will jogged across the field and aimed for the path that cut between the departments for science and maths. Stu glanced back after a moment; Karen was sprinting towards the car park which would take her to the main entrance. Ahead, windows bounced sunlight back at them and Stu wondered how long it would take before someone saw them and reported two men running into the school.

There was nothing left to do but hope they got to Geri before anyone could stop them, and hope Karen could get the kids out.

He and Will ran faster.

Seventy Nine

Kirsty couldn't stop her eyes moving from the rear-view mirror to the silent school. Back and forth, trying to watch both at the same time, trying to watch Phil in the back of the car and look for an escape in the same shot of vision.

It couldn't be done. There wasn't an escape.

Her hope had died about ten minutes before. She'd felt it go. There'd been no one reason for it, no single thing Phil had said. It had just gone. With her in one breath, and dead with the next. No more real thoughts of escape, just the imagination of running, of her trainers on the pavement as she pounded through the streets away from the bastard behind her. No belief she'd see Stu or Lucy again, no hope of telling them what they meant to her. Just her, this car, and the man behind. Just nothing at all but wanting it to be quick when it came.

I'm sorry, Stu. I'm really sorry.

There were no tears. Not even when Phil breathed right beside her ear.

'Drive up there. Right by the main entrance.' He pointed. 'Don't worry. Your car will be fine. This is a nice neighbourhood.'

He hissed a little laugh like a little boy laughing at a dirty joke.

'I hate you,' she said.

His chin brushed her earlobe and Kirsty bit back a groan of disgust.

'I know. It doesn't matter.'

Fully aware her words were nothing but a weak attempt at stalling him, Kirsty spoke as slowly as she could. 'Why here? What's so special about your school?'

He was listening to something she couldn't hear. Although there was only a little light in the back seat, she saw enough of his face to note the dreamy lack of focus in his eyes. Despite it, the pressure on her neck didn't ease. An abrupt mental picture exploded in her head. Bringing her arm up, elbow smacking into

Phil's face as she jerked forward, then to her side and out the door.

Kirsty let the image go. Even if she could move fast enough to injure him a little, he'd be out of the car and coming after her before she'd made it more than a few feet. He was fast. The bastard had proved that back in the house.

In the rear-view mirror, she watched life slip back into his eyes.

'She's here. That's why we are. Now drive.'

Kirsty summoned Lucy's little face and promised herself she'd keep it in front of her as long as possible.

'Drive,' Phil whispered and the knife dug into her skin.

Kirsty turned the key and drove towards the building. It loomed before her, an empty pile of bricks and windows with the occasional light stuck up high and offering no comfort. Even if there was anyone in the swimming pool, they were no help.

She brought them to a stop right beside the edge of the pavement and killed the engine.

'Very nice. And who says women can't park?'

Fuck you. Fuck you. Fuck you.

The thought wouldn't stop. It echoed as if stuck to her brain.

'Okay. Here's the deal. I get out and open your door. You try anything and I'll cut your face. How about that?'

Kirsty let out a sob. She couldn't help it.

'Good. What I hoped for.'

He slid out of the car, stood straight and opened her door. The entire movement took him no more than a couple of seconds. She had time to look at the car keys still in the ignition, but not to reach for them.

He hadn't asked her for them. That's how sure the bastard was she'd do what he wanted.

Her body took over; she stepped out to the pavement and stood beside her car. He eyed her.

'Fast, aren't you?' he said.

Kirsty's mouth stayed shut. Like her legs, it seemed to be acting without any conscious thought.

'Come on.'

He yanked her arm and pulled her tight against his body. The touch of his clothing, the stink of his sweat, they both pushed into her nose and mouth.

'Stay close and don't piss me off,' Phil said.

Moving with quick and oddly light steps, he pulled her to the main entrance. Dark pressed against the windows from the inside. Keeping her head motionless, Kirsty watched Phil scan the windows and doors. None were open, even a little.

'Too much to ask for,' he whispered. 'Should have just driven the car right through the doors.'

He gave her a smile and coldness enveloped her. He meant it. He actually meant they should have driven her car into the doors.

He'll kill me if it means getting in here.

No argument came and that was somehow worse than the realisation itself.

Phil pulled on her again; pain bolted up and down her arm and she bit back a shout. He took her around the side of the main entrance towards a path that led to the open grounds of the building. All of his attention appeared to be on the windows but Kirsty wouldn't let herself seriously consider running. Not here when there wasn't anyone else around.

'Fuck's sake,' he said and spat.

They'd reached the end of one side of the building. It opened into a wide avenue lined with young trees. Kirsty couldn't see what was at the end of the avenue although she had an idea simply from the layout she'd often seen from the other side of the building. Cromwell Road ran alongside the far side of the building from where they stood. That meant they were close to the cafeteria.

Phil shoved her to the nearest window. She bounced off it and stumbled. The impact winded her; she fought for breath and rubbed her chest.

'Sorry.' He smiled again. 'My fault.'

Kirsty found her breath and inhaled despite the throbbing in her chest and back. He pointed to the window she'd struck.

'A lot of give there, was it? Old glass?'

He stared over her shoulder, then met her eyes. A careful look had come to his face, one that said he was considering.

A horror film image struck her as hard as it could: Phil shoving her to the glass she'd hit, bending her head by the neck and using her skull to smash his way into the building.

It wasn't a horror film image. It was a possibility. Right here in the shadows coating the ground of her husband's old school, she was seconds away from having her head used as a battering ram.

'The cafeteria.' Her two words tasted like smoke. They burned. 'It's just down there.'

'So what?'

He glanced towards the darkness at the end of the avenue and understanding flowed into his face. Kirsty had no idea how long it had been since Phil had last been anywhere near the building but as he'd said, it had changed in recent years. The cafeteria had moved.

'Glass all down one side. Windows. Big.'

She could say no more. He was smiling again.

'I like your thinking.'

In one step, he was right next to her. His hands fell on her shoulders and spun her around to face the end of the avenue. He pushed her that way, the cafeteria rushed towards them and the moonlight shone on the glass Phil was still shoving her towards, faster and faster.

Eighty

Stu smashed into the door; it rattled but stayed shut. He kicked it, swearing. The door rattled again and remained locked.

He ran to a nearby window and swore again. The room was empty. So was the next one. He span in a fast circle. They'd come to the side of the science department; wide windows stretched down to a high wall of hedges. They'd come here simply because it was the nearest section of the building. It looked as if they'd chosen the wrong area.

'Where the hell is everyone?' he shouted.

'We need to get moving. Another door,' Will said.

Stu studied the side of the building and smacked his fist into the locked door. It was the only one he could see.

Will ran to the next window and hammered on it. The glass shook and that was all. Will sprinted almost to the end of the block and stopped.

'Fire exit,' he panted. Stu ran to him as he squatted and pulled at the frame.

'Take the top. It's open a bit,' Will said.

Stu pulled at the top of the door while Will yanked at the bottom. Wood scrapped and the door slid open to expose a long corridor. Silence greeted them.

Stu thought of the school layout and hoped the interior hadn't changed too much since they'd last been here. Realising the mistake in his thinking, he barked tired laughter.

'What?' Will said and Stu shook his head.

'In here, through home ec, then through to art, all right?' he said.

'All right.'

They entered the school together and no voices greeted them.

Eighty One

Phil's thought came over the noise of the breaking glass. *Are you here?*

I'm here, she said. *You're close now.*

He punched at the last of the glass from the big window and stepped into the building. The echo of the impact shook in his head. He threw it off and gave the cafeteria a quick look. Not much to see in the dark.

Broken glass and wood everywhere though; moonlight shining on the shards. And how long before the police arrived?

'Up,' he said. On the floor, Kirsty lay still. He bent towards her and her arm rose fast, hand extended to smack into the knife and her fingers were daggers aiming for his eyes.

Phil jerked up his other hand, hit her in the cheek and she cried out. He squatted and pulled her close.

'Try that again and I'll fuck you so hard, you won't be able to walk,' he told her.

Kirsty mewled and tried to pull back. A momentary thought came that she was faking her fear. A quick look into her eyes told him she was for real.

'Up. Now.'

He pulled her. Together they crushed glass as they moved into the wrecked cafeteria, Phil doing his best to disguise his limp. Pain filled his foot and much of his leg and he briefly wished he had shoved Kirsty through the window instead of kicking it in. Best to be safe, though. He might need her.

'We'll be there in just a couple of minutes,' he said and shook his head to lose the last of the echoing crash.

'Fuck you,' she said dully.

He laughed. 'Keep your mouth shut. Move.'

He pushed her ahead of himself but kept a hand on her arm. They took two steps further into the building and he noticed the stains on the wall.

Pulling Kirsty close, Phil clamped a hand over her mouth. She squirmed against him and he ignored her to study their

247

surroundings. The more he stared, the more shapes of stains were visible. Their colours were vague from the lack of light. He leaned closer to the wall and caught an unpleasant scent. He named it immediately.

'Blood.'

Kirsty pushed back against him and he tightened his grip until she was still.

Bloodstains on the walls. He stared at the floor around them. Bloodstains on the ground, the broken glass covering most but not all. Nowhere near all.

Phil moved backwards, dragging Kirsty with him. The shadows marking the paving slabs outside were too thick. It didn't make sense. The moon was bright tonight, the sky cloudless. From what he could see of the grounds, almost no moonlight shone now.

And there were broken windows.

He stared at their surroundings.

Broken windows. Bloodstains on the wall. The school was wrong. The school was—

changed.

'Where are you?' he whispered.

Here, she said. *Keep coming*, she said. *Like you always did*, she said.

Phil grinned despite his apprehension. She always knew the right things to say.

'This way,' he said to Kirsty as if they were walking hand in hand.

'Where are we going?' she asked in her new voice he quite liked.

'This way,' he said again.

They reached a long corridor and although a few windows lined it, only a little light came in. Phil gazed into the shadows and gloom. Something was wrong. Too dark. Too quiet. Where were the police sirens? Why weren't the people who lived across the road coming to investigate the breaking windows? They had to have heard all the noise. There was simply no way they couldn't, and this wasn't the sort of area where people ignored things right outside their houses. For that matter, why the hell hadn't any alarms gone off?

He pulled Kirsty closer and listened. Nothing but the wind blowing through the massive hole they'd created. No voices anywhere.

'You here?' he whispered and Kirsty stiffened against him.

Phil listened and heard his sister's voice.

I'm here, she said. *Just keep coming.*

He moved on, arm rubbing against the wall and there was something unpleasant in the feel of his arm on the surface. Something like a secret whisper.

Phil jerked his arm away and stared at it. Secrets. No time for secrets. Nothing on his arm.

They moved on again and he heard his voice come from far away, far out of the night around the school.

'You are here, aren't you? I wouldn't want to come all this way and be disappointed.'

They passed a couple of doorways, the doors open wide and a little of the interior visible. Broken tables. Overturned chairs. Smashed windows.

She murmured something he didn't catch.

'What was that?'

I'm always here, she said.

For some mad reason, fear made his insides squirm. And wasn't that a joke. She'd never scared him. Never ever. Ever.

'Are you ready for me?' he said.

Always ready.

'Good. Glad to hear it. It's been a long time.'

Too long. Too big.

The same fear, momentarily vanished, returned. He frowned. Too big? What the hell did that mean?

'Forget about it,' he told himself.

They reached the end of the corridor and entered the cafeteria. The place was a mess of wrecked tables and stains on the floor.

'What the hell is this?' Phil said.

She didn't answer.

Phil marshalled his thoughts. Who cared about this mess? This whole business was almost over. All he had to do was get upstairs to Block, hide from the law whenever the hell it decided to turn up and the job would be done.

'Not far now,' he said to Kirsty.

She made no sound. With the faint illumination dropping through a skylight, Phil studied her. She'd been strong and happy and keen to help a stranger if only because doing so might have helped her husband. But that was before. That was back then. Now she was weak and scared and injured. The woman he'd met in Memorial Square was long gone. Someone new had come in her place.

'Nice,' he said and pressed himself against her. She pulled away; he yanked her by the hips and pressed against her again. She closed her eyes. Phil considered taking a break and finding a corner in one of the classrooms. It wouldn't take long.

Come on, she said. *Hurry.*

'Hold on.' Phil smiled in the dark. 'I'm coming.'

I hope so, she said.

Phil smiled again and pulled Kirsty with him.

Eighty Two

Karen yanked on the door; it opened fast enough to smack into her foot. Not giving herself time to feel the impact, she dashed into the school and ran to the front desk, shouting as she moved.

'Hey, you need to get everyone out.'

Her words came to a halt.

There was nobody in the reception. Chairs and desks appeared normal; there was a cup of tea on one of the desks and a bowl of fruit close to a window. But no people.

'Hello?' Karen called.

This is wrong. Where is everyone?

'Hello.'

She raised her voice further, not caring if doing so made her look crazy. It didn't make sense. Although she hadn't run particularly close to any windows on the way from the field, she'd seen kids in classrooms. They'd been at their desks, working, talking to each other and probably thinking of nothing but the summer holidays. So where the hell was everyone now?

'Where are we, Mick? You brought us here, so where the hell are we?'

The answer was implacable and solid. It was like having Mick beside her.

School, you stupid cow.

'Thanks, Mick,' Karen whispered.

She heard, or thought she heard, a laugh touch her ear. Then nothing but her own panting breath.

Karen dashed to the corridor which ran beside the office, shouting again. Nobody replied. She shoved open door after door, saw nobody and ran back to the reception. Sweat dripped into her eyes. Hissing, she rubbed it away and caught a snatch of children's voices. They were moving somewhere close. Through the cafeteria.

Karen sprinted through the reception to the connecting hallway and saw shadows on the ground at the other end. Two or three and the same number of excited kids' voices.

'Hey,' she yelled.

The shadows vanished around the corner.

No time for this. You need to get everyone out.

'What everyone?'

No time to think about it. No time to chase kids through the school. She ran back to the reception and there it was on the wall close to the office window.

The fire alarm.

Karen struck it as hard as she could. The alarm shrieked into life, the noise crashing around her and racing through the corridors.

She raced from the reception, sprinting through long corridors towards the library and the steps beside it. As she passed a long window which showed Cromwell Road, she slowed, then stopped.

'No.'

Dozens of figures were in the street. The same figures that had chased them through the horrible nightmare version of Dalry. Same ragged clothes, same scarves covering their mouths, same makeshift weapons of clubs and bats.

Karen ran again. Whoops and cheers flowed through open windows. Knowing they'd be on her any second, she threw herself into a classroom, smacked into the wall and slammed the door shut.

She whirled around and came within a second of screaming.

She was back in the classroom full of dead children.

Eighty Three

He's fucking crazy.

The thought wasn't new by any means. The feel of it had been in Kirsty's head for hours, circling in the background, but it hadn't come to the front of her mind until now. Even after he'd revealed himself back in the house, she'd been secretly hoping that he was just mad with grief. The idea was nothing but a joke. He was crazy and she couldn't get away from him.

Who's he talking to?

She kept her eyes aimed ahead and listened to him talk to someone who wasn't her. They moved through quiet corridors and Phil told someone he was coming, asked if they were there, if they were ready for him. Occasionally, he pressed his crotch against her. Equal parts fear, rage and disgust raced through her each time he did it, again bringing forth the image of lifting her hand and plunging her index finger deep into the soft muscle of his eyes.

Blind him and leave him screaming and bleeding here in this fucked up school.

Kirsty clenched her hands into fists and summoned Lucy's face again. This was almost over. She knew it. And she wanted her daughter in her mind for as long as possible.

Phil pointed.

'Left at the end, then straight ahead. Then it's just up the stairs.'

Kirsty thought of her daughter and kept her eyes open.

'Been a long time,' Phil whispered. 'But I'm ready for you. You ready for me?'

He paused, then laughed.

'Glad to hear it. Always liked you like that, sis.'

Geri? Kirsty thought and couldn't blink, couldn't shut away the sight of this damaged building while beside her, Phil talked to his dead sister.

Stu. Help me. Oh, Christ. Help me.

Eighty Four

Will and Stu ran into the maths block, the door to the art department swung shut behind them and something let out a low snicker.

Both men froze. The sound was repeated, a sly laugh full of mocking, bitter humour. Will's eyes met Stu's. They were staring, white circles.

'Stu. Stu.'

The voice wasn't even close to human. A whistling noise filled Stu's head. It was the sound of the void they'd come through to get here. His mind attempted to protect itself by throwing itself into that white nothing. If he went into it, he'd never get out.

Terror buried him when the voice spoke.

'Stu. Dear Stu. Lost your way. Lost your friends. Lost your wife.'

It came from the floor and the walls. It came from everywhere.

'She's dead, Stu. Dead as Mick. Dead as Andy. Dead as Geri. Dead as you.'

It chuckled, something well pleased with a good joke.

Needles stabbed Stu's hand. Will was gripping it, digging his nails into Stu's skin. The pain brought a savage focus.

'Fuck you,' he cried.

At once, the laughter vanished. For two seconds, nothing breathed. Then the windows that lined the far side of the corridor exploded in a great volley of flying glass. Will and Stu ducked, shielding their eyes and faces from the glass. It scattered on the floor in wickedly sharp pieces. Fresh air slid in through the holes and Stu smelled a chill at odds with the bright day. His mind lurched and nausea claimed his stomach. The outside chill was a complete contrast to the sunshine and made him feel as if he was in two places at once.

'What the fuck was that?' Will whispered.

This place. Dalry. Where we were.

Stu's words wouldn't come out despite the need to scream them, to grab Will and run.

The chill was growing stronger. Sunshine mixed with the fresh air and it was all the good sun of summer just as it was something darker at the same time.

'Stu,' Will said. 'We have to go.'

The fire alarm brayed at them.

'Shit.' Stu lifted a hand to cover his ears. At the same time, the crash of breaking glass broke from somewhere close.

'Where was that?' Will shouted.

In response, Stu grabbed his friend's arm and they ran to an alcove which led to toilets. Together, they squatted close to the boys' toilet door and listened. The ringing alarm made it impossible to tell where the breaking glass had come from or if anyone was running through the corridors. Desperately, Stu tried to think through his panic.

Nobody here, no kids. This isn't the real school and we're away from the fucked up version of Dalry, so who's breaking in here?

The fire alarm fell silent and a surety hit Stu. Someone had turned it off deliberately. He stood. 'We need to keep going.'

The men ran as quietly as they could to the next junction of corridors. When the soft slap of their trainers on the floor stopped, an echo of it came.

Not an echo. Running feet. Coming, fast.

More glass broke from somewhere much closer than before. It was immediately followed by more, then a scrape of wood on wood.

'Run. Get to Block,' Stu whispered.

'What?'

'I'll make some noise, distract them.'

'No fucking chance.'

'Run.' Stu shoved Will. 'Get to Geri and talk to her. She's our way out.'

'There's nobody here. She can't shoot anyone.'

Stu shook his head as a door banged open.

'Doesn't matter. This is about her.'

He sprinted back towards the doors they'd passed through a moment before and shouted over his shoulder.

'Get to Geri.'

The crash of Will's trainers echoed as he ran the other way. More glass broke, followed by the sound of many voices jeering and calling.

All of them were shouting Will's name.

Terrified, Stu whirled around. The voices changed as he did so.

Some shouted Will's name.

But others now shouted his.

Eighty Five

Karen crept backwards until her back hit the wall. Not taking her eyes from the rows of dead children, she listened to the sounds of the people in the corridors. They didn't sound any closer but nor were they any further away. Her best guess was that they were in the corridor to the left of the room she was in. If that was right, they could be on her in thirty seconds.

Holding her breath, Karen crossed to the nearest desk. The two dead boys sitting there gazed at her with blank eyes.

At least they don't smell, she thought and had to swallow a horrified laugh.

Gripping the desk at both ends, Karen lifted it and staggered backwards under the weight. Sweating, Karen lurched to the door and placed the desk against it with as little noise as she could make. She took a few breaths and listened. The footsteps were no closer.

She ran to the next desk, avoided looking at the dead girls and took the desk to the door. She placed it on top of the first and told herself she couldn't move any more. It was a thin defence but better than nothing.

Karen ran to the windows, pulled at the blinds so they moved away from the glass and peered outside to the edge of the school field. Dull surprise hit her when she saw the twenty or thirty children on the playing field. Twelve year olds by the looks, all playing football and everything right with their worlds, everything as it should be.

'What the hell is this?' Karen whispered and couldn't take a guess for an answer. They were back in their last day; she knew that but it seemed that last day was outside the building. Inside, it was ...

The icy cold of a winter night filled her nose, a fierce chill that shoved thoughts of loneliness and hurt into her mind, thoughts of being lost in dark places with the light of home far away.

It was the smell of Dalry and all its secrets. It had bled through into this version of Dalry, come here to corrupt it, turn all this heavenly summer light into the permanent night they'd escaped from.

It had come back for them.

Sweating, Karen pushed the window open, wincing as the scrape of it sounded in the still quiet. She boosted herself up, slid halfway out and a hand grabbed her shin.

Karen slid back into the classroom and grabbed at the window. Her mind one white noise of horror, she stared into the room and came close to simply being unable to accept the sight of dozens of lifeless children come from their seats to pull her back inside. Two held her by the shins, a boy and girl in their uniforms, their mouths open and stupid saliva drooling from their lips. Another boy placed a hand on her thigh and squeezed.

Revolted terror shoved into Karen's muscles. She pulled herself on the window, made it half a foot and they pulled her.

Daylight blinded Karen. She thought of Will, of his smile.

They pulled her again. Only her head and shoulders jutted out of the window. Hands were all over her body; her t-shirt had rucked up to her breasts and cold fingers prodded her stomach. A sexless hand rose from her shin to her knee, then higher. Eager fingers squirmed against her crotch and a barrage of images assaulted her: fourteen, a party, her mouth full of the taste of cheap wine and Sam Radford's hand sliding up her skirt, hot on her thigh, her crotch a pleasant ache; sixteen, music from her stereo loud enough to drown out her gasps and Andy's nonsensical words against her mouth as his middle finger slid deep inside her; twenty-three and pulling Will on top, his hand a lovely weight against her stomach and her body rocking against him as his hand dropped and she was ready for him, oh God, she was ready for him, she was open for him, she was here right now and *it's touching me oh Christ oh Christ.*

Outrage consumed her and she barely heard her own thought.

Geri, I'm sorry, I'm so sorry but this isn't my fault, so get these fucking things off me.

Karen's scream broke free. She yanked on the glass pane and shot out of the classroom to drop to the concrete below. The ground scrapped her forearms and the cuts sang. She ran in a lurch, trying to stand at the same time and not looking back until she was at the edge of the now empty field.

The window was shut, the blinds up. Even from a distance of thirty or more feet, Karen could see the rows of children at their desks. They were all writing and studying and listening to their teacher.

Karen rubbed at her crotch and legs, desperate to lose the feel of the violating hands.

'You bastards. You fucking bastards.'

She welcomed her anger and wished for one, just one, of the dead kids to be right in front of her now. She'd tear them apart.

No time for that. This is almost over.

The voice in her head wasn't quite Geri's. Nor was it far off.

Struggling not to weep, Karen ran through the school grounds.

Eighty Six

The stairs.

Kirsty saw their outline. There wasn't enough moonlight to make out the stains on the walls and floors particularly well, but she could take a guess as to what they were. The same as they'd been on the way here, splashed everywhere. Blood, everywhere. Broken furniture and windows on all sides. This wasn't right. This wasn't the school. They'd come somewhere else.

If Phil had noticed, he wasn't showing it. He pushed her along and talked to someone who wasn't there, someone he was eager to see, someone who was apparently eager to see him.

Geri. This is all about Geri, Kirsty thought and a meaty hate of a person she'd never met enveloped her.

'Almost with you,' Phil said.

He panted as if running and his sweat coated her mouth and neck. With dull horror, Kirsty realised that the stabbing lump against her was Phil's erection. Her stomach clenched hard. She focused on her feet until the nausea in her mid-section passed but couldn't ignore the lump against her.

Phil pushed her against a wall and leaned in close to her face. Blood from cuts on his cheeks had trickled to his jawline.

'It's just up here. Then through the doors. Then it's all over. Think you can go a bit further?'

She didn't react. He shook her so her head bounced off the wall. The centre of her face exploded and she screamed.

'Think you can go a bit further?' Phil repeated.

'Yeah,' she croaked.

He pressed his groin against her.

'Yeah?' he said, and the bastard was grinning. For an instant, Kirsty's one wish ceased being her survival. She wanted nothing more than to make Phil scream as she had.

'You'll like my sister,' he whispered. 'Everyone does.'

He pressed his face to hers and his sweat was on her lips. Kirsty clamped her mouth shut and ordered herself not to vomit.

'Up the stairs,' Phil said and pushed her. She stumbled on the first step. He pulled her upright and held her by the hips as if guiding a close friend.

Kirsty did her best to ignore the feel of his hands by counting the steps that took them to the second floor. Fifteen. Then the outline of the doors ahead, a rectangle in the gloom. Phil stood beside her, still panting, and she watched him from the corner of her eye. He stared at the doors and although she couldn't be sure, she thought he was whispering.

Wanting to hear his words just as much as she didn't want to, Kirsty tilted her head towards him and strained to hear. His words were hisses in the dark.

'I told you, didn't I? I told you I'd come back for you and you know why, don't you? I love you. Always did. Every day. And you knew that, really, didn't you? Even when you said you didn't. You knew it. I proved it. And I came back like I told you I would. And you're back like I knew you would be. It's because we can't stay away from each other. But you knew that already, didn't you? Didn't you? Didn't you?'

Each repetition had a little more emphasis and volume than the previous, a little more life. Kirsty pulled away from him and he didn't appear to notice her move.

'I remember your blood,' he said and his erection pulsed against Kirsty's leg. Her vision greyed for a moment.

Gripping Kirsty's hand hard enough to make her sob, he pulled her close and ran to the doors.

Kicked them open.

Light everywhere. And warmth. The light and warmth of a summer evening.

Kirsty saw.

Eighty Seven

Stu shot through the doors into the art department, dashed past displays of drawings and paintings and stopped in an open plan classroom. The shouts of whoever was coming after him rang out loud. They'd be through the doors in seconds.

He sprinted to the far right corner and ducked behind a high shelving unit. A moment later, the doors crashed open again.

Stu lifted the bat, held it with both hands in front of his face and listened.

Something whispered, then giggled childishly. He couldn't tell how many there were. Maybe three. He scanned what he could see of the classroom. Nothing that resembled an obvious weapon. He tightened his hold on the bat.

Come on, you fuckers. Mick. Andy. Come on and try it. I'll bash your fucking heads in.

Another whisper. Stu stood straight.

'Where are you?'

The voice was somewhere between a laugh and a shout, and while it came from a man, it wasn't a man's voice. The sound of it made Stu think of children pretending they were adults.

'Are you here?'

Another voice and the last word dragged out in a sing-song voice.

'Come on, you fuckers,' Stu breathed.

They moved a chair out of their way, then kicked it. It flew into the centre of the room, knocking others aside. As soon as the echoes stopped, a few steps slid over the ground.

They were coming towards him, moving along the shelving unit.

Stu gazed at the bat and a brief wish came that he still had the knife which had stabbed Andy instead of forgetting it when they ran from Geri's house

One last giggle and they ran at him.

Stu swung his bat and jumped forward at the same time. It struck something that howled. Something else clattered to the floor. Stu swung the bat again and the man ducked. The bat hit the unit behind him and glass exploded.

The second man ran at Stu, knife coming up. Stu smacked his bat into the man's elbow and the blade clattered to the floor. Stu screamed wordless noise at them and the sound seemed to come from someone else's mouth.

The first man raced at him; Stu hit him in the face and he dropped. The second man, holding his elbow and screeching like an animal, ran. He sprinted to the corridor that led back to the doors and vanished from sight.

Stu kicked one of the knives away and tried to find his voice. It was buried below the roar of blood in his ears.

'Who the fuck are you?' he spat.

The man grinned. His hand shot out from under his leg and the penknife he'd palmed slammed deep into his eye.

Gagging, Stu jerked back as the man's legs shook and blood ran down his cheeks from the ghastly wound in his eye. He was dead, gone with horrible triumph.

Still gagging, Stu brought his bat down on the man's head and face until there was nothing but blood and bone above the neck. Exhausted, he collapsed against a table and fought for his breath.

'Geri,' he whispered.

Stu pushed himself upright and ran to the corridor. As he turned the corner to the doors, a blurred movement flew at his face.

Stu fell back, dropped, and the man's fist swung for his face.

The blade struck the wood of the bat and a knee struck Stu's thigh. He screeched and his flailing hand found the hot, grimy skin of a face. He struck the man's nose; cartilage twisted and Stu shoved hard. The attacker squawked and his knee missed Stu's testicles by inches. Stu bellowed into the man's face and something set a detonation of agony off deep inside Stu's leg.

He looked down.

The knife stuck out just above the knee.

Spit flew from his mouth as he screamed at the man who reached for the handle of the knife. Stu did the same; his assailant got to it first and Stu swung the bat as hard he could. At the same time, the man shoved the palm of his hand against the handle and Stu's leg exploded into fire.

His bat glanced off a narrow shoulder in a weak blow. The man jerked back, clearly expecting a harder blow and Stu bucked beneath him. He rolled, hit his wounded leg against the floor and cried out. Hands crashed down on his throat, fingers met each other and his head hit the floor, once, twice, again and again.

Blood filled his eyes. Black closed in.

Then screaming came, shrill and horrible. A thud. The fingers fell from his throat and he coughed blood and spit even as he tried to inhale. Fire blossomed in his neck and mouth. He pushed himself over and Karen was there, tall and glorious. She still held the chair with which she'd hit the man. He lay on the floor, unconscious and bleeding.

'Stu, Jesus.'

She fell against him and pulled him upright. Her tears dropped on to his face and he blinked until she came into proper focus.

'Karen?'

'Will, Stu. Where is he?'

'We split up. He went to find Geri. What happened to you?'

Each word was a blade in his throat. He coughed more blood, swallowed some and gagged. He spat to the floor.

'I was in the reception. Nobody's there, Stu. The school's empty.'

'I know.'

He swallowed and coughed more blood. Some spattered on to Karen's hand and she didn't let go.

'I ran; people came after me so I hid.' She was babbling and Stu had no energy to tell her to calm down. 'The dead kids, Stu. Like before. They came after me, grabbed me but I got away and ran here.'

She wept and embraced him. He pressed into her breasts and accidently shifted his leg. He screamed.

'Fuck.' Karen reached for the handle. Stu steeled himself but couldn't keep another screech inside as Karen yanked the knife free, the meat of his leg splitting further around the blade. Everything from his waist down was on fire. Blinking furiously, he reached for her.

'Help me up,' he panted.

The agony grew as she supported him under the armpits. He leaned into her and eventually made it upright. The stink of sweat and blood stuck to him. He prodded the unconscious man with his bat and the man didn't move.

'Who the hell are these people?' he whispered.

'Give me that,' Karen said and extended a hand.

She took the bat, Stu rested against a nearby table and Karen lifted the bat high.

She spat on the unconscious man and brought the bat down on his head. Bone split. He let out a bubbling squeal and slid to his side. Karen spat on him again and handed the bat back to Stu.

'Let's go,' she said.

Stu leaned into her and froze. The mess that had been the dead man's head had changed into a black fog. It ran from his wounds like a murky stream and sank into the floor. A moment later, there was nothing before them but a corpse.

'What the hell was that?' Karen whispered.

A chuckling laugh answered her. As before, it emerged from the ground and the walls.

Stu whirled to face the nearest wall. His wounded leg screamed and he screamed back.

'Come on. Fucking come on.'

The words tore in his throat and blood coated his teeth.

The laugh faded.

'We have to go,' Karen said. She was trembling but her grip on him remained strong. Stu stared at the dead man, at his mashed head and the patch of the floor which had swallowed the black fog.

'It's Dalry. These shits here. They're Dalry. The bad side. It's come here,' he said.

'I know. There are more of them.'

'Good. I want to kill them.'

Using the bat as a makeshift crutch, Stu leaned further into Karen and they moved towards the doors.

A tremendous rumbling shook the outside, a shaking in the ground.

'What the hell is it?' Stu whispered.

They staggered to the nearest window. Out on the street, scorched with light and cooking in mid-morning heat, the houses on the other side of Cromwell Road were collapsing. Windows, bricks, roof tiles fell to the grass and road as if dissolving. Clouds of dust flew, blocking trees and hedges from sight. The rumbling grew louder and something not too far away exploded. Cars rolled from driveways into the road, struck each other and metal crumpled. Glass broke and the smell of smoke choked his nose and mouth. With it, the heat of the day faded. Winter air closed in. Through the rising dust, the sun was still visible but its light was murky, fading. Darkness crept into the day and cold air swirled in over the grass.

The grass was turning black.

'It's here,' Stu said and he managed to keep a steady voice.

'It's come for us, hasn't it?' he said to her.

'Will, Stu. Geri.'

A heavy explosion roared towards them and fire ate at the remains of the house directly opposite them.

Karen dragged Stu to the doors as the buildings on Cromwell Road continued to fall apart.

Eighty Eight

Kirsty stared into Block. The sixth form room wasn't there. Nor was moonlight.

She saw.

Oh God.

She saw.

A bedroom. The window open wide and evening light slipping inside to cover the sill, the mess of books and clothes on the floor below the window. The light rising and falling in beams towards the posters of New Kids On The Block on the walls. A small chest of drawers with pots and tubes of makeup. A drawer open a couple of inches and underwear visible. Cotton underwear. Small bras. The light touching the garments with gentle fingers and falling into the shorts tossed to the carpet.

A bedroom pregnant with summer light even if it's the light of sunset, and night will be here soon.

She was on the bed, under the covers and they were pulled up to her neck. She stared at the ceiling and tried to think of something other than his words. She couldn't. They were stuck in her head in an endless loop and the secret part she could only just admit to herself is there was something in those words she liked. It was a secret thing. More than that, it was their secret thing and while that was a strange thing, new and full of possibilities, she knew enough to know she liked it. Liked it because it was a secret and it wasn't allowed. She knew that much even if she couldn't have said why.

It didn't matter, though. He'd be here soon and he'd tell her the rest and whatever game this turned out to be, it would be their game. He'd said so. A game for her birthday next week. Had to be tonight. Had to before her birthday. It didn't matter about him, he told her. Fourteen or fifteen, he could do this at any point. What mattered was her and playing this game before her birthday.

A door closing somewhere. Footsteps rising. Summer light and her warm bedroom. Then him in the doorway, close to filling the doorway.

'Are you ready for the game?' he said and she said yes she was. He smiled and the first warning alarm rang for her.

The smile didn't work. It was like when Mum shouted at Dad about something and he smiled to say he didn't mind the shouting.

The light at the window. Warm.

He came to her bed, sat beside her.

'Are you really sure about playing this game tonight?' he said.

She said yes she was.

'Really sure? I mean, it has to before your birthday but it's our game. Can't tell Mum or Dad. They'd ruin the game.'

She asked why.

'They're too old for this game.'

That didn't make much sense but she let it go.

He took hold of the top of her duvet and pulled it down an inch.

She asked him what he was doing.

'It's hot in here. Don't want you getting too hot under the covers.'

His words made sense. The last fortnight had been a hot end to a long summer and the approaching night hadn't cooled a great deal.

He pulled the cover again and eased his face towards her.

'This is our game. But we don't have to play it tonight, okay?'

She said she wanted to but didn't know if that was true. His face seemed too big. His breath was hot on her mouth and nose.

'Do you really want to play this game?' he whispered.

She said she really wanted to.

Then her covers were off and he was whispering against her ear.

'You can't tell anyone about our game. This is our secret game and we'll be in trouble if you tell.'

She pulled her face from his, opened her mouth to speak or shout—she didn't know which—and his face was half an inch above hers, blocking out the last of the daylight and robbing her voice. Something tickled her knees, then the skin above her knees, then it tickled higher.

Something oddly pleasant in that, something secret, something new.

A single second of time span around her head, chasing itself and marking its prints over her mind, making its home in her head. This moment raced ahead of her, filling the days, weeks, months and years with its sad weight. Her life shrank to an infinitesimal dot; she lived inside it and called it home even though it was a home of hurts.

The tickling came again, higher, and that second that seemed to have lasted for years was long gone. Nothing pleasant now, only fear.

She squirmed, felt her t-shirt rise over her stomach and the ghastly sensation of her shorts now around her thighs. Warm air kissed her thighs, kissed higher and all at once it was more than warm. The air burned her alive and her scream at this shock remained locked in her mouth.

Then he was on top of her and then the room was far too hot, the light of sunset too red, too ...

red

too red ...

too red down there, oh mummy, oh it hurts, oh it's ...

red.

Eighty Nine

The stairs. The fucking stairs.

Will staggered towards them and tripped when the mammoth rumbling shook everything. He crashed into an open door and fell through into a classroom. Dropping beside the teacher's desk, he used it to pull himself up into a crouch.

'What the fuck is this?' he shouted.

The rumbling had grown louder in the last few seconds. Panting, Will managed to stand and stare outside. The grass beside the building was no longer visible. Flying debris filled the air and coated the green as far as Will could see. With delicate, frightened steps, he moved closer to the windows and made out the wrecked buildings across the road. He attempted to cross reference the sight with the familiar. The best he could do was the idea of an earthquake. He seized on it, aware it wasn't true. Earthquakes didn't work like this. They didn't eat into buildings this way; they didn't break windows with a deliberate pattern. Nor did they leave buildings looking much older than they were in the space of a minute.

'Dalry.'

The word gave the scene flesh and brought a sickening fear. Any minute now, the sun would vanish, turning the familiar street into an endless night. And then they'd come, the people, the *things* who'd killed Andy and Mick. They'd come to finish their work.

Will stared, unable to move. Cracks in the road spread rapidly to meet and form holes. Trees collapsed to block the road. Cars rolled from driveways to crash into the fallen trees. He watched the growing chaos, mouth open wide and feet unwilling to move.

Karen.

The single word came from somewhere far away in his mind and brought Karen's face to him.

Realisation of his situation smacked into him. He drew breath and roared his wife's name.

'*Karen.*'

The windows coughed inwards, glass flew towards him and he threw himself down and away in an ungainly movement. Broken glass pattered on the floor and table. Will crawled to the door. He stared.

The glass had missed him by less than a foot. He splayed a hand on the dirty floor, realising the kitchen knife he'd taken from Geri's house was long gone. For all he knew, the blade had fallen between their last seconds with Mick and their arrival at the school.

'Fuck this,' he said and ran back to the corridor. Other windows had exploded. Pieces of brick and road lay in loose piles on the floor; dust rose and filled his mouth. He coughed and spat the taste away. The corridor shook; Will slapped his palm against a trembling wall to steady himself and did his best to believe this was just a picture, this wasn't his school or his past. The floor trembled, spilling him against the wall. Dizziness filled his head and he forced his eyes to focus on a classroom door. With no surprise at all, Will realised he was looking at the door to his year ten class. A barrage of memories assaulted him: sights, sounds and smells from his past come back as if they'd never been away.

'Bollocks,' Will croaked and ran with lurching steps. 'Geri.' He coughed hard. 'Coming, Geri.'

He tripped on the third step and struck his head against the wall. Blood ran into one eye. Groaning, Will used the wall as a guide and ascended as fast as he could. The stairs curved at the tenth step, there were another six, then the floor, then the doors he hadn't seen in twenty years.

The ground shook hard enough to drop him. He bashed his shin against a step and bellowed. Limping, he pulled himself up to the floor, stared at the doors, both so brown and old just as he remembered them. Even the faded metal of the handles was the same.

Will let out a mad, raving laugh and ran in a lurch to the entrance. A deep, savage chuckle ran through the entire school as Will ran, the laugh emanating from floors and walls and doors.

Dalry, bad Dalry, bad fucking Dalry.

Will's hands struck the doors dead centre and they flew open to crash into the wall. At the same time, the day's glorious sunshine winked out and night pooled in through the wrecked windows.

Red. She's red.

Then he was running to Kirsty even as the man holding her swung his arm upwards and moonlight shone on something in the man's hand.

Ninety

Karen heard the laugh. Even with the horrendous noise of the buildings falling apart and the school rupturing, she heard it.

A scream tore out of her and she came within a second of throwing Stu to the wall and running the rest of the way down the corridor to Block.

'Faster,' Stu yelled and for a few painful steps, he was ahead of her. She gripped him as tightly as she could and they staggered onwards. Stu's wounded leg dragged behind him like a club and fresh blood stained Karen's jacket the faster they moved.

Whatever had caused the destruction outside appeared to be growing stronger. The cracks in the walls rose into the walls and spread to the ceiling. Plaster rained and clumps of it fell when the school trembled. Karen didn't think of it or its cause. She thought of Will.

They drew level with the little corridor that ended at the cafeteria. The windows collapsed at the same time with a shriek of breaking glass; plaster fell on Stu's shoulder. He leaned into Karen and she pulled him forward.

The doors were in sight, both hanging loose from the frames. Stu and Karen reached them and she saw the debris covering the stairs. Getting up there would be close to impossible.

'Stay here,' she shouted and Stu shook his head. 'You can't get up past all that shit.'

He shook his head again and let go of her. He dragged his wounded leg, blood now dripping from the makeshift bandage Karen had made from an old cloth. He made it up two steps before falling. She ran to him, caught his arms and couldn't halt his downward movement. They fell together and a stair jabbed hard fingers into her back. She cried out, pulled Stu upright and tried to holler over the noise.

'Up.'

He nodded and she had no idea if could hear her or not.

They moved up another couple of steps, Karen's muscles howling in protest. As she lifted a foot to move to the ninth step, Stu slipped from her grip and dropped.

Karen saw the next few seconds with a horrible clarity: Stu falling, his wounded leg buckling beneath him and his head connecting with the stairs. She heard the sound of the impact as clearly as she could hear the school falling apart.

Her slow, stupid hands reached for him and they were much too slow, much too stupid.

Stu's wounded leg jerked upwards. It rose an inch, two inches, and Stu rose with it. Karen realised he was screaming just as she was. Stu came down on the next step and fell against her. She caught him.

He tried to speak against her ear. He had nothing but his panting breath.

A hand touched hers. Karen looked down and saw the shape of a hand already fading to a shadow. With the shadow came a name.

Andy? Are you here?

She was crying, heart bursting. Andy was here. Andy was gone. Andy was gone. Andy was here.

Karen dragged Stu to the tenth step, still weeping. It seemed she could do nothing but weep. Andy had come. Dear, sweet Andy.

Stu's mouth brushed her ear and he wheezed a laugh.

'Got a free period. Want to go for a fag?' he whispered. Karen gazed at him, eyes wet, and saw his exhausted smile.

'Later,' she said and kissed his cheek.

They kicked through the piles of rubble on the steps and made it to the second floor, Stu shaking and sweat dripping off his head and Karen unable to stop her tears.

'Fucking hallelujah,' Stu whispered and there was a moment, a glorious second between only them when it seemed the rage eating into the school's fabric paused and drew a breath.

Silence filled the world.

They walked, staggered, ran to the doors of Block and those doors opened as they moved and the world was made of tears.

The world was made of red.

Ninety One

Geri is on her bed.

Geri is aged eleven and her childhood is over.

Over and dead and buried inside a scream she keeps inside.

The summer light fills her bedroom. There aren't any shadows at all and that means nowhere to hide, not here, not in the safest place she knows and loves. There's just one big open hole and she's deep inside it, looking to the light at the top and she knows it's a billion miles away. It's as far beyond her reach as anything in the world because that is where her happiness lives now, where it went. She'll be looking for it for the rest of her life. She knows that just as she knows that life is going to hurt, going to do nothing but hurt for as long as it wants. And it makes no difference that she wants that happiness and that she wants to love. It's gone from her just like the sunlight is gone from today. It doesn't matter about the last of it falling through the window in little drops of red and yellow and pink and green, coming to her bed in red, so much horrible red. None of those things are real for her now. What matters is what's here, what's come to her.

Nothing.

Nothing left.

She curls up on her bed and listens to the sound of her heart beating. It beats in time with the terrible throbbing between her legs. She counts those beats, one after the other, as night closes into her bedroom and the time slips away until her mother calls up the stairs that it's time for bed.

One beat after the other. Time flowing past her and her bed. Time like water. Like blood. Like all the red between her legs.

Let it go, she thinks. Let the pain go and stay here, stay as far away from it as you can. It'll go away if you let it. If you let it. If you stay here and the pain goes wherever it wants. Stay here in bed. Stay red.

Beat after beat. Thud after thud and she's eleven and the world hurts her and the last of the daylight fades into black.

Now she's crying again and it's her fourteenth birthday and he's here. Stu's here and he's talking to Karen, not her, and she knows why. He wanted to talk to her. Made that pretty clear at school yesterday and she was so far away, stuck in her bed, stuck in the nightmare there, so now he's talking to Karen and pretty soon they'll be kissing. Pretty soon they'll find somewhere private upstairs and that won't be with her.

She faces the stereo and turns up the volume, not reacting when Andy shouts that he loves this song, not wanting him or any of the others in the room to see she's crying. The music covers her hitching breath and that can only be a good thing in this warm room, warm house, warm with too much sun. She leaves the room as quickly as she can without running, grateful nobody is near the door. Motes of floating dust touch her in the hallway, the frosted glass of the front door ushering in the light outside and someone says her name. Her sister Leigh is halfway up the stairs, ten years old and smiling, asking if she can come downstairs and join the party. Geri tells her no, tells her to go back upstairs to her bedroom and not talk to anyone. She doesn't wait to see if Leigh does as she says; the tears come back when she hears Stu laughing above the sound of the music. She runs to the downstairs toilet, locks the door and sits on the lavatory. Rocks back and forth, hugging herself and forcing her mind to close off its images, memories, forcing her head to stop. Just stop. Just fucking stop.

Fucking stop, she says aloud and the word she's spoken only a few times before is darkly exciting. She says it again and again and her tears cease. Control has come. She's in charge and that's the best thing in the world. It's a present. She gave it to herself. The tears aren't with her anymore. She's smiling in the toilet. In charge.

And she's smiling because she's with Will. She's twenty and Will is here with his uneven smile and his hands all over her, and oh God she loves it when he's like this. She loves being twenty and his house is theirs and theirs alone. Late January outside, stupid, dead January with its bare trees and wind and all the joy of Christmas already long gone. It's all outside and so what? Who cares? It's out in the night and she's here in the light and heat of Will's bedroom, pillow below her head and the stereo on, volume not too high, just high enough to cover them.

This is it, this is what it's all about, she tells herself. Happiness here in this room, dead winter locked away. They're safe from it because they're inside and it's out. She's safe with him; she's in charge of him.

Now he's on top of her, blowing into her ear and it makes her laugh and down there, she's hot. Jesus, she's hot. Her new denim skirt is high, much higher than her thighs, and it's frustrating in a strangely pleasant way that her tights around her knees prevent her from opening her legs any further. Frustrating. Annoying. But pleasant. He likes her like this, she knows. Sort of slutty. Open but not completely. Showing a bit. Open.

She relishes the heat that comes with this thought. She's in charge. She gave this to him. She does this to him. Her. Her. All of her. What power. What heat.

Will's middle finger trails over her thighs, then higher, and she shifts to let him in. She feels herself let go when he enters her as deeply as he can; it drips when he pulls his finger out, pushes it back in and oh my God, oh my God, it's blood, it's blood everywhere, it's red, it's red between my legs.

She's crying out of nowhere. Dead January is here. It's broken in. Now Will has jerked away from her, his mouth stained with her lipstick and he backs away over his bed, staring at her, wanting to speak. She can see that, even if she can't see anything else. Eyes full of tears and she staggers out of Will's bedroom and across the hall to the bathroom. She sees herself through his eyes as she lurches away from him: skirt up around her waist, tights nothing more than a torn second skin stuck to her legs and she's still wet, still dripping.

The bathroom door is closed, locked. She's leaning against it and her hand moves down there to her heat, the terrible pain. She's crying as she does it, as her orgasm eats into her, thinking of nothing but her bedroom flooded with red. And worst of the worst, worse than four nights later and finishing with Will, worse the other guys in the pub, all three of them one after the other, worse than the pain, exhaustion and shame she feels in the morning, worse than anything there could ever be is her right now, right here at Leigh's funeral.

Leigh, dead. Leigh, gone from the world and only seventeen. Not fair. Not fucking fair. Leigh, pregnant, and the car hitting the wall hard enough for flying chunks of glass to take off her face.

Not fucking fair.

Not fair.

Not her. Shouldn't have been Leigh. She didn't deserve this, not her little sister, not the one she should have protected for all this time.

This is the worst of the worst. Leigh, dead. Leigh, pregnant. Leigh in the car and it wasn't out of control, she wasn't drunk; there was nobody else, just Leigh in her car, belly still flat despite what slept inside, and her car hitting the wall fast enough to end everything.

The worst of it all.

Is right now.

Because she knows everything.

What he did to her. Just once.

What he did in her bed just once.

What he did to Leigh for ten years.

Geri stands on the edge of the car park and Christmas shoppers are miles below; the Christmas lights watch her stand on the edge, watch the wind whip through her hair. Dirty Christmas. Dirty lights. Dirty air, full of winter and cold and there's nothing left but below, but Dalry, but her home and she knows it as well as she knows her own name, knows it's a dark place, full of ugliness and hurt and rage: streets and roads filled with secret things as ugly as what he did to her one time, what he spent ten years doing to Leigh and Leigh never said a word.

Not fair. Not fucking fair. So fuck you. Fuck you.

Fuck you, fuck me, fuck me, that's what she said, Geri, when she told me to, she told me fuck her because she loved it, she loved me and we did it all the time, for all that time, I fucked her, I fucked her like I never fucked anyone else, like I made her believe it, believe me and for that all time, all those years, all those ten years until she was seventeen and she was pregnant so do it, you bitch, fucking do it, see if anyone gives a shit because they'll know you wanted it like she did, you asked for it so you fucking well do it.

And the world, made of Geri's tears, of rage, of red exploding out from between her legs.

This world is red.

Geri brings Leigh's face to her mind and she is sorry, she is so sorry she never told anyone what he did to her.

Geri jumps from the carpark, sails down towards the Christmas shoppers and Christmas lights of Dalry.

Ninety Two

Phil let go of the woman. His hand free from her arm felt strangely sad.

'Go,' he told her.

Kirsty ran to Stu and Karen; Karen let go of Stu. Kirsty caught him. Karen lifted Will and supported his head. His hands fell on his stomach. His blood coated her when she lifted his fingers from the wound.

'Karen?' he whispered.

She lifted her head, marked Phil and the depth of her rage surprised him.

'You fucking bastard.'

Her shriek managed to bury the noise outside for a second. He waved the knife at her.

'Stay there,' he said.

She held Will, talking to him and burying his head against her breasts.

'Will?' Stu croaked.

'He's fine,' Karen sobbed. 'He's fine.'

Phil watched this, idly interested. Stabbing Will hadn't been part of the plan. It had just happened when the idiot came running in here, running right at them. It had just happened like so much other stuff.

Will raised a bloody hand a few inches; Stu dropped, wounded leg jutting from his body at an odd angle. Will's hand slapped against Stu's arm. Kirsty embraced Stu as she wept and Stu took Will's hand.

'You're not going anywhere, Elton,' Stu said.

Phil watched them, wondering who'd be first.

Will. It'll be Will.

He was right. Will lifted his head with obvious effort and stared at him. Blood covered his stomach and chest.

'Geri.'

It wasn't much more than a whisper. Phil heard him, though.

'You raped her.'

Phil lifted his hand and extended the blood stained knife towards Will.

'Say that one more time.'

Will's mouth trembled and it wasn't with fear, Phil realised. It was anger. His words flew from him in a terrible bellow and blood poured from his stomach at the same time.

'You raped her, you bastard. Leigh, too. You raped them, you piece of shit.'

The windows in Block collapsed. Phil ducked as glass rained. Momentarily forgetting the group on the floor, he shielded his face. Freezing air coated his skin. The night outside finally registered even though a distant part of his mind had noticed it moments before. The crash of the collapsing roads and buildings also reached him. Faraway panic came closer and told him to get out of here, to leave the people on the floor and get somewhere safe.

No. This is my place.

Phil stared at the little he could see of the school grounds, frowning. This, his place? His school, yes, but he hadn't been here in years. He hadn't been back to Dalry in God knows how long and until he'd seen her, he hadn't given much thought to Geri for a long time. Not until the girl, of course. Whatever her name was, she was the spitting image of Geri. Same hair, same eyes, same potential.

Telling the woman, Kirsty, about her, hadn't been a good idea. He knew that now. But nothing to be done about it. Nothing but deal with this and get out. Nothing but this place and *her* coming back to him.

Letting a slow smile spread over his face, Phil faced Geri's friends and welcomed what he saw. Their faces were all aimed towards him, their mouths open.

The moonlight between him and them was moving. It danced just like she did.

She was here.

'You came.'

Told you I would.

'I did wonder.'

I didn't lie.

The light around her grew and the noise of the town falling apart belonged to another world.

Here, it was their world and their world alone.
Phil moved towards his sister.

Ninety Three

The storm in his stomach had faded to background noise. Karen's hand was in his and they were all together in this nightmare. And the light was here. Inside the light, Leigh.

Will's mind raced backwards in time, taking him with it through his and Karen's relationship and back before that to home, to family and Dalry and school. And now Geri.

He stood in his past, buried with it, and saw Leigh as she'd been as a kid, a figure in the background of his teen years, only gaining flesh and colour when he and Geri had become closer friends, then more than friends. Leigh, always behind, always young and always there but never quite as solid as anything else in his life.

Here she was as solid as she'd been back then, as alive as she hadn't been since she was seventeen.

Realisation fell into him. The girl. Andy's flat. Looked like Geri. Could have been her cousin.

Or her sister.

Or Geri and Leigh inside one body, the face belonging to neither and shaped from both of them.

I knew you. Will couldn't speak. All he had was the thought. *I knew you. I knew you.*

He heard her talking even if her mouth didn't move. She spoke to Phil and her words broke through the noise outside now racing through the school and heading up to Block, and even if her face and body said she was seventeen, Will saw her as a child in her bed, blood between her legs as she wept for what her brother had done to her, would keep doing to her until she died: her scream, one constant noise all around her, a hand resting on her stomach and the *thing* growing inside her, the thing he put there; and her car crashing into a wall at seventy miles an hour.

Then those bleak times for him and Geri when some unnamed horror had been eating her, some horror that gained a name after Leigh's death. It all came back and welcomed him like an old friend. Will was conscious of the others around him, Karen's hand in his and the distant pain in his stomach. They were all with him but none as solid as the lost years of before, lost with Geri and her grief for her dead sister and her lost past.

Her childhood. He took it, he fucking stole it, he ...

The thought descended into noise. Will returned to his body and his pain. Block was here; school was here and *they* were all here with their blood and their grief of lost time.

Back here in Dalry.

Back home.

They're coming, Will. Those outside. The forgotten. They're coming here.

Will's free hand dropped to the shaking floor, palm flat and ready to support him.

Glancing down, he saw Karen's hand sliding towards Stu's jeans pocket, and Stu and Kirsty were looking down, a frown crossing Kirsty's face and an exhausted smile filling Stu's.

In front, Phil and Leigh; Phil smiling at the sight of his sister back again; Phil's smile a monstrous beast as Leigh crossed to him; Leigh, seventeen, and forever there with her arms opening and the light that enveloped her a dark, pulsating heartbeat.

Two heartbeats.

***

The diary flies from Karen's hand.

It lands without a sound on the carpet.

The diary opens.

The light around Leigh falls into it, slips inside the pages as if made of ink. The crash of the school falling apart reaches the door to Block; wood splinters and collapses, the cracks race across the floor in lines and the moonlight bellows in through the holes in the windows and walls.

And the diary.

Geri's diary.

A shape coming out of the pages, rising, full of light, the pages giving birth to light and it's there for all of them: Will, Karen, Stu and Kirsty see her emerge from her pages, standing over them and smiling as she did in life.

Geri.

Leigh.

Phil.

Sisters face brother and Leigh is away from Phil without moving a step. He's left alone on the floor, eyes moving between them, tasting them. The wind blows into a gust, then a gale. Debris spins around Phil, blocking his body but not his face from view. The ground falls away from him. Chunks of building drop into nothing and it isn't nothing below. It's the same void that brought them to this version of their school and the laughing thing from the river, the thing that keeps the doors closed between what is past and what is now, that thing is there, peering upwards. Its great mouth opens and it swallows the falling chunks of building and the beams of moonlight.

Phil tries to speak, to say his sister's names and nothing is there. What is there is movement behind him: figures coming in waves. They walk on nothing. They fill the holes in the building, clamber through the wrecked windows and cross towards him.

The dark things with their clubs and bats, their hands stained with blood. All the dark things come from the underside of Dalry to this little world.

Leigh screams.

The sound splits everything in two. The sound echoes from death to life. The rage of her monstrous life torn in two by her brother flies into what remains of Dalry, falls below the hungry holes into the mouth of the laughing thing below to land in the lost Dalry.

All the light starts to fade. The moon is gone. The clouds are here. The people advance on Phil; hands reach for him and he speaks, calling Leigh, then Geri and the hands are on him, fingers digging into his skin, tearing open his flesh and he's still calling to his sisters, still saying he loves them, always loved them and fingers move to his face, higher to his eyes. Fingers pierce them, eager to blind him, eager to unleash his blood and screams and he falls down into the Dalry he created, the Dalry he owns, the dark things falling with him.

Leigh falls with him, a Leigh forever seventeen and Phil shrieks that he loves her, that he always loved her and always wanted to prove it.

There's a pause, pregnant with wonder and terror. Phil's horrified scream breaks out of one world to crash into Block. A scream of realisation.

One final sound comes from the lost side of Dalry.

The sound of a crying child, calling for its father.

Ninety Four

It's been so long since I've seen them. They're older now. They're not the people I remember and they're just the same. Stu, this new woman, this good woman Kirsty. Karen, our Will. He's bleeding. His blood is on us. He's still breathing, still here.

Sunlight is coming back and that's all right. It's welcome here. The mess is gone. The things are gone. Leigh's gone, too, and I miss my sister. Always loved her. Always wanted to protect her and I didn't. Not my fault, though. Phil hurt us; he hurt me and that wasn't my fault. It was all down to him and I won't hurt, anymore.

So I sit with my friends while the sunshine comes back to us and I tell them I love them, that I always loved them, and I hold their hands. They hold mine. We hold one another for as long as we can while the light comes back in and their world comes with it.

Our sunshine. Our days. I miss them. I miss them all. And Mick is with me. Andy, too. We're here in Block and this is us right here, right now.

Too much blood. It's on our hands and Will is breathing; he's breathing to Karen, still breathing and still loving her and now he's coming with me.

Coming with us.

Coming with all of us.

Coming home.

***

'Will?' Karen whispered.

Stu and Kirsty were beside her. She knew it and didn't care. The school as it was had gone and they were somewhere else. Where didn't matter. What happened didn't matter. The only thing in the world was Will. His bloody hand was still in hers and that was only because she was holding him so tightly. Her jacket was wet with his blood and no more pooled from the wound in his stomach.

'Will?'

A touch on her shoulder. Kirsty. She was crying.

'Karen, he's ...'

'No, he isn't.' Karen ran her fingers through a few loose strands of Will's hair. It was getting thin on top. Needed a trim around the sides. 'He's not. He's not. He's not.'

She held his body and she wept for her husband.

***

Later.

Kirsty rocked with Stu in her arms. He hadn't spoken in what might have been hours. She hadn't wanted to but had forced herself to speak to Karen. Nobody had said a word since. Sunlight was here, the windows, doors and floor were whole. No ghosts. No *things*. Just them.

There was just her, rocking with Stu.

Back and forth.

Together.

***

Later, again.

Stu stared at nothing and tried to think of nothing. His eyes saw Block and while a fraction of his mind noted that it was all as normal as it should be, he didn't think of it in any deeper way. It didn't mean much if anything.

A spark grew inside his chest. Pain came with the spark. Grief welcomed him and he said their names in his heart.

Andy. Mick. Will. Geri.

He said their names over and over as grief took him.

Stu stared at the floor and tried to think of nothing.

***

Later, the last.

The school sat where it had for four decades. Its field rose up in a bank to the tennis courts and the grounds and the languages department. It stretched its pathways in and out of the grounds and its newer blocks grew side by side with the older ones, fresh bricks with old. In Block, three people sat on the floor as close to each other as they could. The school knew two of them and welcomed the third just as much as it welcomed the others. It felt the body of a fourth and was sad for the life gone. It wished for it back and knew it couldn't return.

The school breathed.

It breathed and the world of real things returned to it. The world how it should be, how it is, not what it was.

Police sirens sang.

And the school breathed.

It breathed and one dead day returned to its place in the past, leaving the present with its grief and its hurts and its future.

Ninety Five

Stu paused with his hand on the fridge door as the voices and from the garden came through the living room into the hall and reached him in the kitchen. The kids' voices, their happy shouts. Letting himself smile a little, Stu reached for a fresh beer from the fridge. His fingers closed around the cold bottle and the memory bloomed as it always did: quick, sharp and pained.

They're at Mick's and it's hot, so hot. The party's here and they've got weeks ahead of nothing, of parties and all of them together. He's in the kitchen and he knows Mick is coming up behind him, ready to try to make him jump while the girls watch from the doorway. He sees Mick's shadow sliding over the kitchen floor and he times his move perfectly. Mick comes at him and Stu whirls around, beer in hand and he shouts a meaningless word into Mick's face and Mick jerks back, laughing, swearing at him. He steals Stu's beer and Stu laughs hard. He takes another beer from the fridge and walks with Mick, Karen and Geri through the house to the back garden. Will's there, fiddling with the stereo, skipping tracks on the CD until he gets to Oasis and Mick tunelessly sings Wonderwall *and Stu sees Karen's smile just as he sees Geri studying Will in a way Will hasn't yet noticed. Stu has. He notices a lot and that's a fine thing. It's his. And they are his.*

Stu let the memory go. It slipped away with a little promise it would return whenever it wanted to, return to prick at him whenever it wanted to.

He let out a trembling sigh and swallowed it when he sensed someone behind him.

'You all right?' Karen said.

He nodded, not trusting himself to speak at least for the next few seconds, then faced her.

Wordlessly, Karen extended her hand. He stared at it, not understanding. She didn't move, only smiled a little. Laughing, Stu handed Karen the beer and took another from the fridge.

'Kirsty says can you bring Lucy some squash,' Karen said. 'And she'll have another splash of wine.'

Stu set his bottle down and poured squash into Lucy's favourite cup. He concentrated on pouring the liquid, conscious of Karen's eyes on him.

'Sure you're all right?' she asked quietly.

'Yeah.'

'Thinking about it?' Karen said.

'Sort of. Mick. Fat bastard.'

She clenched her jaw for a moment. 'Yeah.'

'He'd love this. Always liked a party.'

'Yeah.'

Stu forced himself to smile. Standing in the kitchen and getting maudlin with Karen would do neither of them any good.

'Always liked getting drunk and blocking the toilet with puke,' he said and Karen giggled.

'That was you, wasn't it?'

'Never.'

He diluted the squash and kissed Karen's cheek. She squeezed his arm and he welcomed the good weight of her hand.

'Thanks,' she said.

'Any time. But I draw the line at snogs.'

She smiled, lips not parting. It was perfunctory, Stu saw, but that didn't matter. Any smile was better than no smile these days.

Stu limping only a little and Karen keeping close to his side, they joined the others in the garden, Stu gave his daughter her drink; she ran to join Susan and the two boys in the paddling pool, and Stu handed the wine to Kirsty. She blew him a kiss. Stu took the chair between her and Jodie, stretching his leg with a little grunt. Karen seated herself and opened her beer.

'Cheers,' she said and Stu wondered if the other women had noticed the little shine in her eyes.

Of course they have, Will whispered to him. *They're women, you knobhead.*

Stu bit his cheeks to stop his laughter and opened his beer.

'Cheers,' he said and lifted his bottle.

Jodie and Kirsty did the same; the group drank and for a little moment, the only sound was the children in the pool and birdsong. Then Jodie shifted in her seat and Stu glanced at her. She was watching the kids and Stu thought that might be on purpose.

'Any of you heard about the new Tom Cruise film?' she said.

Stu shook his head and knew at once where this was going. He stayed silent and waited for Jodie to continue.

'I read about it the other day. Andy's last screenplay, it's the film. They bought it a few months ago.'

She fell silent. Stu sipped his beer and felt Kirsty's eyes on him. He knew what she'd be thinking: he was the man, he'd been Andy's friend long ago and it was down to him to reply to Jodie.

'He'd be pretty chuffed about that.'

It was weak. It was much too small but it was all he had.

Sorry, Andy.

Stu kept his eyes on the hedge at the end of his garden. The occasional bee flew in and out of the greenery.

'Jodie?' Karen said.

'Yeah?'

'The boys. What have you told them?'

Stu took a long swallow of his beer and wished it was all easier than this. Two years, a handful of days like this when they all got together, got their kids here, drank too much and talked too little; two years of that and talking about Mick, Will, Andy and Geri was like digging knives into each of them.

Although tears were in Jodie's words, her voice was surprisingly strong.

'I told them their dad was a good man and that he died helping a friend who was in trouble. They cry sometimes but they're not old enough to understand what it means. Not yet.'

Stu glanced at her around the rim of his bottle. She saw his look and attempted a smile. It almost appeared genuine.

'They're good boys,' Karen said.

In the pool, Mark and Kevin splashed water towards Susan who goggled at them, then splashed back.

Good boys. Good boys with good girls.

Stu's thought was a pleasant one. It was easy to watch the kids in the pool and think about them as they'd be tomorrow or next week or next month. Beyond that was a featureless grey world.

Stu only realised he'd spoken aloud when Kirsty said his name a few times to get his attention.

'Yeah?' he said.

'What did you say?'

He blushed. 'I don't know. Thinking out loud.'

'Too much beer,' Karen said and Stu snorted.

'Never too much beer.' He patted his stomach which jutted over the waistband of his jeans. 'Fat and forty. It's the way ahead.'

Kirsty laughed; Jodie threw a crisp at Stu. It landed on his chest. He threw it back, laughing. He knew why Karen wasn't laughing, why she was watching him. It was simple.

She knows you in old ways.

The thought wasn't his own. Nor did it belong to Andy, Mick, Will or Geri. All of them talked to him occasionally. He replied but only if he was drunk enough.

The thought was cold but not without feeling. It was easy to think of the voice announcing bad news and regretting having to do so.

Stu glanced at Karen. She winked at him and he flashed back to the last day of school again.

Geri.

Geri noticing his appraisal as she watches Will at the stereo. She meets his gaze, eyes cool, a little smile sitting at the corner of her lips. A second spins out into something longer; she lifts a hand, brushes her hair back from her forehead and winks at him, a sly gesture of amusement. Another second comes between them, long enough for Stu to see Geri as he never has before, and long enough for him to want to tell Will to do whatever Geri tells him to, to be whatever she wants him to be. She crosses over the patio to the grass and stands with Will, and then Karen is there, talking to Stu, blocking his view of Will and Geri and he knows what this is, he knows where he is and he knows what is coming in the weeks ahead.

Stu watched Karen place her drink on the little table beside her and lower her hand to her jeans pocket. Jodie and Kirsty also saw the movement and their conversation fell into silence.

'I wasn't sure if I should bring this,' Karen said and touched her back pocket. In the pool, the children played.

'What is it?' Jodie said in a voice too light to be real.

'I put it in a box when I got home the day after,' Karen muttered. 'Not looked at it since. Didn't open the box, didn't even go in that cupboard.'

'The diary?' Kirsty said.

'Sort of.'

Karen pulled a sheet of paper from her pocket. It was folded in four. Its frayed edges fluttered in the wind.

'I went in that cupboard last week. Been thinking about it since we arranged today. Thought it would be all right to bring the diary and ...I don't know. Give it to one of you. Throw it away.' She shrugged. 'The thing is, when I opened the box, this was all that was left. Just one page.'

'Where was the rest of it?' Jodie asked.

'Gone.'

'What?'

'Gone. No trace of it. Just this left.'

'What about the photo?' Jodie said.

Karen didn't speak and Stu pictured Block as it had been during their dark time there. Them, huddled on the floor, bleeding, the carpet sticky with patches of their blood. Karen's hand had crept to his pocket, pulled the diary free and there had been a second of wonder, then panic when he'd realised the photo wasn't with him.

'Don't know,' he said to Jodie. She studied him. 'It went at some point. I don't know if we lost it or what, but it went.'

Stu extended a hand which shook a little. Karen didn't offer him the page.

'Do you believe me?' she said.

'About what?'

'About this being all that's left.'

'Why wouldn't I?'

She considered that, then handed him the page.

'When's it from?' Kirsty asked.

'There's no date and it's not the full entry. I think that's the last half of it,' Karen replied.

'Can I say something?' Jodie said.

'Of course,' Kirsty said.

Jodie studied the children. 'I never met Geri, obviously. Mick only talked about her a few times. He mentioned all of you, but he only brought her up when he was proper drunk.' She smiled and it was bitter. 'I know what she meant to him and to you but I still wish sometimes you'd never been friends.' She stared at Stu. 'I'm sorry.'

'Don't be,' Karen muttered. 'I know what you mean. We all lost our friends, the babies lost their father.' Her voice broke and Stu recognized the stumble. Karen wasn't about to cry; she was holding onto her anger. 'Phil didn't just hurt Geri or Leigh. He hurt us. We paid for what Leigh wanted to do to Phil. We didn't have a choice about getting involved or getting Phil face to face with Geri and Leigh.'

Stu found his voice. 'It's not about Geri. Not all of it. It was Leigh. I don't want to know what it was like for her. Ten years. Christ.' He swallowed a large mouthful of cold lager. 'What he did to her, I hope he's still screaming. For what he did to both of them.' He met Jodie's steady gaze. 'It was Leigh. With the gun. At the school. Then in the bushes. Then following us to Monk's Cave, I think. Leigh wanted to hurt people. It was Geri's diary, her writing, but Leigh writing through her.'

'She didn't care what happened to us. She cared about getting to Phil. We were just things she could use to make that happen,' Karen murmured.

'I think Geri let her,' Kirsty said. 'I think she wanted you all back together like you used to be so maybe you could stop Phil. I told you what he said about being a teacher, about a girl in his school. If Leigh used you all to get to Phil, then maybe Geri used you to stop Phil from doing anything to that girl. And I blamed her. When I was stuck in the house with Phil. I blamed her. It was all her fault to me, and that's not fair. It's not true. It was all down to that son of a bitch. God knows what would have happened if Geri hadn't come back. If she hadn't got you all together, Phil would have hurt that girl. I know it.'

Stu reached for his wife and held her hand. The sun had warmed her skin. Stu welcomed the sensation and ran his fingers over her wrist.

'He was a monster,' she said.

Kirsty kissed Stu's fingers and let him go. He held the page of Geri's diary, aware the women were watching him. He didn't move. His wife, his friend, his friend's partner: they were here, he was here and how he wished the others were here, too.

For no reason at all, he looked across the garden, beyond the pool and children to the hedge.

There were no ghosts and no visions. There was only the hedge and Stu's wish that his friends, all his friends, were here at the party that wasn't a party without them.

Geri came back. So why can't the others be here now? How the hell is that fair?

293

Stu closed his eyes for a moment. Fair? What did that have to do with anything? Nothing about the whole shitty business had been fair. So why should it surprise him that his friends couldn't come back?

A memory whispered to him. Karen's voice from outside Geri's house with Mick come back to them.

Maybe things, maybe they just have to be in the right place.

Maybe she'd been right. Maybe things had to be a certain way. Didn't stop it hurting, though. Didn't stop it feeling like they'd lost so much to stop Phil.

Mick came back to you, remember? He came back to help you. Don't you forget that.

Stu listened.

So did Andy. On the steps. He saved you from falling so you remember that. And you remember why you did this. You remember that when you think about if all this was worth it.

Was it Geri talking to him in a scolding way? Was he talking to himself?

Does it matter?

And that was all himself. He knew why they'd gotten involved. He knew what they'd been to each other.

Andy. Mick. Will. Geri.

He said their names in his head. He said them in his heart and he wished they were with him.

In the pool, the children played together.

Stu unfolded the page and read.

Ninety Six

She's Geri. She's nineteen. She's the girl looking in the mirror.

Geri reads the page she finished writing a moment before. She reads it again and again and she lets the breeze play on the back of her neck. Nice. Comforting. Warm.

The clock radio beside her bed. Quarter to seven. Time to get ready, to get dressed. Time to put on her new skirt and think about him while she does, time to get ready before Karen arrives and they go to Mick's. She stays on her chair and touches the pages of her diary. Putting the words on paper is like locking them up. They're in a secret place and while they're hidden, she doesn't have to think about them or what they might mean.

Breeze on her neck. The wonderful sensation of the wind on her skin.

'Will.'

The name spoken aloud and it's full of promise and potential.

Geri traces a finger over her words and reads, her voice a whisper in her bedroom.

'Will. I'm going to tell you tonight, going to say it right to your face. And what I hope more than anything is that I can get all the words out. I hope that more than I hope you'll kiss me tonight. Isn't that odd? I hope I can speak, more than I want you to feel the same. Because saying it all tonight means I'm in charge of what I feel and what I do about it. If you kiss me, if you feel the same, then that's going to be so good. If you don't, I can deal with that. I won't like it but I can deal with it. But if I can speak and say everything and say it all to your face, then I win. Even if it's just a little bit, I win.'

She falls silent and resists the need to touch her flaming cheeks. How much she blushes. How much she can't hide what she's feeling right now. The thought makes her laugh at herself and doing that makes her laugh even more.

Geri stands and crosses to the mirror beside her bed. Her smiling reflection watches her and she looks at herself as if with new eyes. With his eyes.

Will he see her? Will he look at her face and at her eyes? Her beautiful blues. She heard him say that to Mick back near Christmas, the boys talking in Will's kitchen with no idea she'd been in the hallway, listening.

Geri flexes the long muscles in her legs and presses them together. Tendons stand out. She inhales and her breasts rise. She touches them with new hands, with his hands and heat strokes her. It slips inside her stomach and she relishes the sensation. It's something new. It's something clean.

The clock. Five to seven. Twenty minutes. Geri drops her towel to the floor, pulls on her underwear and slides her new skirt up her legs. The whisper of the material on her skin, the tickle of it and she thinks of Will again, and again the same heat lights her.

'Will,' she says and finishes dressing. Clothed, she studies herself in the mirror one last time. 'Going to tell you, Will. Going to say it to your face.'

And maybe the evening will go as she wants it to. And maybe she'll get what she wants.

Back here.

Back here tonight. The two of them. And what a thought that is. What a picture filling her head. Geri lets out a small laugh, tells herself to calm down and a car pulls up outside: Karen early as usual. Geri pads across to the window and Karen is getting out of her car. She looks up and waves and Geri waves back. Karen walks to the pavement and looks up just before she moves out of sight beyond the fence at the edge of Geri's garden. She sticks out her tongue, a childish gesture that makes Geri laugh. Then she's gone and Geri gazes at the pavement and the pretty gardens and the little section of Oakfield Walk visible from her bedroom window. A couple of cars pass each other. Maybe people heading out on a Friday night, maybe people going to see their friends just like she is. Maybe. Maybe. All the maybes in the world.

Geri pulls her window in, leaving it open enough to let the night air cool the room, and again studies herself in the mirror.

Not too bad, she thinks. Looking good. Looking in charge.

The doorbell rings and Leigh answers the door, then calls Geri's name up the stairs.

'Looking good,' Geri tells herself and hopes and wishes Will thinks the same later.

At the party.

Mick's house.

That's where they're going, that's where they'll be tonight. All of them. Together.

Out the door, to Karen's car, pull out of Oakfield Walk to the road and the sun will be bright in their faces. They'll need to put their sunglasses on and they'll drive together, car eating the road towards the roundabout, over it, head past the school that was now just an empty building asleep forever for her now instead of the place she'd gone to almost every day for years and years; past it and its playing field and turn into the little snaking roads that will take them to Mick's house. Out of the car. To the paving slabs at the side of the house, through the gate and to the back garden where they will all be, all drinking, all in the garden and there'll be music and her friends.

All together.

And the sun will still be out for a little longer. And she'll feel it on her head and her hair.

All together. All happy together.

'Geri.'

Leigh's voice, calling up the stairs. The light sliding through the window with the scents of grass and flowers still strong. How warm it is. How bright.

'Geri. Karen's here.'

Geri shouts her reply to the open door and it carries down to the hall below.

'Down in a sec.'

All together. Like they always would be.

He'd know that. He'd see her.

And he'd know her even if she didn't say a word.